Praise for *Dog Days*

"*Dog Days* is everything I love in a book—funny, tender, beautifully crafted, and cleverly plotted, with a perfect twist of an ending I didn't see coming. The touching tale of two lost souls finding each other has been given fresh life by the talents of the very gifted Elsa Watson."   —Susan Wiggs,
#1 *New York Times* bestselling author

"A delightful story that readers should relax with and just enjoy. Anyone who loves animals and has ever imagined what they might be thinking will find this to be a wholly amusing tale. Those who haven't may see the world from a different point of view."
—*RT Book Reviews* (4 stars)

"A doggone good story, told with humor, warmth, and insight."   —Sheila Roberts,
bestselling author of
On Strike for Christmas

"I savored *Dog Days* for its humor, beautiful prose, heartwarming story line, and quirky, unusual perspective. Elsa Watson writes with compassion and deep insight."   —Anjali Banerjee,
author of *Haunting Jasmine*

TOR BOOKS BY ELSA WATSON

Dog Days
The Love Dog

The
Love Dog

—ELSA WATSON—

TOR®

A TOM DOHERTY ASSOCIATES BOOK
NEW YORK

This is a work of fiction. All of the characters, organizations, and events portrayed in this novel are either products of the author's imagination or are used fictitiously.

THE LOVE DOG

Copyright © 2013 by Elsa Watson

A Tor Book
Published by Tom Doherty Associates, LLC
175 Fifth Avenue
New York, NY 10010

www.tor-forge.com

Tor® is a registered trademark of Tom Doherty Associates, LLC.

ISBN 978-0-7653-6809-6

First Edition: February 2013

Printed in the United States of America

0 9 8 7 6 5 4 3 2 1

For Lucky,
a very sensitive soul.

Acknowledgments

I've sometimes thought this book should have a sticker on the front that reads "Produced by People, Inspired by Dogs." It took a fleet of hardworking people to create this book, beginning with my wonderful editor, Kristin Sevick. Not only does Kristin have a terrific editing eye, she has a great sense of what a story needs (and doesn't). Best of all, she's very funny. It really says something when a person's editorial letters make you laugh.

Kevan Lyon is the fabulous agent who has guided me through many complicated decisions. As a person who hates decision making and complication, this is worth more than I can say. Thank you, Kevan!

Many, many thanks go to my fellow writers for their advice and critiques: Susan Wiggs, Sheila Roberts, Lois Dyer, Kate Breslin, and Anjali Banerjee, and to Suzanne Selfors for her endless encouragement and for making me laugh and laugh. Thanks to both my parents, Jim Watson and Carol Watson, and to Dawn Simon, Kristin von Kreisler, and Marcie Gwiazdon for their support.

Diedre Johnson helped me understand the world of tabloid reporting. Joseph E. Miller (of Miller-Gregson Productions, Inc.) and Michael Rosenblum explained the ins and outs of reality television. I deeply appreciate their help. Any mistakes in this book are mine, not theirs.

I'd also like to recognize Sunny, a gorgeous, spirited, delightful blond dog who was the physical model for Apollo. Sunny shared many of Apollo's quirks—given the chance, he would have stared at our cat for days. Without blinking. We miss you, Sunny.

Most of all, I'd like to thank my husband, Kol, and our dog, Lucky. I want to thank these two together because they're inseparable. Lucky wants to go where Kol goes, and Kol always wants to have Lucky with him. Our Lucky is a sensitive dog who feels things deeply—he's the model for Apollo. When he's alone, he tends to worry about things, but when Kol is near he kicks up his heels and frolics with joy. Neither his life nor Kol's would be as rich without their connection. They're so beautiful together.

The
Love Dog

Samantha

Popcorn?
  Check.
  Fuzzy slippers?
  Check.
  Skeptical attitude?
  Double check.
  I plopped down next to my sister, Cassie, and clicked on the TV just in time to see a graphic of a giant pink heart—made out of tiny paw prints—materialize on the screen. Schmaltzy music poured out of the speakers. The screen flashed with a close-up of a beautiful golden dog, while over its head formed the words we'd been expecting: *The Love Dog.*
  Cassie gave a heartfelt sigh.
  "Give me a break," I grumbled. My cat, Zephyr, walked across Cassie's lap and settled onto mine.
  My sister rolled her eyes. "Do you have to be like that? Is it something they teach you in paralegal school? At least let the show get started before you tear it

down. Ooh!" Cassie pulled one of my throw pillows close. "There he is."

And there he was—the show's leading man, Mr. Love Dog himself: Mason Hall. Smiling into the camera as if he knew each viewer personally, as if he were best friends with all fifteen million of us. I could almost hear the thud as half the women in America swooned. Technically, I reminded myself, he wasn't perfect looking. His nose was dented a little on the left side and he had a white scar that cut through his eyebrow. His auburn hair was styled in that purposeful-messy way that made me think of surfers and extreme rock climbers.

"I think his hairline's receding," I said. Cassie thwacked me with the pillow, making Zephyr flick her ears. I laughed, because deep down, even I knew I was being ridiculous. "What?" I said, chuckling, "I really do. In three years he'll have to comb those bangs over from the center of his head."

Cassie gave me the evil eye, but when she saw me laughing, she smiled, too. I turned back to Mason and let a tiny, begrudging piece of myself admit that, flaws or no, he was an absurdly attractive human being. Which he probably knew perfectly well.

On-screen, Mason stood in front of a midnight-blue wall, his thumbs hooked boyishly into his belt loops. "Love," he told us, with a quirky little smile, "is a universal truth. It's something we all long for, but it isn't easy to get or to keep. As a wise man once said, the course of true love never did run smooth. But tonight on *The Love Dog,* Apollo is going to show you something that has to be seen to be believed." He paused for dramatic effect. "Tonight you're going to meet the dog who mends broken hearts."

The camera panned back, showing Mason standing on a typical talk-show-type stage, artfully arranged with a comfy velvet chair, a red velvet couch, and a tiny table that held a vase of yellow tulips. "I give you," he said, with a sweep of his hand, "the Love Dog."

As the music rose, I dropped my chin and mumbled into my collar. "Who writes this stuff?"

"Shh!" Cassie's eyes were glued to the screen. "Here he comes."

Zephyr gave the screen a wary look as Apollo, the show's canine star, trotted onstage, his blond locks flowing. He cruised in, his furry paws flicking across the carpet. The breeze created by his own movement fanned his hair back like Farrah Fawcett's.

At Mason's encouragement, Apollo leaped onto the red velvet couch and settled down, paws drooping over the cushions, his big brown eyes meeting the camera without blinking.

Not even I could deny Apollo's beauty. He was truly gorgeous. He was lightest-haired golden retriever I had ever seen. Long, stunning waves of champagne-colored fur flowed behind him whenever he moved. I might have had my issues with Mason, but I had to hand it to Apollo. He deserved to be a star.

Of course, that didn't mean I believed he was a "love dog," whatever a love dog was supposed to be. No such animal existed. Neither did mistletoe magic or Cupid or fairy godmothers. I knew this from experience.

While a recording of an audience hooted and hollered for Apollo, Mason walked over to the dog and rubbed the side of his head, just below his ear. Apollo beamed up at Mason, giving the impression that the two were old buddies. I quirked one eyebrow at this.

The blogosphere—one of my favorite places—was full of speculative questions about whether Apollo belonged to Mason. As with most things, I had my doubts. They probably did this little routine to add to Mason's likeability. After all, if the dog adored him, he had to be a great guy, right?

"It's just such a sham," I mumbled to Zephyr.

Next to me, Cassie stiffened. "If you think it's so fake, why do you watch it? I swear, you do this every time."

"Do what?"

"Ruin the whole show with your snarkiness."

I looked down at Zephyr and lifted her paw onto one of my fingers, balancing it gently. "I'm sorry. I don't mean to ruin it. Hand over the popcorn—it'll help me shut up."

I meant what I'd said—I didn't mean to ruin the show for Cassie. It was a hazard of my chosen vocation—not what I did for a living, filing paperwork for a law office, but what I did to put meaning in my life. I, along with two other women, wrote a blog that warned about the dangers of believing in fairy-tale love, the kind of love that only one person in a million ever experienced. On our blogging team, reality television was my purview. I watched *The Love Dog* because it was one of the most popular reality shows on television that focused on romance. This show was the enemy. If I could poke holes in its façade, my battle would be halfway won.

I hadn't been successful yet, though, in persuading my own sister that *The Love Dog* was a pile of hooey. Cassie loved fantasies of all kinds, especially ones that involved true love and living happily ever after. I didn't want to quash that in her; I just hated to see her so dreamy-eyed and vulnerable. Her blind trust in love had already driven her into trouble more than once.

When the show took another commercial break, Cassie and I both got up. In the kitchen, I filled her water glass, added a slice of lemon, and pushed it across the counter to her while with the other hand I hid a pile of rejection letters. Cassie knew I'd sent out some of my short stories, but I wasn't ready to broadcast my mountain of rejections.

"So," she said, taking a sip and smiling brightly. "What's new?"

Poor Cassie. Every time I saw her, she bravely asked this same question, even though all I usually had to talk about was work, or Zephyr, or the song I'd been practicing that week. I was trying to learn every song in the *Beatles Songbook* on my little Gretsch guitar, and nearly every week I bored Cassie with another long story about the chord changes in "Blackbird." But this time, things were different.

"You'll never believe who sent me an e-mail," I said, leaning on the counter. I'd been waiting so long to share this with someone, my pulse picked up in expectation.

"Who?" Cassie's eyes searched my face. "Wait. No." She stared at me. "No way. He wouldn't."

"Yes way. He did. Richard. Can you believe it?"

Cassie set her glass on the counter and shook her head. "What did he say?"

I shrugged, though nonchalance was the last thing I was feeling. "Not much. Said he felt bad about the way things ended and just wanted to say hi. Wondered how I was doing. That sort of thing."

"He felt bad?" My sister's shoulders dropped in disbelief. "He felt *bad*?" She slammed her glass down on the counter, her face turning beet red. "That ass-hole. That blooming *king* of assholes!" She snatched up her glass again and thrust it toward me to under-score her words, sloshing water onto the counter. "Unbelievable! Un-be-lievable. Clearly he has no sense of decency. I mean, gnats are more self-aware." She leaned in and stared at me. "Doesn't it freak you out to think how close you came to being tied to him for-ever? Forever, Sam!"

I nodded, elated by her indignation. "I know. It is terrifying, isn't it? And he was so bland in his e-mail— almost like nothing had ever happened. Can you be-lieve it? Yeah. He said he got a new research grant. As if I care."

Cassie swung herself onto a bar stool, her face still pink. She grabbed one of my kitchen towels and wiped up the water she'd spilled, shaking her head. "I'm so stunned I don't even know what to say. But what about you? How was it to read all that? What did you do?"

The truth? I'd ranted around my apartment for half an hour, shouting at the top of my lungs. I'd thrown balled-up socks at the computer. I'd terrified Zephyr with the evil things I screamed about Richard and his entire family. And then I'd sat down and read the e-mail again.

"I deleted it," I said, as coolly as I could, fanning my finger across a smudge on the counter. I wasn't above faking strength and superiority for my big sister. "No way am I writing back."

"Yeah, but that's it? You didn't plant a virus on his hard drive or something? Nuke his entire neighbor-hood?"

If only I knew how. Actually, I'd printed the e-mail and lit fire to it with great ceremony on my apartment's little deck. The ashes were still scattered in my geranium pot. And before I burned it, I tried to get Zephyr to pee on it, but she's not the kind of cat who takes orders.

"I don't want to hear from Richard ever again," I said, hoping I looked noble as I sipped my water. "That chapter in my life is closed, and I am glad, glad, glad."

Cassie shook her head again. "At least you're a writer. You can put Richard into one of your stories and make him suffer a thousand awful fictional deaths. You can whack his balls off and have him get eaten by piranhas or something."

I gave a little sigh. "Yeah, maybe someday I'll be ready to write about it. Just not anytime soon."

Cassie picked up her water glass. "Then here's to someday," she said, clinking her glass against mine.

The show came back on, and we hurried to the couch in time to see Mason give Apollo a final scratch. Then he stood and turned back to the camera.

"Apollo is a unique dog—he specializes in broken hearts. Broken relationships. Without speaking a single word, with nothing but his heart and his soul, Apollo brings love back to those who have lost it. Tonight he's going to do that for a very special couple that's come here all the way from Colorado. I'd like you to meet Jonathan and Keisha Tate."

We cut away from Mason and Apollo to a video montage of two people, a husky football-player type and his dark-skinned, dark-eyed bride. We saw photos of Jonathan removing Keisha's garter at their wedding, pictures of their honeymoon in Hawaii, shots of the two of them out with friends, martini glasses in hand.

"Jonathan and Keisha began their marriage with the best of intentions," Mason's voice-over told us. "They vowed to love and honor each other. But every relationship has its rocky moments, and theirs was no exception."

We cut to a recorded scene of Jonathan and Keisha fighting over whose turn it was to do the dishes. Apparently it was Jonathan's turn—it had been for the past five nights, but he kept skipping out to the garage to watch wrestling instead.

Cassie snorted. "I'd like to see how Apollo's going to fix that. He can't genetically alter Jonathan, can he?"

Next we saw a clip of Keisha on the phone, talking about how Jonathan left his dirty socks on the floor and spent the whole weekend watching football. Then the camera turned to Jonathan, who said, "She calls her mother every day. Every single day. I think she spends most of the call complaining about me. Whenever she gets off she's in a nasty mood for hours."

"Well," Cassie turned to me and said, "we've never had *that* problem."

"No way," I agreed. "Our apron strings got cut a long time ago."

On the screen, Mason brought Apollo out to meet the couple on a pale beach with a promenade that looked like the Santa Barbara boardwalk. We saw Apollo playing one-on-one at the beach with Keisha, heard her tell him how she worries about her mom. "She's been so lonely since Dad died," she said, stroking Apollo's silky blond ears. "It hurts to hear the sadness in her voice. I want to tell Jonathan about it, but he always thinks the calls are about him. He might be what we talk about, you know, day to day, but that's not what our talks are really about."

Later, Jonathan and Apollo spent time shooting hoops with Mason. We heard Jonathan confess that he feared he'd never be good enough for Keisha. "Ever since her dad died, I feel like she's comparing me to him in her head. And I just don't measure up."

As the show broke away for a commercial, Cassie exhaled in a heavy way that let me know something was on her mind. My sister was a single mom, so I started by asking the obvious question.

"How're the kids? Is Lulu excited about school?"

"Super excited. She's had her first-day outfit picked out for weeks. Oh, that reminds me." Cassie threw a piece of popcorn into her mouth. "Can you babysit on Friday? Just for Lulu. Jacob's going to his dad's."

"Of course. What's up?"

She smiled coyly and slid her hand behind her neck. "I have a date."

I tried to smile for her—honestly, I did. But it took some serious effort.

"Who is it?"

"His name's Liam. And don't go giving me that look." She leaned closer and bumped me with her arm.

"What look?" I had hoped I looked supportive.

"That overprotective little sister look. I know you're suspicious of every guy I date. But you don't have to be that way about Liam. He has a son. He knows what it's like to be a single parent. We aren't going to do anything impulsive."

I considered mentioning her second husband, the one she ran off to Vegas with. He had also been a single dad who should have known better than to do anything impulsive. But love was like that. It made people lose their heads.

"I just don't want you to get hurt," I said, aware of

how trite I sounded. How many times had I heard people say that in movies? Just because I really meant it didn't make it sound less canned. But that was my role, to be the supportive character who frowns when the leading actress starts gushing about her new love.

"I know you don't. But this time's gonna be different," Cassie said, looking starry-eyed and confident. "You'll see."

Back on the show, Apollo was in full swing. The show (twenty-two minutes of actual footage after subtracting the time for commercials) had entered act 3. If Apollo was going to transform Keisha's and Jonathan's lives, it had to be now.

His first move clearly had everything to do with the show's producers and nothing to do with Apollo. The show flew Keisha's mom to L.A. where she had a heart-to-heart with Jonathan. We saw two minutes of it. Next, Apollo walked with Mom on the beach and "helped" her meet a few single older men. Back on the set, Mason played this footage for Keisha, who let out a Himalayan-size sigh of relief. "Mom looks so happy! Good work, Apollo!" Fake audience cheering filled my speakers. I rolled my eyes.

Apollo trotted onto the set carrying a dish towel in his mouth. He took it to Jonathan and set it on his lap. "I know, I know," Jonathan said, laughing. "I'll do the dishes!"

While the audience roared, Apollo trotted offstage and returned with two slips of paper in his mouth. He took these to Keisha. As she looked at them, she leaned toward Jonathan and smiled. "You're gonna love this. It's tickets to see the Broncos play the Rams.

I guess if you do the dishes, I'll have time to watch football with you. As long as you tell me what's going on."

"Babe, I'll make you a football expert," Jonathan told her, grinning like he'd just scored a touchdown.

And just like that, they were fixed.

"There, isn't that sweet?" Cassie asked. "They made up. What's not to like?"

Ah, a quandary. Should I assume her question was rhetorical and keep my big mouth shut? Or say what I really thought? I waffled, and I was just about to choose the former when she went on to say, "I wonder if Apollo could have fixed things between David and me."

"No, Cass, no. Don't even go there. This wasn't a real fix." I waved at the TV screen. "You can't fix a marriage by handing out towels and football tickets—you know that. This is just TV, period. Real relationships can't be patched up in twenty-two minutes of on-air time. You've been married and divorced—"

"Twice."

"—twice. You know the issues go a whole lot deeper than one person not doing the dishes and another talking to her mom too often. That's surface stuff. Made-for-TV nonsense. Excellently rehearsed, scripted, and acted for an audience that isn't even sitting there."

"Acted! What do you mean?" Cassie looked horror-stricken.

"I mean Keisha and Jonathan are probably actors. Nice, out-of-work Hollywood types who're happy to play these parts on a reality show. Heck, they might not even be paid. The publicity alone is worth thousands of dollars. But I'd bet you anything that they know how to act."

Cassie clutched the pillow to her stomach and turned

back to the TV screen, which was airing a commercial for a lawyer you could call at 1-555-DIVORCE. "I'm never watching this show with you again. Ever. You're such a cynic, Sam. Can't people enjoy some dreams once in a while? What's the matter with believing in love?"

I paused, not sure what to say. "Every time we talk about this you get mad at me."

"Okay, so this time I won't. I want to know. Why do you hate this show so much?"

I shrugged, as if that could take some of the punch out of what I was about to say. "I don't hate it. I just think it's fake. And not just this show—all of these reality love shows. *First Date. The Fiancé. Loves Me, Loves Me Not.* They're a bunch of bunk, and they do people a real disservice."

"Disservice." Cassie snorted softly and took a drink of her lemon water. "They're just TV shows."

"Sure. But they feed people's hunger for that big myth in the sky." She looked blank, so I connected the dots for her. "Love. They make people think all that hokey stuff is real. That couples like Keisha and Jonathan are real. I hate to tell you this, but these couples don't stay together after the show."

She crooked an eyebrow at me. "How do you know?"

I sighed. "Have you *never* read our blog?"

$$-2-$$

 Apollo

I stared at Lucas's mouth, my tail wagging softly, and tried to absorb his meaning.

"Take this towel in your mouth and put it on Jonathan's lap. Jonathan, the man." I looked at the towel, looked at Lucas, and back at the towel again. The scent coming off Lucas was of sweat spiked with that metallic odor that meant he was anxious—which made me anxious, too.

He held the towel to my lips. "Take it."

I opened my mouth and accepted the towel, then looked at the area where Lucas was pointing. It was my favorite part of the set, the place with the comfy chairs where Mason and I sat and talked with people. Mason. I watched Mason working and for a minute forgot everything else, even the towel in my mouth. When Mason talked, everyone listened. He had such confidence. The people onstage listened; the people offstage listened. Even the people wearing big headphones and holding large pieces of machinery listened.

I felt honored to get to work so closely with him.

Sometimes, when we were onstage, Mason touched me on the head or the back. Never on the belly, which I wished for, though I wasn't about to push my luck. He didn't touch anyone else. Not even on the hand. But he touched me. We worked together.

A fresh wave of metal smell brought me back to Lucas. I had to focus, had to get this right. I looked at Lucas again and tried to make the position of his cheeks, the tone of his voice, and the way he was standing—with one arm outstretched—resolve into some piece of instruction I'd learned before. I watched intently as he spoke again.

"Take it to Jonathan." His lips curled, as if he was trying to draw my attention to his mouth. Was I supposed to put the towel in his mouth? "That man right there." Lucas turned away from me and stared intently at the end of his finger. Should I put the towel on his finger? Drop the towel and grab Lucas's finger instead? Sometimes my job involved dropping the thing I held— I knew that. But other times I was supposed to put it somewhere. Or keep it. So many choices, so few clues.

The people in the comfy chair area had stopped talking. From time to time, one of them looked toward us. The woman played with her hair. Lucas's metal smell grew stronger. I looked at Lucas—I really wanted to get this right. For him. So many hard things had happened to him—I wanted to help him get to good. If we got this right, maybe he would whistle on his way home, and maybe that would lead to good dreams, which would lead to smiling at work tomorrow and a cheerful smell, like blueberries, coming off his skin. That's what I wanted for Lucas, and it all began here, with my understanding what he was asking.

I was panting, eager. Lucas's tone was insistent. I took a step toward his finger, then paused, unsure. If I got this wrong, Lucas would never know my happy chain of events. He would stay mired in his own misery—a sadness that made my heart feel swollen. I took another step, my breath coming hot out of my mouth. I looked out at the comfy chair area, and that's when a miracle occurred.

Mason's hand had dropped to the side of his chair (the best chair, the biggest one, the one that smelled like him). He wasn't looking at me, he was looking at the man and woman sitting near him, but his fingers wiggled the way they did when he wanted me to come over and be touched. It was a clue. Mason, my colleague, was prompting me.

I trotted to the comfy chair area, the pads of my feet damp and slick from worrying about Lucas. My belly still felt cramped, but I breathed freely through my nose, confident that Mason was leading me true. When I arrived, I paused, looking at Mason. He didn't move, so I concentrated all of my energy on sending him this thought: *Tell me what to do.*

Tell me what to do.

Tell me what to do.

Without moving more than a paw's-breadth, he tipped his head toward the other man. The hand at the side of the chair flicked one finger out toward the man, as if he was tossing something. I breathed once. Twice. Then I took a gamble and tossed my towel into the man's lap.

Instantly, everyone relaxed. The woman giggled. The scents changed, growing warmer, sweeter. I sat down and wagged, relief warming my belly. This was why

I loved my job. I wanted to stay right there in that happy glow forever, soaking up joy from the guests, from the crew, from Mason.

Somewhere offstage, I heard a squeak, and my ears perked up off my head. Squeaky toy? Was that a squeaky toy? My nose quivered with hope. My mouth opened, ready to bite at any squeaky toy that might come flying through the air. But then I heard the noise again, and it was just someone's chair creaking. Sigh.

Click-click. Click-click. That was the sound of the little black box Lucas held in his hand. When he clicked it, I was supposed to return to him for more instructions.

I looked at a patch of floor far away from Lucas, pretending I hadn't heard anything. What a fascinating bit of floor—I'd never seen anything so interesting. It was shiny and glossy, with little pieces of wood—

Click-click. Click-click.

I dragged my eyes away from the floor. I was a professional, after all—I couldn't hide from Lucas. He was my trainer. So, as much as I hated to leave the cozy set, I forced my feet to move. As I turned, Mason set a finger on my back. I stopped immediately, honored by his attention.

"We have a lot of shooting yet to go today, buddy. Do your best, okay?" I watched his lips move, saw the set of the skin around his eyes and the way he held his jaw. The weight of his finger on my back warmed my spine. He spoke seriously, with a tone of calm and encouragement. I felt that he was trying to strengthen me. That he was asking for a sacrifice. If I could figure out what he wanted, I would gladly do it. I would do anything.

* * *

Lucas was moving fast, making me sail down the dim hallway. His metallic smell was so strong, I barely noticed the buzz of the fluorescent lights or the click of my nails on the linoleum floor.

Ping! Ping-ping-ping!

I jumped, my hackles up, and tried to crane my neck overhead to the source of the sound, but Lucas kept me moving forward while I shook inside, wondering what sound was going to attack me next. I hated this hall. Pipes and tubes lined the ceiling, and every time I walked there, one of them pinged or hissed and made me jump, wondering what was about to snap at my tail.

Mrrrrrr-rrrrrrr.

I started again, my ears cocking wildly from side to side. That sound I knew. It was an engine, one that belonged to a big vehicle. I tried to calm myself down. I needed to focus. The metallic smell coming off Lucas was stronger than ever, and that meant he'd been thinking negative thoughts. Remembering. While my ears listened to the sound of the engine, I let my brain send him soothing thoughts: *Shh. Soft. Happy.*

Soft.

Shh.

Happy.

Lucas kept walking, looking forward. Sometimes it worked when I sent people thoughts, and sometimes it didn't. I hadn't had very good success with Lucas— yet.

He pushed through the heavy metal door at the end of the hall, which opened with a phoomp of wind. I didn't like that door. In the hallway I felt like a professional. On the other side, I was just a dog. Lucas's dog.

He heaved a long sigh, and my heart slumped to the floor. I hated disappointing him. Somehow, even when I was sure I had done everything right on the set, I felt that I had let him down. "I looked like a dumbass today," he said. His face was tipped toward the floor, mouth in a slight pout. He clenched his fist until his knuckles went white. "What the hell am I doing here? Training a dog to carry a stupid towel?"

He strode into our room, and I followed, keeping my head bowed low. I never knew what to do when Lucas got down on himself like this. How could I help? I tried to slink into my crate, but Lucas started pacing around between me and the door. Instead, I sat down where I was and sent Lucas my thoughts. *You're a good man. You're strong and tall. You can be happy. All you have to do is let yourself.*

"Jesus Christ, don't look at me like that. You're the saddest damn looking dog, you know that? Sometimes I don't think I can spend another second around you. You bring me down."

Poor Lucas. It made my heart hurt to see him like this. I'd tried to help him, just like I'd tried to help the guests who came on the show. They were my projects. Every week two of them came, and every week Lucas asked me to do silly things like carrying pieces of paper in my mouth. I took them little gifts—flowers, envelopes, a towel. But what I really wanted to do was to help them mend their hearts. Mason had explained my job to me. People came to me damaged, and I was supposed to fix them. If only Lucas didn't keep me so busy carrying things around, I might have time to really work with them.

As it was, all I could do was send my thoughts. Send my thoughts, and watch guest after guest leave the studio in the same messy, foul-smelling state they'd arrived in.

"Bite the towel," Lucas was saying in a simpering voice. *"Take it to the man.* How hard can it be? Half the actors in this town would give their balls to have a role as big as yours, and you can't even follow a simple direction." He gave that chest-heaving sigh again and went to the wall, where he started moving collars and leashes, his shoulders slumped low. He shoved things into a bag.

Then he shook his head sadly, as if the air in the room felt too heavy for him to bear. I wanted to run at him, to bark and wag until I teased him out of his misery, but I knew from experience that it wouldn't work. He couldn't play with me, not anymore. Something inside him was broken. Nothing I'd tried could make him smile. Maybe if I took him a squeaky toy? Or a cheese cracker? Cheese crackers always made me happy.

Lucas turned off the lights and went out the door. I heard the click as he locked me in, then I sat and listened while his heels thumped across the floor. He went through the heavy door, then it shut behind him.

I was alone, in the dark. My room was white, with all white walls, but in the dark it looked like endless night. And it kept me jittery because it wasn't completely silent or noisy. This part of the building had pipes in the walls, just like the hallway. They clanged sometimes, and groaned, and whined. In between these noises were long stretches of absolute silence. Sometimes I panted out of my mouth just to hear myself breathing.

Lucas had left me in the dark, but I wasn't in my crate, where I belonged. I was still in the middle of the room, the same place I'd been when he was pacing around the room. I needed to be inside my crate—that was the only safe place in this room—but I was trapped out here, in the dark. It would kill me to sleep in the open all night with those noises squealing overhead. I wanted to panic, but I made myself stay calm. One thing I'd learned from being on the set was that pretending to be calm was almost as good as *being* calm. I knew this room. I could close my eyes and picture every part of it, looking just the way it did with the lights on. I knew where my crate was, where the door was. It was open, I knew that. I kept my eyes squeezed shut and backed up until my rump hit the door to the hall. Then I walked in as if I was walking straight into my crate. My shoulder grazed the side of the crate opening; my head hit the top. I ducked down and kept moving forward.

Relief. There was my blanket. It smelled like sleep and safety. Like me. I was in. I nosed around the back of my crate and found my prized possession, a bit of rope Mason had given me once. Lucas had been away the day Mason gave it to me, so I was able to sneak it back here to my crate. One of the men with headphones had brought me to my room and let me walk right into my crate with my rope. I always made sure I hid it in the back, under my blanket, first thing every morning before Lucas came. If he found it, he would take it away, just like he'd taken the stuffed dog the intern-girl brought me and the rawhide one of the guests brought.

I nosed my blanket until I had my rope in my mouth. Then I turned around three times and lay down with a sigh. The door of my crate was open, which I didn't like. Scary things could attack me in the night if the door wasn't closed. It would be hard to sleep—I'd have to be on my guard all the time. I chewed my rope a few times and reminded myself that the door of my room was shut. Even though it was dark, I was okay in my room, no matter what noises the building made around me.

After a while, I dropped my rope onto my paws and rested my chin beside it. I closed my eyes and got ready to do my most important work of the day. I started, always, with Mason.

Breathing deeply, I gathered all my best intentions, drawing energy from my entire body, even from the tips of my hairs. I drew and pulled until a warm feeling swirled in my chest, warm like when I had cuddled with my mother and the other puppies in my litter. I held the circle of light in my body for a minute. This was my love, all the love I had in my entire being. I closed my eyes and thought of one person, one face, one scent. Mason. Then I let my love go. I imagined my circle of love spinning, transparent, out of my room, down the hall of pipes, out the building, and across the night sky to wherever Mason was at that moment.

After a short rest, I began to gather my love again. This circle of light went out to Andrea. Three times, Andrea had taken me outside the area where I relieved myself. Andrea held the leash gently, and she smelled like horses and ink pens. It always made me happy to send my love to Andrea.

Next came Joe. Joe was half of one of last year's guests, part of a couple that couldn't stop arguing. While he was here, he once snuck into the backstage area to pet me. When Lucas showed up, he sent Joe away. Joe had been gone for a long time, but ever since that moment, I've remembered him in my night-time thoughts.

I only had two more people to send my love out to, beginning with the Dog Lady. I didn't know her name, but the Dog Lady was part of the crew, and she carried the scents of three different dogs. One was small and older with terrible breath. Another was a dog in its prime, good-sized, and clean. The third was a puppy who liked to roll in the grass. His scent was my favorite—I loved the smell of grass. The Dog Lady didn't come near me very often—she was busy being part of the crew—but when she did, I always strained to get close so I could sniff her shoes and coat. Wherever the Dog Lady was, she and her pack deserved a message of love.

After this, I took another rest. The last one I had to do was also the hardest, and it took more concentration. When I felt ready, I closed my eyes and summoned the sparks from every part of me, pulling them slowly together to build the biggest circle of light yet. I took a deep breath and focused hard. Then I sent my love across the nighttime to Lucas.

🖳 Samantha

Blogging late into the night came with its hazards. There was the urge to snack, the eyestrain, the battles with Zephyr, who always wanted to sit on the keyboard. But the very worst was how hard it was to wake up on time the next morning.

The Love Dog aired on Tuesday, and I had a lot to write about after watching the producers rig "love" between Keisha and Jonathan. The blog I write for is called *Unvarnished,* because my coauthors and I tell the honest-to-god truth about the fairy tales of romance. It's our duty to help women understand that no hero is going to swoop in on a white horse and change their lives.

There are three of us, each scheduled to blog at least twice a week. I usually take Tuesdays and Thursdays, since those are big TV days. Livy O'Neal takes the weekends, when her kids are with their dad. Our third teammate, Essence Johnson, is in college. She blogs at random, but her posts usually come between midnight and 3 A.M. Livy lives in Dublin and Essence is in Boulder. Long live the Internet.

We all take our blogging seriously, and it requires a lot of typing, so it's no wonder that I woke up exhausted on Wednesday morning. Hitting the snooze button didn't help—not the first time, the second, or the third. By the time I rolled out of bed, I was already half an hour behind schedule. As a paralegal in a law office, I couldn't wear sweats to work. I threw on one of my legal-eagle uniforms (black dress pants, low-heeled black shoes, and one of the tailored button-down shirts my mom gave me for my last birthday). In an outfit like that, I was always professional and unremarkable—just the way I liked it. I raced out the door, skipping my usual peanut butter toast and calling out my good-byes to Zephyr.

My tiny apartment in Burbank cost me a fortune, but it was worth it most days because I could take the bus into the city and sink into a good book on my way to work. That day, being late, I had to drive. Naturally, the Ventura Freeway was clogged with its usual dose of Los Angeles morning traffic, and the 405 was even worse. Peering up at the haze overhead, I could almost feel the nastiness pouring out of my exhaust pipe, adding to the smog that cloaked the city. As I drummed the wheel, I stared at the back of a bus, which was plastered with a giant *Love Dog* banner. MEET THE DOG WHO MENDS BROKEN HEARTS, it said in garish pink letters. Curse that Apollo and his cute furry face. And double-curse pretty-boy Mason Hall for putting his face on a bus that was making me even later.

As I turned off onto Wilshire Boulevard, I tilted my chin purposefully to the right, so I wouldn't have to look at the mass of white high-rises to the left that was

UCLA. Deep in that maze of roads and higher learning stood the building where Richard, my onetime fiancé, worked. As a matter of fact, that was where Richard had proposed, at a little café with wire chairs and wobbly tables. Richard was probably at work already, invigorated by his new research grant. Damn him.

I wrenched my thoughts away from Richard and back to my upcoming day. I knew from experience that letting myself dwell too much on Richard was a recipe for disaster. I'd start by dusting off all my old injuries—the breakup, the canceled wedding, the humiliation—then I'd move on to long, imaginary shouting sessions that started with "Ten Reasons Why You're Such an Ass," and ended with "Horrible, Disgusting Things That Should Happen to You." My face would turn red, my skin would grow hot, and I'd spend the rest of the day in a bright, angry haze.

Instead, I turned my mind to my job. A job I hated. I'd have given just about anything to be able to quit this life-draining job and write instead. I'd write anything—everything—fiction, nonfiction, memoirs, song lyrics, advertising jingles, whatever people would pay me for. I wasn't picky. I was just tired of the recycled-air stuffiness of legal work.

After I found a parking place, I dashed up the block, through the doors, and into the elevator, my heart jumping. The problem with getting up late is that you wind up feeling late all day, even when you're right on time. I was still breathing quickly as I scarfed a bran muffin and settled in at my desk. My pulse was still racing as I sped through my e-mails two hours later. I jumped when my phone rang. And when Gene Camp, the managing partner, appeared at my door at 1:30, I nearly had a heart attack.

"Debbie's sick," Gene said. "Join us for the Stone-street arbitration hearing. I could use you to handle the paperwork. The arbitrator's a retired judge—he likes to keep us on our toes."

I jumped up, pulled on the black blazer I kept hanging on the back of my door, snatched my bag, and followed Gene into the hall. Together we speedwalked to the elevator. Gene's arms were loaded with files, so I took half of them from him. As we waited, he gave me a long look, as if he was trying to remember who I was.

We hit the ground floor and hurried three-quarters of a block to the Pitts Building, the site of the day's mediation. The bright sun made me sweat in my blazer as I struggled to keep up with Gene's pace. He always walked fast, wherever he went. Inside the Pitts Building, Gene led us up the stairs to the conference room, where I found a seat at the table, took charge of the massive accordion file that held most of the case documents, and tried not to look at the two people who were there to reach a divorce settlement.

Still, of course I looked.

Valerie Stonestreet, our client, sat on one side of the table opposite her soon-to-be ex-husband. Valerie, I knew from the file, was forty-seven, though she could pass for thirty-nine. Today, on the day of her divorce, she looked immaculate. Her pale hair fell in graceful waves, framing a face that was so beautifully made up it took a second glance to see the pain in her big, brown eyes. Love scars.

Of course, she came by her beauty skills naturally. Our client, the file told me, was an "independent stylist," an in-demand makeup artist who worked on a number of hit reality shows that were filmed in Burbank. I nearly snorted out loud when I saw *The Love Dog* on the list. If Valerie only knew what I'd been blogging about last night, she'd kick me off her legal team.

Valerie's ex-to-be was Donald Stonestreet, a Hollywood mogul who dressed the part. He wore a three-piece suit of dark navy blue that coordinated perfectly with his ice-gray tie. I wondered if Valerie had picked out the suit for him. Donald was a small guy, balding, but the suit made him look sharp and cool, like the king of the world.

As I looked at these two, visions swirled in my brain. I saw them coming home after a night out, arguing over his flirtations with the waitress. Or sitting across the table from one another on a Sunday morning, not saying a word. Back stories bloomed. In the space of a blink, they became characters, players in whatever scene I imagined for them. How I longed to shoo everyone out of the room so I could spend half an hour writing about their breakup. They could star in a short story. Or maybe a novel.

But I didn't have the luxury of stopping work to write. These two weren't characters in my fiction— they were real people in the middle of a divorce.

The hearing began, and it didn't take long for things to turn ugly. Gene Camp accused Donald of incurring debts that Valerie hadn't agreed to. His attorney shot back that the boat and Maserati were purchased within the scope of the marriage, so what Valerie knew or didn't know was irrelevant. The boat talk went on for nearly half an hour, then we took a short break.

"We'll get to her spousal support next," Gene said. "This is where you can expect some really wild shit to fly."

"It looks like we have plenty to fire back with," I said, nodding at the file. I hadn't had time to read the whole thing, but I'd seen plenty—his anger-management classes, her fertility treatments. His drunk driving arrest. Her depression.

Gene shook his head. "A marriage is a black box," he said as the judge came back into the room. "No one knows what really went on. The judge isn't interested in anything other than income and expenditures."

He sat back in his chair with the jaded look of a man who did this for a living. When we started again, things heated up quickly. Speaking in an overloud voice, Donald's attorney claimed Valerie didn't deserve spousal support because, "for two years during this five-year marriage, Ms. Stonestreet contributed nothing to the good of the household."

That made Gene Camp speak up.

"Nonsense. She maintained the household for the good of both parties. And during those years, the parties were trying to have a child. Clearly that endeavor was in the interest of both."

Our opponent leaned forward, his jacketed elbows resting on the tabletop. "My client maintains that during this time, the respondent abused him verbally and sometimes physically. He maintains that the house wasn't kept, meals weren't made, and that, quote, 'living with her was like living with a she-demon.' He's seeking an exception due to extreme emotional distress."

Valerie's face turned chalk-white under her makeup. I leaned closer to Gene Camp and whispered, "That's absurd!"

He glared at me to be quiet while the opposition

started listing dates and times of supposed abuse on Valerie's part. I grabbed the legal pad that sat in front of Gene and scribbled, *"Can't you stop this? Where's the proof? Hearsay!"*

He shot me a poisoned look. I was pushing him too far, I knew, but I couldn't help it. Valerie's face was a picture of agony. Even without hearing her say so, I could see exactly what had been going on. This was a made-up stunt to protect his precious money.

I felt the familiar angry haze sliding over my vision. Five years ago, Donald had probably pledged undying love to Valerie. *Together forever. Till death do us part.* Utter bullshit. This guy and Richard were two assholes of a kind.

Heat crowded into my face. I had to say something in her defense—in the defense of all women who found themselves in a position like this. It was so unjust. If I didn't speak up, I might explode. As an *Unvarnished* author, I had a duty to say something. Paralegals weren't supposed to make a peep—I knew that. *I should be smart, be still, and keep my big opinions to myself.*

This is me, not doing the smart thing.

"Your Honor," I said, raising my hand, "we have records to show that during those two years, it was the petitioner who sought anger-management treatment, not our client. Also, Ms. Stonestreet went through monthly cycles of hormone shots in an effort to get pregnant. Given the stress of the treatment and the trips to see fertility specialists all over the country, plus the addition of the hormones themselves, I think it's reasonable to expect some snappishness and irritability. I wonder if the petitioner can actually document any of this so-called abuse?"

Silence spread through the room. I might have been right—well, *of course* I was—but that didn't matter. Paralegals weren't supposed to speak up, ever. I'd just sunk my own battleship.

Gene Camp looked aghast. He reached over and took the accordion file that sat in front of me. Then he cleared his throat. Twice.

"I'm sorry, Your Honor. That won't happen again."

"See that it doesn't," huffed the judge. He turned back to the opposition.

Gene leaned toward me, his face red to the roots of his hair. "Get out," he whispered. "You're fired. I never want to see your face again."

Blood rushed to my head. "I—"

"I've never been so embarrassed in my life. There's a right way and a wrong way to present the facts, and your blurting has just bungled the whole case for us. You think the judge is going to listen to me now when I bring up the anger management? Do you know how powerful this judge is? He knows half the people in L.A. Don't even think of using us as a reference. In fact, don't think about working in law again. I won't have you shaming any other attorneys like this. Get out of here—don't come back."

*I*t's amazing the way your body continues to operate even after your brain has shut down. Somehow, I got up from that table, left the room, and stumbled down the hall to the ladies' room. Leaning over a sink, I gasped for breath. The room was a wheeling kaleidoscope of fluorescent lights, white enamel, and mutated reflections of my own face. I spun around and plunged into the nearest stall, where I dry heaved over the toilet.

That was it. I'd lost my job. I wasn't even sure why I'd done it, except that I couldn't help myself. *Besides,* I rationalized, *all I'd done was broken with stupid, arbitrary legal-world protocol.* How was it a firing offense to say something logical in a hearing? I wasn't in the military—following the chain of command wasn't a life-or-death issue in the legal profession. Why should it matter if I spoke up when my point was a perfectly good one?

I stood and pressed my head back against the stall's cold, metal wall. I'd embarrassed Gene Camp—that was why it mattered. His pride had been injured. I groaned out loud as hot tears started flowing out of my eyes. All these years I'd managed to stay invisible at work. I'd filed my paperwork, kept my head down, and held onto this job that I so desperately needed. And now, in the space of five seconds, I'd blown it all.

I started to sob in earnest. I can't even say how much toilet paper I went through, blowing my nose and mopping my eyes. When I finally breathed my last shaky breath, I felt as dried out as the Gobi desert.

Exhausted, I leaned my forehead against the wall and tried to get it together. I'd been standing like that for about five minutes when I heard the bathroom door swing open. Heels pattered against the floor, and I heard the unmistakable sound of someone else sobbing.

Taking a deep breath, I opened the door to my stall. Valerie Stonestreet stood over the sink just as I had, her hands braced on either side as she cried, bent over, air pouring out of her in thick rasps. I was about to sneak out and give her some privacy when she stared to hyperventilate.

"Hey there, shh," I said as I came up behind her and

put a hand on her shoulder. She spun around and fell into the hug I wasn't sure I had offered. "It's going to be okay," I said, letting her weep on my shoulder. "Everything's going to be okay. You'll see."

Valerie's breathing calmed. She sniffled, and I felt her shoulders relax. When she raised her head, I got her a tissue from the box on the counter and averted my eyes while she dried off her face.

"Thank you," she said, her nose stuffy. "I wanted to be tougher than that. I swore I wouldn't cry today. But—I just loved him so much."

I nodded because it seemed like the appropriate thing to do. Inside, though, my heart was screaming *Why? You're a smart and beautiful woman—why would you bind yourself to that scumbag in the name of love?*

"I should have protected myself better," she said.

This time I nodded with real gusto.

"Well, I've learned my lesson now. I won't walk into that trap again. No more type-A dickheads for me. The bastard."

Valerie blew her nose and got a fresh tissue from the box. She looked at me for the first time. "I really appreciate what you did in there. You stood up for me a hell of a lot better than dickhead Gene Camp. I hope you didn't get in too much trouble."

I started to shake my head no, so she wouldn't feel bad. But then I stopped. I just didn't have the heart to lie about it.

"Oh my God," she said, watching my fallen face. Mascara runs had made black tracks under her eyes. "You did. You did get in trouble. You've been crying, haven't you? Did that bastard fire you?"

I nodded slowly. "I shouldn't have spoken up. It isn't

my role. I'm just a paralegal." *Was* just a paralegal. Now I was nothing, nothing at all.

"No! Oh, no—it's all my fault!"

"Of course not," I said firmly, resting my hand on the arm of her jacket. "It was mine. All mine. I knew I wasn't supposed to speak up. It's no one's fault but mine."

"But you were doing it to help me . . ." Her voice trailed off. She leaned against the sink again and was quiet for a minute, then she looked up, straight at me, as if she was seeing me through new eyes. "When I first saw you in there, I thought you were lucky, you know? You're above all this—men, makeup, having a ring on your finger. Trying to look good for someone else. Good for you, that's what I thought. Trying to look pretty is a loser's game. It's all pointless anyway."

She bent to blow her nose again, while I stood there, stunned. Above looking good? Beyond trying to look pretty? My eyes flashed on my reflection in the mirror, and I shuddered. I looked like a tomboy who'd had to put on go-to-work clothes. Everything about me looked sexless and drab. Cropped hair, a boxy jacket, shapeless pants. No jewelry. No makeup. I was all function and no form.

Valerie sighed heavily and leaned against the counter. She caught me looking at myself and ran a critical eye across my face.

"But you're really quite pretty," she said. "Too pretty for those boring clothes. And way too nice to be a paralegal for a dickhead divorce firm." She fished a card out of her purse. "I'm an image consultant. Looking good is what I do. If you're thinking about a change, give me a call. Really. It'd be good for your job hunt. You'd get a new look, new confidence. Plus, to be honest, a new client would be a nice distraction for me right now. I'd do it—what do you legal people say? Pro bono." She gave me a weak smile. "Let me do this for you, okay? So you can start your new life. I'm starting one—we might as well help each other out."

When I reached the parking garage, I dumped the cardboard box that held my work life into the back-seat, climbed in behind the wheel, and sat with my head in my hands for a long, long time. What was I going to do? I wasn't rich. I'd been saving as much as I could, but between rent, groceries, and my gigantic student loan payments, I couldn't make it more than a few months. What if something happened to my car? Would I be able to pay for my own health insurance? What about Zephyr's next trip to the vet?

I was working myself into a nice bit of hysteria when I decided to use a lifeline and call my mother. The cell coverage in the parking garage was nonexistent, so I started the engine, put my headset on, and started driving as I told my phone what to do. Within thirty seconds, Mom was on the phone.

"Hi, sweetie, what's up?"

"Hey, Mom. What are you doing? You sound out of breath."

"Just taking some hay and sawdust into the Schroom Room. We're getting ready to start a new colony."

"Why isn't Tim helping you?" Tim was my mom's second husband, a retired fitness-club owner who usually spent his days following Mom around the house, getting underfoot.

She made an exasperated sound. "I sent him outside to work the aloe bed. He's been driving me crazy. Did I tell you he wants to get bees now? As if the goat and the hens aren't enough. You know, we'll never be able to go on vacation at this rate."

I rolled my eyes. Mom could complain all she wanted, but I knew she was just as much into their home farming experiment as Tim. She was the one with the quarter-acre herb garden. And now they were growing mushrooms. Next they'd probably try hydroponic peanuts.

"Sometimes I think your stepfather is trying to drive me into an early grave. Do you know he had his buddies over here all night last night, down in his man cave? I think one of them was smoking pot."

It always meant big trouble when she referred to Tim as "your stepfather." I knew better than to take Mom deeper into this conversation. I'd had about enough of other people's bad relationships for one day, and once I opened that door, Mom would give me a list of Tim's flaws that was so long it would seem as if she made things up just to keep me listening.

"A really bad thing happened to me today, Mom," I said, trying to get her attention off Tim's pot-smoking friend. "I lost my job."

"You what? Wait, I can't hear—this stupid machine. Did you say you lost your job?"

I told her all about it, this time with details. "I was really stupid, Mom. I can't believe I spoke up like that. In a hearing, of all places. I know better!"

"Oh, but, sweetie, you were defending the client— how can they fire you for that?"

I spent a few minutes trying to make Mom understand the hierarchy of the legal world. At the end, she just sputtered. "Sam, you were doing the noble thing. I don't care what's expected and what isn't. I think you should be proud."

Aw, how nice. That was my mom. She might not understand how the business world worked, but she was always ready to put a positive spin on things for me. And, to be honest, she did make me feel better.

I breathed out a heavy exhale. "I'll have to go home and come up with a plan for something new to do. I need to find some work right away. But it's scary, Mom!"

"Of course it is, sweetheart. Times of growth are always scary. But this is your big chance to find out what color your parachute really is. I never thought your work at the firm really fulfilled you. This is an opportunity. Are you still writing short stories?"

"Sure," I said, faking nonchalance.

"Well, maybe you could sell some of those. Just send them out and see what happens."

I shook my head and stared blankly at the taillights of the car ahead of me. Just send them out and see what happens. As if it were that easy. As if I hadn't sent each of my three best stories to more than twenty magazines. And what did I have to show for it? Sixty-plus rejection letters. I had a new story out making the rounds right now, one that had only been rejected five times.

"You just have to be tough and be brave," Mom was saying. "It'll all work out for the best. You'll see."

I nodded, but inside, I didn't believe a word she said. This was a nightmare. An absolute nightmare. I had to believe Gene Camp was as good as his word when it came to blackballing me in the legal world. I couldn't ask him for a reference, and without it I surely couldn't get another paralegal job. "If I can't find something soon, I'll probably end up crashing on your couch, Mom."

When she laughed, I detected only a trace of nervousness. "Don't worry, Sam. You can do anything you put your mind to—you always have. And here, I tell you what. If I kick Tim out of the house, you can come live in his man cave."

That evening, I sat down at my computer with a cup of lemon tea and logged into our blog, *Unvarnished*. The masthead showed a paper heart torn in two next to a photo of a woman eating chocolates out of a heart-shaped box. I responded to the comments about my *Love Dog* post and read the three paragraphs Essence had put up on the new study that showed physical desire really does cloud our brains.

Then, after stretching my arms and rubbing Zephyr's ears, I opened my work in progress, a short story about a girl on a Montana farm who rescues a wild colt. Even though she dreamed of keeping it as a pet, of turning it into the beautiful mare that would impress her father and sniping sister, she decided to send it back to its herd. Soon my mind was filled with the scent of sagebrush, and the Montana night air seemed so real, I could almost feel its chill on my face.

—4—

🦴 *Apollo*

I knew it was morning because I heard the sound of car motors outside the building. I jumped to my feet, hid my rope under my blanket, and waited, my ears alert to the sounds of the studio waking up. Someone heavy, wearing boots, walked down the hall outside. The pipes groaned and whooshed overhead. I heard the *beep-beep-beep* of the little yellow cart that hauls the garbage away, and that's how I knew it was Friday. Garbage day number two. We had two garbage days, Tuesday and Friday. Friday was the worst day of the week, because at the end of Friday's workday, Lucas took me back to his ranch.

The thought of going *there* made me creep farther into my crate and I had to shake myself to calm down. That was hours away. In the meantime, I had a full day of work ahead of me. A million wonderful things could happen between now and the time I got into Lucas's truck. Mason might even touch me again.

Lucas said nothing when he came for me. He hardly looked at me, only busied himself with latching the leash to my collar. I was relieved that his metallic smell was faint, but troubled by the fact that he smelled like his ranch, the way he always did in the mornings. He also smelled of cigarettes.

As we sped down the hall, I distracted myself by listening to the sound of the vehicles pulling up outside. A small rattly car. A truck. A growly sports car. A heavy four-door. I liked to guess which crew member arrived in what vehicle. I assumed Mason drove my favorite, a Jeep that always played music as it pulled into the lot.

We stepped outside to the area where I relieved myself, and I went about my business. My area was lined with gravel and walled in with cinder blocks. I was the only one who ever relieved myself there, so there wasn't much sport in peeing. I covered my own spots, consoling myself with the idea that if another dog *did* ever come here, my markings would stand out like neon signs.

I ate a quick breakfast, had a fish-oil pill for my coat, and stood still while Lucas brushed my teeth. Then I did one of my favorite tasks, trotting on my treadmill while Lucas went away to smoke another cigarette. He came back smelling strongly, with a cup of coffee in his hand. He slurped from the cup as he brushed my hair, yanking through the snarls. I flinched and had to squeeze my eyes shut, but I didn't object. Instead, I turned my thoughts to chili dogs.

When Lucas straightened and put the brushes away, I started wagging because I knew what was coming next. We were going to walk among the crew! Lucas held my leash high and tight above my head, and I followed close behind him as we headed down another hall. My heart doubled its beat when I saw my first pair of jeans approaching. Just as we passed the jeans, I lunged, dragging in air through my nose, praying for a whiff—but I got nothing. Lucas yanked me back into place behind his heels, and we moved on. Seconds later, I saw a pair of khakis. Even though my paws were twitching with anticipation, I made myself wait until the khakis were right beside me before I arched my back, leaning in their direction. I pulled in all the air my lungs could hold.

Aha! A musky smell, like old tennis shoes. And a very faint smell of some small, furry animal. Plus wood shavings. A rodent, maybe.

On we went. At every pair of legs, I leaned as close as I could and breathed so deeply I thought my lungs would pop. It was a good day. I collected mysterious, incredible smells like car grease, peanut butter, baby powder, and lipstick. A host of wonders.

In time we arrived at the little corner to the side of the set where Lucas and I usually worked. He had me practice walking up to the smallest chair on stage and sitting down, facing the camera. I learned to put my paw in Lucas's hand when he held a treat that smelled like liver. I practiced sitting on my haunches and waving both paws in the air. This was my work, and I tried to take it very seriously. Even when a cameraman walked by with wet grass stuck to his shoes. Even when I saw Mason standing in front of the stage, talking with the crew.

Minutes later, Lucas stopped me in the middle of my paw-waving work and tugged me in close to his heels. I looked around, wondering what was going on, and was delighted to see Mason coming toward us. He always walked with purpose, as if he knew what he was after. He came closer and stopped right in front of us. I looked up at his face, a million miles up, and felt a cold loneliness wash over my belly. If only he would reach down and rub it.

Instead, he spoke with Lucas. I did my best to look serious—tongue in, ears alert. I knew I was well groomed, so that was a relief. Sometimes, when Lucas's frustration and metallic smell were so strong I could barely stand it, I sent him love by remembering how kind he was to brush my coat and keep me looking clean. I wouldn't have my job if my fur didn't flow behind me like a curtain. And I would be nothing without my work.

I still remembered the day we first came to the studio, when Lucas and I walked down the long hall into Mason's office. I sat on the floor while Mason and Lucas talked. Then, while Lucas scratched with a pen at Mason's desk, Mason crouched down beside me. He looked into my eyes—straight in, the way Kim used to do.

"You have important work to do here," he said. His voice was so hushed I could feel his words echoing in my heart. I didn't always understand what people were saying, but Mason's meaning was as clear as a bark on a still night. "Beginning today, you are the Love Dog. Your mission is to help people find love. You'll have the power to change their lives. Can you do that?"

The Love Dog. I thought about this while Mason waited, sitting quietly. Love had always made me happy. I loved a lot of things: Kim, Lucas, walks, cheese. Salami. If I could help people find new loves, loves as powerful as my love of cheese, that *would* make their lives better. That would be a real gift. And I could do it. Me, Apollo.

I was honored. I told Mason so by licking his face.

"Good," he said, rubbing my ears. "Then the Love Dog you are. You're going to be great at it."

Almost every time I saw Mason, I thought of that day, and it made me stand a little taller. That day, I also stood taller because I detected a whiff of chocolate coming from Mason's pocket. M&M's, to be specific.

"How's it going?" Mason was talking to Lucas. The words floated over my head in a muddled clump, but I understood Mason's stance and the way his eyebrows lifted. There was a faint disarming smile. This was an alpha dog checking in with one of his officers.

Lucas shrugged, which made me shift on my feet. He didn't look at Mason, and I had the feeling that he wasn't giving our boss the full respect he deserved.

"Okay. Fine," Lucas said. "But there's something I wanted to tell you. You know Apollo isn't my only property." Mason nodded, and Lucas kept talking. "Well, I've been getting other calls, for some of my other dogs. And my chimp. Calls from movies, offering a lot more than Apollo's making. I gotta tell you—either you pay me more, or you're going to have to find help for me with Apollo. It just isn't worth my time being here anymore. Not full time. If the chimp gets called to do a movie, I have to go, to train him."

Mason's reaction was subtle—I would have missed it if I hadn't been watching. But he stiffened just a tiny bit. Straightened his spine and reset his jaw. He glanced up and down Lucas's face with an expression I couldn't quite understand. Then he surprised me by reaching down to stroke the top of my head. I closed my eyes, absorbing the feeling of his fingers on my skull. I exhaled slowly, carefully, afraid I'd frighten him away. But instead of leaving, he crouched down in front of me and moved his hands to my ears.

I could barely hear—his fingers made a sound like blowing wind in my ears—but I'm pretty sure he looked up at Lucas and said, "Apollo's a great dog. We all love him around here. And I think it's obvious that he's critical to the success of the show. He *is* the Love Dog. I'm sure you remember, too, that both you and he are under contract for the full season—Apollo as the talent and you as the trainer. We need you to teach him the skills for each show."

Mason straightened up. "But if you have other commitments, we should work something out. Maybe the show could hire a handler for him, someone to take care of the little stuff. Walking him, brushing him, taking him out to pee. Then you could just come in to train him, nothing else. Or," he said, giving Lucas a level look, "you could find us another trainer who would do the job as well as you do." He bent down and touched my ear again.

I leaned against his left hand and lost all sense of sound. All I could feel was the exquisite glory of Mason's hand rubbing that deep, impenetrable spot where my ear constantly itched. Itched so badly I didn't even know it was bothering me most of the time, but it was always there, like a hunger. And Mason, *Mason,* our great leader, was tending to it for me!

I think Mason and Lucas continued to talk, but I was oblivious to everything except the cooling sensation deep in my ear. Metallic tension wafted off Lucas's arm, but I blocked it out, focusing on nothing but the relief in my head. Until, that is, a small woman ran up to us and Mason stopped what he was doing.

She was shorter than most, and at first I thought there was something wrong with her face until I realized she was wearing a headset that sank into her black curls.

"There you are!" I was glad to see that she addressed Mason immediately, showing proper deference to the alpha. "Everyone's gathered for the morning meeting." She was slightly out of breath. Whatever she was saying seemed extremely important. I stood up in case I might be needed. Was it an emergency? Did anyone need to relieve themselves? Because I could show them right to the place for that kind of business.

"I'll be right there, Rebecca." Mason smiled at her kindly, and I was struck by the differences in their body language. She was bright-faced and eager to please, while Mason looked patient, like a leader dealing with a particularly excitable pack member. He looked at her the way he looked at me, with extreme kindness. When she looked at him, she reminded me of myself, wagging my tail at the big boss man. This Rebecca and I had a lot in common.

I stared at Mason and Rebecca for a long moment. There was energy between them—I could feel it. Was this love? I usually sensed it right away when the spark of love flew anywhere near me, but my fascination with Mason might be clouding my judgment. *Should they be my next project? Should I be helping them come closer together?*

I never got my answer because Mason and Rebecca suddenly turned together and left, and Lucas and I went back to our practice. Later in the day we took a break while Lucas had lunch (I lay down on the gravel in my area), and then we filmed some short segments that didn't involve any cast members. Toward the end of the day, Rebecca returned with two new people.

"This is Cara and Tyshawn," she said to Lucas, motioning to the pair of people before me. I wagged—it's always polite to wag when you meet someone. The man crouched down and tried to pet me, but Lucas jerked me back into the heel position.

"He's a working dog. Giving him attention will ruin him—it'll undo the training we've been practicing all morning." Lucas had his legs apart, chest out. I noticed he never stood this way when he talked with Mason. He did with nearly everyone else, though—like a dog who wants to show his dominance by putting his chin on other dogs' shoulders.

The new people took a step back.

"Well." Rebecca went behind them and clapped a hand on their shoulders. "They're our couple for the week, so start thinking those love thoughts!"

All the humans laughed. The two new people leaned in toward each other and made fake kissing noises. It was revolting. My stomach clenched, feeling sick. There was absolutely no love here. This fake love felt childish and pointless—and the way the people laughed made me feel like they were all agreeing to be in on the same lie. Were they lying to Mason? To the rest of the crew? Should I let him know?

These people were the new guests, I knew that much. And I also knew that for as long as I was near them they would make me sick. They'd act out their fake love while we were onstage with Mason, and I'd get that terrible feeling in my belly, the same one I got when Lucas shouted at me. I looked down at the floor and tried to ignore them. I wasn't sure which was worse—enduring these two with their pretend kisses or spending the night at Lucas's ranch, locked in a kennel in a place that love never touched.

Samantha

The sound of the phone ringing startled me so deeply I felt as if my heart had just been jump-started.

For the past forty-eight hours, my apartment had been silent. Except for the rumply sounds of Zephyr purring or my fingers clacking on the keyboard, I'd been living the hushed existence of a researcher at an Antarctic station. I'd cooked, I'd eaten, I'd slept. Once I went out to buy chocolate soy milk and ginger snaps. Then I came home, devoured them all, and was too ashamed to go out again.

I'd never been fired before. I'd hunted for jobs, of course—after college I worked as a barista at a coffee shop for five months before I got my first paralegal job. And I'd put a lot of time into the search that led me to Camp and Donahue. But I'd never been cut loose without a safety net, not like this. And I'd certainly never been blackballed from an entire industry. In general, I wasn't a rule breaker. But here I was, enduring the fallout from breaking a major tenet of the paralegal's code.

Zephyr walked across my keyboard, demanding attention. I ran my hand down her back and along her fluffy tail.

"Zeph, why can't my life be as simple as yours?" I sighed and made myself click one more time onto LoveMyJob.com. Immediately, a nauseous feeling boiled up in my stomach. I sat back and pressed my fingers against my temples. The night before, in a bleary-eyed haze, I'd actually applied for a job at *Enchanté* magazine. The only problem was that *Enchanté* would never hire me. That was an absolute dream position—nothing I had any chance of getting.

Zephyr turned her head and slid her cheek along my nose, marking me. "Mm-hmm, that'll help. Now that I'm clearly marked as yours, I'm sure the job hunting will be a snap. Thanks, baby."

I stared at the LoveMyJob home page until my head started to hurt, but I couldn't get myself to click further. Even offering myself a cookie bribe didn't work. When Zephyr swished her tail in my face, I caved and clicked back to *Unvarnished*. At least blogging was something I could get myself to do.

*T*wo weeks later, everything was exactly the same. I still had no job. I still had rent to pay, and an electric bill, and health insurance. The feelers were out there—I'd sent out résumés each day—but the net result was a big zero. Worse still, I'd already applied for everything that made even remote sense. Now I was down to things I wasn't really qualified for.

To distract my mind, I worked on *Unvarnished*. Livy and Essence were happy to let me take on a few extra posts, and they also kindly left all the mail to me. I'd just finished answering our latest string of comments when Zephyr meowed, asking me to throw her crinkle-ball. After a few minutes of play, I pulled my bathrobe tighter and went down to check the mail. A trek to the mailbox was an awfully adventurous step for someone in my state of hermitage, but it was also the only way to get a new Sudoku puzzle. Some things required sacrifice.

Back inside, I flopped on the couch and sorted through the pile of envelopes. There were four letters from charities I'd supported in the past (no more of that for now!), a letter from my college inviting me to socialize with the Burbank Alumni Club at a local bookstore, three envelopes from literary magazines, and my credit card bill. Great. I held the magazine envelopes in one hand and my credit card bill in the other. Surely there was some good news here somewhere. I squeezed my eyes shut and tore open the three from the magazines. *Dear author, I regret to inform you that while I enjoyed your story, "Goodbye to Love," it just isn't right for our publication . . .* I sighed. More rejections for my pile. They said that every no was bringing me closer to yes. I wondered if that was really true.

I sat still on the couch for a long minute before I turned to the credit card bill. Finally, I bit my lip, ripped open the envelope, and unfolded the bill.

My face turned cold. Then my neck froze, and my armpits, and something near my duodenum. Then the skin on my face became fiery hot. Gripping the paper in both hands, I scanned the list of charges to see what absurd fraud had made my balance so high. My eye ticked down the list—groceries, normal. Phone bill, normal.

There it was. Sitting there in all its glory—my latest student loan payment. Thanks to my great job at the law firm, I hadn't ever consolidated—I'd been happy to make larger payments and work down the principal faster. Now I was about to pay the consequences. Between rent and these payments, my savings were shrinking fast.

I started to cry. I could manage one more month, maybe two in my apartment without a job before I freaked out and did something drastic. The future loomed before me, and it was carpeted in brown shag. I was going to have to move in with Mom and Tim. The man cave was about to become my new home.

After a while, I got up, shook myself off, and headed for the bathroom. I ran a bath, stepped in, and cried some more. My solitude suddenly terrified me. I was totally alone—I could die in this apartment, student loans unpaid, and no one would know for weeks.

I'd started to howl—crying can really get out of hand when no one can hear you—when I thought I heard a noise. A ringing noise. I wiped at my face with my wet hand and listened. What was it? What was that jarring sound? Aha, the phone! My phone! Another human was reaching out to me in my time of need! I bolted out of the bath so fast that a small tsunami splashed out onto the bath mat.

"Hello?" I pulled my towel closer as I dripped onto the kitchen floor.

"Hello, Ms. Novak?"

My heart sank. It was a telemarketer. I could tell by the hesitation in the man's voice. He wasn't a friend calling with a soup offer. He was a man sitting in a small cubicle with a three-foot-long sheet of phone numbers, all of which had to be called before he could go home and see his adorable baby daughter. And there I was, standing like a schmuck with all my hopes for human connection dripping into a puddle on the floor.

"Yes, this is she."

"Ms. Novak, I'm Vern Heller with the *Telltale*. We're an entertainment journal based in Hollywood. Maybe you've heard of us?"

Had I ever. My wet feet, which had been steaming

hot and now were turning to ice, began to itch. I'd seen the *Telltale* a thousand times at the checkout line in the grocery store. "Entertainment journal" was putting it generously—the *Telltale* was a tabloid, a gossip rag. They made their money off Botox gone bad and people who built ten-acre shrines to pigs.

"Sure," I said. "I know what the *Telltale* is."

"Great," Vern said. I pictured him—balding, wearing jeans and a sweatshirt. His office was probably heaping over with stacks of paper and old takeout boxes. "I wonder if you know that we're affiliated with *Enchanté*?" I stood stock still, waiting for him to explain. "They sent your résumé down to me. I take it you're looking for a writing job."

"Um, yeah, I am," I said. "But you're with the *Telltale*? Not *Enchanté*?"

"That's right. I'm an editor here, and I have to say that we were impressed with your résumé." *They were?* Instantly redressing Vern in khakis and a button-down shirt, I tidied up his office a little. "I checked out your blog, *Unvarnished*. That's some great stuff. Nice lot of followers, too. I was calling to ask if you might consider doing some pieces for us."

"For the *Telltale*." Never in my life had I pictured myself writing for a gossip magazine. But a job was a job, right?

"Look," Vern said, "why don't I tell you a little more about what we're looking for? We want to do a series on *The Love Dog,* exposing all of its dirty little secrets. I saw the posting you wrote after the last show. You said everything Apollo did seemed staged, and I think you're on to something. We want you to get all the dirt and let our readers see the show for what it really is."

Oh. Wow. "Um, this would be paid work?"

"Absolutely. We'd pay you our usual writer's fee, which is a per-word rate." He threw out some numbers. I fumbled for a pen and paper, still dripping wet. Zephyr ran in to see what the commotion was about and started twisting in and out between my ankles. While I scribbled, Vern kept talking. "We're looking for four submissions of twelve hundred words each. If you want your piece in Friday's edition, it has to be in to me by the Monday before. But the Friday before is better—that gives us more time. You can write them back to back or turn them in when you have something— whatever. Those pieces would be the minimum, but we could add some sidebars and companion articles if you're digging up good stuff."

I wrote those last words on my paper, *"digging up good stuff."*

"What would count as good stuff?" I asked.

"Oh, anything about how the show is preplanned, how Apollo doesn't really have anything to do with the outcome. And Mason Hall. Anything about Mason Hall will sell. Who he's dating, if he has any deadbeat relatives or a drug habit—that sort of thing."

Whoa. The hairs on my arms were standing up, and I wasn't sure it was just from being cold and wet. "A drug habit? Seriously, that's the kind of thing you'd want me to find out? I'm not sure I really feel comfortable getting into someone's personal life like that. I don't even know him. Our blog's really more of a cautionary voice, warning women about the perils of getting carried away with love and losing their heads. I'm not an investigative journalist."

But, a little voice whispered inside my head, *I am a writer.*

I started to shiver. My eye fell on my note paper, the one with the figures written on it. Three articles would pay a good chunk of that ugly credit card bill. Was I being an idiot? Hadn't I always said I'd be happy to do writing of any kind?

On the other end of the line, Vern took a slurp of coffee and spoke again. "The drug habit was just an example—we don't really expect you to get dirt like that. I mean, he'd have to *have* a habit for you to find out about it, right? We're just looking for anything about him. Mason Hall is an enigma in Hollywood. The only interviews he'll give are about the show—he never talks about himself. Anything you could do to paint a picture would sell. Even if you came back and said he dedicated all of his free time to helping kids with cerebral palsy, that would be something. Not as racy as a drug habit, of course, but something!" Another chuckle, another coffee slurp.

Well, okay, that sounded better. If I could expose someone as a good person, I wouldn't feel too bad. And I had no qualms about disclosing anything that was preplanned about the show. That was truth that should come out. A lot of women would benefit from knowing there was no magical dog who could fix their relationships. Including my own sister.

"But how am I going to find these things out?" I asked, wrapping my free arm around my middle. I was getting seriously cold. "None of the crew will talk about the show—I know. I've tried interviewing them for my blog."

"You'll just have to figure something out," Vern said cheerfully. "We won't start the series until you're ready, so you can take your time finding a source. Maybe a

past contestant or something. You'll work it out. Just
don't wait until the season's over. Tell you what—call
me when you're ready and we'll get you paid. Up front.
With a contract. Then all you have to do is deliver
your articles." He gave me his number, which I jotted
on my paper. "Look," he said, "I've read your stuff. I
know you're a serious writer and that you probably
never pictured yourself writing for a tabloid. But try
not to think of it that way. Our parent company,
NewsGroup, is one of the biggest publishers in the
U.S. If you establish yourself as a solid writer for us,
then you have a foot inside the door. It's way easier to
move up to, say, one of our magazines. We publish
Enchanté, Principles, Sixes. Or you could move to a
big-city paper—we run five of those."

"Really?" I could barely keep from drooling. Working at *Enchanté* would be more than a dream—it was
the biggest women's magazine in the country. And I'd
been reading *Principles* for years. I took a deep breath.
He had me. I would do this. A byline, payment, and the
potential to write for a bigger and better publication—
it was everything I wanted. Vern couldn't have sold
this better if he'd gotten my wish list straight from
Santa.

"Really. Writers get their start at the *Telltale* all the
time. From here, the sky's the limit. So, you are interested, right? And you won't take your story to anyone
else, will you? I need to get your word on that."

"Oh, yeah, I'm interested," I said quickly, visions of
credit card bills sparkling in my head. "And no, I won't
go to anyone else. If I can get what I need, the stories
will be yours. Let's have a verbal handshake on it, and
then we can work on getting everything in writing

later—after I find out what kind of information I can dig up."

A minute later, I was off the phone and sinking back into the bathtub, which felt nearly boiling to my frigid skin. *Well,* I thought, *that was a crazy turn of events.* Who would have thought someone would offer me the chance to be published—to be a writer? A paid writer. I dunked my hands in the bath and did a happy little wriggle. Zephyr came in, hopped onto the side of the tub, and demanded to lick warm water off the back of my hand.

A real, live, honest-to-goodness writing job. I leaned back and let the first wave of excitement crest over me. Amazing. Incredible. I was employable. In spite of all my fears to the contrary, I could be hired. I could support myself in this insane world.

And for writing! Someone actually wanted to pay me to write. Not be a paralegal or do anything remotely connected with a law firm or contracts or mediation. Someone wanted my creative product. They'd seen my blog, my labor of love, and had asked me to produce more for pay. Absolutely unbelievable.

I sank down and let the water swirl around my neck and up to my face. Zephyr was conducting one of her kitty science experiments, popping at the water and lifting it up on her paw, then shaking her paw so the droplets flew all over. I closed my eyes and thought about writing for a living, first at *Enchanté*, then at the *L.A. Times,* then at the *New Yorker*. What a dream. And it all started here, now, with turning my blog into articles for the *Telltale*.

But wait. My eyes flew open. Where was I supposed

to dig up dirt about *The Love Dog*? I didn't know anything more about it than any other viewer. To do this I'd have to find someone on the inside who was willing to spill the beans, something a person wasn't likely to do without a big cash offer. Or else I'd have to get myself inside somehow. And how would I do that? I didn't have any skills in television production. I wouldn't know a boom from a key grip. What was I going to do?

—5—

Apollo

I loved Mondays. Mondays were my favorite day of all. On Mondays, Saturday and Sunday were both over. The long weekend at Lucas's ranch was done. On Monday mornings, I'd ride in the back of Lucas's truck, secure in my crate, and think about the long, glorious hours to come. My work week stretched ahead like a trail through a forest filled with musty smells and colorful humans. I could frolic my way down the path, never thinking about having to go back *there*. At least not until Friday.

Lucas and I arrived at the studio early, before the sun had fully risen. He clipped a leash onto my collar and took me inside without a word, never stopping, as I did, to breathe in the miraculous concrete-and-human smell of the studio. It was like no other place on earth. My own hair still smelled of *there,* and if I bent down and caught a whiff of my feet, my stomach heaved, like I was about to lose my breakfast. So instead I raised my head and panted as I looked around at my beloved work zone. There—those were the banks of seats where people sat to watch us work! That over there—that was the door Mason and the crew came through when it was time to start filming! I saw the towering, skeletal frames of the cameras, the set with its comfy chairs, and the folding chairs where important people in headsets spent their time.

Soon, I told myself, *my fur will smell like this place.* Not like desperate, frightened dogs. Soon the crew would arrive and new, exciting odors would fill this room. Soon I would be asked to work again. Soon I would help someone fall in love.

*L*ater in the day, after my treadmill trot and two visits to my outdoor area, Lucas and I went to the place offstage where we rehearsed. Lucas wanted me to run through a flap in a piece of plywood. The flap swung open when my head pressed against it, then slammed shut behind my tail—but if I didn't move quickly enough, it would hit my back. I practiced it while Lucas held the door partway open and learned the speed I needed to make it through without injury, but every time the door closed, it became invisible again—just part of the solid wall. Facing that closed door, I lost my nerve. What if I ran at the wrong part and bashed my head? What if this time the flap didn't move? My nose—the second most important part of my body, after my belly—would take the brunt of the impact, and I knew from experience that it would sting for days. I wouldn't be able to sleep at night. And what if something happened to my sense of smell?

Lucas's metallic odor was growing stronger by the

minute, and he also had that yeasty smell he sometimes picked up at lunch when he left the set with a few of the sound guys.

"Come on," he muttered, "just do it! What's the problem?"

His words floated high above me in a cloud of gibberish, but I couldn't mistake his narrowed eyes and the disapproving set of his mouth. He was getting frustrated. I was going to have to be supremely brave and rush through, no matter what happened to my head.

Just then, a commotion on the other side of the set caught everyone's attention. The Dog Lady, one of the people I sent love to at night, had just entered, and my tail wagged faintly at the sight of her. I wondered if she knew I sent love flooding to her every evening?

Right behind the Dog Lady came a man, and behind him was a dog.

A dog. *A dog!* Unbelievable! I danced on all four feet, I was so excited. We'd never had a dog in here before!

I started to move toward the dog, wagging hard, but Lucas caught my leash and held me tight. "Oh, man," he said, his voice growly, "not a dog! What are they thinking? He'll never focus with another dog in here."

I lunged on my end of the leash, desperate to get to that dog. It was large, about my weight, but taller, with curly black hair all over its body. It had a sprightly, prancing way of moving that I found entrancing. But only one question burned in my mind—was it a male or female? Male? Or female? Which one was it? I stared hard, but none of the usual clues (head size, height, the glimpse of a private part) told me the answer. I had to know. If that dog left the set before I found out, I would regret it forever.

While the black dog skipped around, sniffing the set and meeting the crew, Lucas tugged on my leash.

"Come on, Apollo. We still have work to do. Come on, I can't go home until you get this." He jerked harder. The last thing I wanted to do was to keep working, but as I watched the Dog Lady petting the black dog, I considered the state of my relationship with Lucas. It was miserable. We fought and strained every day, no matter how hard I tried to understand what he wanted me to do. There weren't many things I could do to make things better between us—maybe this was one of them. If I was obedient now, maybe he would be happier.

With great reluctance, I turned away from watching the curly haired dog and came back to Lucas. "That's right. Good boy," he said. I sensed a grudging approval that made me satisfied with my decision. Really, it was a small sacrifice to make. There would be other dogs, right? Just because no dog had ever come on the set in the whole time I'd worked here didn't mean Curly Hair wasn't the first of many.

Lucas and I continued our work with the flap door, and eventually I noticed that a few of my hairs had clung to the front of the flap, marking the spot I was supposed to hit. Once I saw that, the work flowed. I lost my fear of the flap, Lucas relaxed, and we made progress.

"Okay," Lucas said, as he set the flap door up between the wings and the stage. "This time you'll go through it, onto the stage. You'll be like a football player busting through one of those paper signs." He always spoke like this when he was giving me direction, though I was never sure why. The words distracted me, and I always knew what he wanted from the props he held. For instance, it was clear from the way he set up the flap door that I should go through it, onto the stage. I lifted my tail high and gave it a nudge.

I burst out onto the stage, which was empty and dark. From there, I could see the whole room, from the side doors to the highest seats in the back. A cluster of people was gathered on the left, focused on something I couldn't see. Suddenly, in a burst, Curly Hair shot out of the crowd and raced straight for me.

The dog leaped the low steps onto the stage and came to an abrupt halt, right in front of my nose. A female! I could tell instantly, now that I was close enough. We sniffed noses, tails wagging, then I moved to her left so we could each check the other's gendered parts. A female in good health, not too old, who slept on a cedar bed. Or on a cedar floor. She let me sniff her parts for a decent interval, then she jumped away and spun her body so our shoulders were almost touching.

She smelled incredible. And not just because she had that warm, earthy doggishness that was like all the forces of life compounded into one super scent. More than that, Curly Hair smelled like grass and wind, like hot asphalt and chewing gum, and tennis balls. The outside world clung to her hair and body in little packets of wonder. I couldn't get enough of her.

We stood there wagging, locked in our own world . . . until I realized that the sounds I was hearing in the distance were people shouting. Lucas was shouting the loudest of all, and his tone was sharp and unkind. Suddenly, Dog Lady appeared and caught Curly Hair by the collar.

"Come on, Jasmine, you're not supposed to be up here. Come back down and let Apollo do his work. I know he's handsome, but his daddy doesn't want him to play right now."

I watched, panting with amazement. Dog Lady's manner was so gentle, so soft. She took Curly Hair away with a calm step, guiding her rather than pulling her. When they were off the stage, Dog Lady bent down, gathered Curly Hair's head in both hands, and kissed her on the bridge of her nose. That kiss left me gasping. I could feel traces of it shimmering around me, even though they were five or six steps away. This was a real kiss, made of real love—nothing like that distasteful fakeness I'd seen from Cara and Tyshawn.

The Dog Lady's friend came over to join them, and when he looked down at Curly Hair, his expression was so full of love a whimper escaped me. I'd never seen anything like this. I'd felt true love spilling out of my own heart a thousand times, but I'd never seen it from someone else—and certainly not for a dog.

My heart felt strangely swollen, and when Lucas called me, I found it hard to move in my usual way. I walked stiffly back to him and sat down, looking up at his face. I'd worked for Lucas for five years, and in that time he'd never once shown me a fraction of the love the Dog Lady gave Curly Hair. Not even back in the early days with Kim. I didn't think he was capable of that kind of feeling. Even Mason, who admired and respected me as a fellow professional, had never shared that level of emotion with me.

I sat there, looking up at Lucas, and felt a dangerous question bubbling up in my belly, the source of all true things.

Where was the love for me?

* * *

🖳 Samantha

I woke up the next morning, ready to get to work. The night before, I'd e-mailed Livy and Essence, letting them know about my opportunity to write for a print publication. They were fully supportive—Livy said she hoped my articles would give America the slap on the ass it needed. She loved pointing out the incongruity of our high divorce rate combined with the over-abundance of American dating websites.

After feeding Zephyr, I threw on shorts and a T-shirt and went to the corner store, where they sold every local paper available. I bought a copy of *Casting Call* and perched on a bench outside while I flipped anxiously through the pages. Overhead, palms swayed in the breeze. The rich scents of chorizo and quesadillas drifted down the street from Alejandro's Taco Cart, which was parked up the way.

I quickly found and thumbed through the advertisements for actors, voice artists, and dancers. Toward the back I hit pay dirt—the real jobs for nonactor types. This was where it listed the jobs with titles I didn't understand: the scenics, riggers, PAs, DPs, FCP editors, and sound mixers. None of that sounded like English to me. But I scanned for the words *Love Dog*, and after reading two incomprehensible listings for a line producer and a shooter, I hit solid gold. "The Love Dog *reality show, dog handler wanted*," it said. "*Calm, patient, experienced handler needed. Must have ability to focus in a hectic work environment. Extreme responsibility, willingness to learn on the job, and love of dogs a must.*"

There. I sat back against the bench and took a deep

breath. It wasn't the opening I'd expected—frankly, I didn't think they'd be hiring for the show at all. And if they did, I figured I'd have to sneak my way in as a gofer or an administrative assistant, should I be so lucky. But this was a job I could do. At least, I was pretty sure I could do it. I understood all the words in the ad, anyway.

I grabbed a quick breakfast burrito at the taco cart and headed back to my apartment, fueled by my discovery. I could do this. Sure, I might not be an "experienced" dog handler. But I was calm and patient most of the time, and I was determined to make this work. That had to count for a year or two of experience at least.

It took me a few minutes online to find the location of the *Love Dog* studio. Like many shows, it filmed right here in Burbank. Then I made myself wait until nearly lunchtime before driving to the studio—that was the only way I could spy on the people going in and out for their lunch breaks. I parked across the street from the entrance and trained my binoculars on the massive warehouselike building. After a while, the red-and-white striped gate lifted, and cars began to dribble out. I used the binoculars to spy on the occupants of each one, my heart sinking with each passing car.

These were mighty pretty people. Of course I couldn't tell if they were cast or crew, but some of them had to be crew, right? And all of the women looked, well, nicer than I did. They wore dangly earrings and pretty tops. I think I spotted lipstick. There was no way I'd fit into this crowd, not in my legal eagle uniform or at-home sweats. These people had polish. Yikes.

Back in my apartment, I paced the floor, waiting for my sister to pick up her cell phone.

"Cass—I need you! Call me back, okay? It's—don't laugh—it's a fashion emergency."

Online, I looked up do-it-yourself makeovers, but they confused me just as much as the job listings in *Casting Call* had. How could I make myself over when I didn't know how to use bronzer or lip liner in the first place? I didn't even know what undereye toner was. Where was the help for the totally clueless?

At last I gave up and went to work on my application and résumé. By the time I was finished, I'd decided what to do. I'd been planning to ask Valerie Stonestreet—the woman whose divorce had gotten me fired—to act as a reference. I didn't want to ask her for two favors at once, but it looked like I would have to. She was a makeup artist. If she was willing, she could put in a good word for me *and* make me fit in at *The Love Dog*.

I ran to my bag before I lost my nerve. Deep in the outside pocket, I found the card. Valerie Stonestreet had crossed out her former last name and written *"Martz"* above it. I held my breath as I dialed her number. Would she help me? Would she even remember who I was? She answered on the second ring.

"Hi, Ms. Martz? This is Samantha Novak. I was the paralegal at your divorce mediation?"

"You're who?"

My heart pounded in my throat. "Samantha Novak. We spoke in the bathroom, after the hearing?"

There was a long silence. I licked my lips and closed my eyes, praying that she'd remember me.

"After your divorce," I said. "In the bathroom."

"Oh, right. You're the one who got fired." She sounded distant, distracted, as if that day was the last one she wanted to remember. I felt terrible for dredging it up.

"Yes," I said quickly, "that's me. One and the same. Do you have a minute?"

"I guess so." It sounded like she was outside, walking. Seeing friends and having fun, no doubt. Living a life.

"Um, I'm sorry to do this, but I was actually calling to ask you for a favor. You mentioned that you work on *The Love Dog* and, uh, I'm applying for a job there. I wondered if you'd be willing to help me put together a look for the interview? You said you do makeovers sometimes . . ."

Valerie's voice brightened. "I do! I love doing them. Right, I remember you—in the boring legal work outfit. So you have an interview? Is it with Mason Hall?"

"Well," I said, swallowing hard, "I don't have an interview yet. But I'm working on it. I sending in my application today and I'm hopeful. I just don't think my boring legal outfit will cut it in the television industry."

Valerie snorted. Then she started to laugh. "Oh, you poor kid. If anyone deserves a makeover, it's you. Look, I really appreciated what you said at the hearing. You were the one bright spot in a shitty, shitty day. I'd be happy to make you over, and hey, maybe I can help get you an interview, too. Go get your calendar—let's make a date."

One week later, on the morning of the makeover, I woke up nervous. The few times Cassie had made me wear makeup, I'd felt like I had a plastic mask on my face. I didn't really want to be fussed over by a stranger.

And, frankly, I thought I looked okay. Not great, but okay. Sure, I didn't get a lot of praising glances, but who did?

"I just don't like being the center of attention," I told Zephyr, who purred loudly and tilted her head for better rubbing. But, I reminded myself, this was my calling. I owed it to all womankind—heck, humankind—to debunk this show. If doing that took me out of my comfort zone, so be it. Wearing makeup was a small sacrifice, after all. I'd already sent in my résumé and cover letter—prepping myself for the interview was the least I could do.

When Valerie's knock came at the door, Zephyr ran ahead of me to greet her. I opened the door and let Valerie in, trying not to be intimidated by her chic sense of style. She wore a bright white wrap top above a pair of perfectly fitting jeans. I'd never had a pair of jeans that hugged me that well.

"Great news," Valerie said as she came through the door. "I talked to Mason Hall. You have an interview Monday morning at nine. With him."

"What—you're kidding!" I was meeting Mason Hall? Me? Monday? I stared at her, stunned. "Wow, that's great—thank you. Thank you so much."

"I was happy to do it." Valerie gave me a warm smile and dropped two giant tote bags onto my couch. "I'm so excited to get started. I just love doing this." She was beaming, her skin glowing with health and happiness—the opposite of what I'd seen the day we met. "There's nothing more fun than giving advice."

An hour later, Valerie had turned my entire belief system upside down. Before she came, if you'd asked me to reach into my closet and pull out the outfit that suited me best, I'd have grabbed my navy blue suit, the one that hit just below the knee and looked so sharp with a white top.

Wrong, wrong, wrong, according to Valerie. "We all have either cool tones or warm ones underlying our skin. Yours are warm, which means you need to stick to warm colors. Taupe, tan, ivory. Yellow and orange. Deep rusts and tomato reds. I'm sorry, Samantha, but navy is just not your color."

To prove her point, she draped a swatch of navy cloth around my neck and then swapped it out for a piece of camel-colored fabric. "See? Your skin looks smooth and creamy. And your short hair is so dramatic with something at your neck."

I took a deep breath. Valerie had already impressed me with her skills. With her help, maybe I really could get this job. I had to get everything I could out of this process—I wouldn't get a chance like this again.

"Speaking of hair," I said, "what about mine?" We both looked in the mirror at my short tomboy haircut.

"I like it," she said, surprising me. "Why do you ask?"

"Well, my sister Cassie's always on me to grow it out. She thinks it looks unfeminine." That was minimizing things, actually. Cassie's exact words were, *You'll never get a date with boy hair like that.*

"No, I like it," Valerie said again. "A pixie cut's great on someone with delicate features like yours. Think how fabulous Halle Berry looks with short hair. Besides, your hair is so dark, and your skin so pale, it really draws attention to your eyes." She started patting my face with a light foundation that she swore would not harden into plastic.

"So," I said, "what's *The Love Dog* set like?"

Valerie shrugged. "Typical. Crowded, busy, too much going on. Everyone's always in a hurry, but that's normal for television. The cast is small, so the makeup work isn't much. Plus, Mason Hall's a cutie"—she grinned—"so that makes it easy work."

My stomach gave a lurch. Gorgeous people made me nervous. "What's he like to work with?"

Valerie chuckled. "Well, he's a kitten in the makeup chair, but almost everyone is. No one can afford to piss off the makeup person." She stepped back to scrutinize her work on my face, then got out her blush and started dusting my cheeks.

"What about Apollo? Have you ever met him?"

She shook her head. "Nope. His beauty is a hundred percent natural. He's absolutely amazing. Did you see the very first show, the one where they explain how Mason found him?"

"My sister saw it," I said. "They met on *Race of a Lifetime,* right?" *Race of a Lifetime* was the show that had made Mason Hall famous. It had been killed by scandal after the fifth season—someone found out that the winners were preselected by the show's producers. The whole thing had fizzled and died. But by then Mason was famous enough to have paparazzi follow him to the gym. His face was more familiar to America than the president's.

I'd seen *Race of a Lifetime* a few times. Couples went on the show and took part in all kinds of weird races—camel trots and land sailing, that sort of thing. Cassie watched the last season religiously. She said the finale involved a kind of race called land mushing, where people run through the woods while leashed to a dog. Apollo made his debut on that episode as the sled dog who was paired with the winning team.

"He was incredible on that show," Valerie said. "The winning couple had some kind of big fight right before the last race, and when they finished, they weren't speaking to each other. Even though they'd won half a million! They just sat there, side by side, not saying a thing. You could tell Mason was pretty miserable about it. I mean, how is that for a host, to have your winners act like they don't even give a shit?"

I shook my head, since I had no idea. Valerie went on.

"But then Apollo came running out of nowhere, right to them. He jumped up and started licking them on the face like crazy. Before you know it, they're laughing and trying to make him sit, but he won't, you know? He just keeps after them. Then the woman fell down and the guy helped her up, and Apollo was right there, nudging them closer together. And after they sat back down, he practically flattened them up against each other. It was genius. She reached over to straighten the guy's collar, and he fixed her hair, and seconds later they're kissing and making up. And it was all thanks to Apollo."

Right. "So everyone believes he's a magical love dog just because he licked these people?"

Valerie looked at me as if I'd just said the sun and moon didn't exist. "If you'd seen it, you'd get it. I bet you can find it online. They showed the clip on the first *Love Dog* episode. Just watch—you'll see what I mean. There was something almost—I don't know— metaphysical about it. Like he knew exactly what he was doing." We were both silent for a minute while she mulled over eye shadow shades. Once she'd settled

on a creamy peach color, she spoke up again. "Do you
have a background with dogs?"

I nodded. "I sure do," I said, trying hard not to
look like a liar. "I've done plenty of dog work over
the years. Volunteering with the Humane Society, fos-
tering dogs, that sort of thing." I exhaled through my
nose. I'd worked hard on my résumé, expanding a
little pet shelter volunteering into what looked like
paid experience. Just thinking about it made me
blush.

"That isn't what you've been doing lately, though,
is it?" Valerie said, deflating my limp balloon of confidence. "Maybe you should amp your dog experience
up a little more. Make it sound more impressive. I
mean, your legal background won't help you any here.
And this is Hollywood. There might be fifty out-of-
work actors applying for this one job."

When we finished, I felt as if I'd been through the
most grueling workout of my life. I was exhausted.
But I looked surprisingly good. Valerie dressed me in
one of my newly rediscovered outfits, jeans with a gold
cable-knit sweater that I'd thought screamed 1970s,
yet looked remarkably modern once I had it on. I
could tell I was wearing makeup, but only barely. Valerie picked out some gold hoop earrings my mom had
given me—a pair I'd never worn, even once—and just
like that, I looked pulled together. My world had just
been rocked.

"There, you look great!" Valerie smiled at me in the
mirror, fiddling with my hair and adjusting the sweater.
"Definitely ready for a job interview."

I blew out a loud breath. Getting the job wasn't

going to be easy, even with Valerie helping me to look the part. "I'm pretty nervous about it," I confessed. "I really, really want this job."

"Well, just be yourself. If you really want it, your integrity and honesty will shine through."

A dizzy feeling filled my head. Integrity. Honesty. Would Mason be able to tell that I was there to spy on the show? I'd never done anything like this before. I was nervous and excited at the same time, thinking about the first article I would get to write. Of course, I had to get through this interview first. Mason Hall. Just thinking about meeting him made the palms of my hands turn damp.

After I heaped my thanks on Valerie, she left me alone with my jittery nerves. I paced around the apartment, conducting my own Socratic interview in a panicky voice.

Logical Me: *What are you thinking?* Are you really going to interview with a Hollywood superstar? And ask for a job taking care of his top-dog talent?

Insane Me: Sure. Sure, I am. I adore dogs.

Logical Me: Dogs aren't the issue. Mason is. Do you think he'll be fooled? What if he asks why you want to work for *The Love Dog*?

Insane Me: I'll just have to lie. It'll be a little white lie, though—for the good of womankind. I'll say I think love is the greatest thing on earth and should be shared with as many people as possible. At the same time, in reality I'll be opening the eyes of thousands of women to the fact that *The Love Dog* is a bunch of scripted hooey.

Logical Me: Well, you make that sound noble. But aren't you really just going to be a spy? A Benedict Arnold?

Insane Me: Not at all. This is for a higher purpose. I'll be going undercover for a good cause, like . . . um. Like . . . Oh, come on—aren't there any famous double agents in history?

Logical Me: No. Because they were all put to death by the people they were spying on.

Insane Me: Whatever. This is my duty, my calling, whether I like it or not. I've undertaken this mission and I have to see it through. Even if it means taking risks. So there.

*L*ogical Me had nothing to say about that. I strode into the bathroom, head high, and checked on my face again. Yes, I still looked like myself, only better. Valerie had picked out a great interview outfit, and I was ready to go. I just needed to spend some time online brushing up on my dog-handling skills and I'd be all set.

*T*hat night, as I tossed and turned in bed, Insane Me forgot all her fine and lofty arguments. The nobility fell away from my plans, and I saw myself for what I was—another tabloid journalist going undercover for a story. For dirt—that was what Vern wanted, wasn't it? Dirt. Love affairs and drug addictions.

"I'm not going to give him that stuff," I muttered into my pillow. Zephyr, sleeping beside me, woke up and started licking her stomach. "Not unless I have to. I'm just going to write the best darned pieces I can about the show, so they'll want to give me more work. I'll make that honking credit card payment. And I'll show *The Love Dog* for what it is. It's all going to work out beautifully. And while I wait to do that, I'm just going to care for a dog. If I get hired. I'll take care of Apollo. He's a dog—I can handle that."

My weary brain swam with pictures of dogs I'd known and loved. Since I was three years old and Cassie walked me down the street to see Jackpot the Jack Russell terrier, I'd been a sworn dog person. "And cat person," I mumbled to Zephyr, who wasn't listening. An all-around animal person.

At last, as consciousness started to drift, my mind settled on one picture, one face. I sighed, pressing my face deeper into my pillow, and dreamed of a face covered in fur, with a long sloping nose and pointed ears. It wasn't until I woke up that I realized I'd been dreaming of Norah, our German shepherd whose face I hadn't seen in years.

−6−

⫶ Apollo

That night, I spent extra time sending my love out to Lucas. I was sleepy, but I made myself stay awake while I focused all the love I had inside and sent it across time and space to Lucas. When I was done, I dropped my head, exhausted, and let my chin rest on my rope.

After such a great outpouring of love, I thought I might notice a change in Lucas when he arrived in the morning. Maybe he would speak to me, I thought. Maybe he would touch my chest as he clipped the leash to my collar.

But he was exactly the same. He strode into my room, slamming the door behind him, and muttered to himself while he got my equipment ready. When my crate door opened, I came out, ready to get to work, my tail wagging. Lucas barely looked at me. He hooked my leash on without touching any part of me. If only he would bring me a peanut butter sandwich. Or a squeaky toy. Or a squeaky toy *made* of peanut butter sandwiches.

The day developed according to our routine. I had

my treadmill jog, my fish oil pill, and my brushing. We reviewed the tasks we'd practiced the day before, and then I sat down while Lucas read the newspaper.

Late in the morning, we walked down a hall (the one that sometimes smelled like pepperoni pizza) and arrived in a crowded room for our Wednesday meeting. At these meetings, everyone—editors, crew, producers, everyone—sat or stood and listened to Mason. It gave me such pride to see all those people standing quietly while Mason paced in the front of the room, speaking in a voice that everyone could hear. I could tell he was explaining something complicated by the way he waved his hands and pointed to different boards on the walls. Sometimes he called on someone in the crowd and they gave a short report. Wednesday meetings were my favorite.

Because of all this, I was wagging even before we entered the Wednesday meeting room. Lucas and I found room in the back. As I took a seat on the floor, I noticed something strange. A curious smell—or maybe it was just a tremor in the air—was wafting toward me from the crowd of legs in front of my face. The smell was deep and rich, like compost, and it swirled up into my nose, making me dizzy. I shifted from paw to paw and craned my neck, straining to sniff where it might be coming from. It was close—I could almost taste it when I licked my nose.

It felt like love.

No, no, more than love. It also felt like desire.

*T*wenty minutes into Mason's talk, I pinpointed the source of the smell. It was the young woman with the dark hair and clanky bracelets who sometimes brought Mason messages. Once she'd brought him a sandwich. She was in Mason's inner circle of colleagues, and I honored her for this.

The scent was so strong, I couldn't pay attention to Mason's speech. I couldn't even watch the way everyone in the room was listening to him, their faces pointed eagerly forward. Instead my nose and eyes were fixed on her, the one with the scent. Every few seconds I saw her raise her head an inch or two, slide her eyes to the side, and look across the room at someone else. My heart quickened. If the person she was looking at also had the scent of love, this could be the start of something phenomenal.

Mason continued to talk, I continued to sniff, and she continued to roll her eyes and dart looks at someone across the room. Then, suddenly, Mason clapped his hands once and everyone stood. People clogged the door. Lucas tried to lead me into the crush, but I hung back on the end of my leash, dallying until the dark-haired woman reached us. When she did, I squeezed up beside her and put my nose in her hand, making her bracelets clank.

She made a little noise of surprise and looked down. "Oh, Apollo! I didn't know you were there—you startled me." She laughed and patted my head. I grinned. We were now next to Lucas, shuffling slowly toward the door, caught in the sea of bodies.

"Apollo's such a sweet dog," she said to Lucas. Lucas nodded, then turned back to look forward at the heads in front of him. He glanced at his watch.

"I'd be happy to look after him if you ever needed," she said. "I know where his outside area is. I'd take good care of him."

I couldn't tell what she was saying, but I applauded

the way she was placating Lucas, speaking to him in that soft voice. If he didn't register the love that came from me, maybe kindness from another human would warm his heart. At first, though, he hardly seemed to notice her presence. He looked at his watch again and shuffled as far forward as he could get without pushing over the large man in front of him.

Then, in a rush, he turned to her, holding my leash in his open hand. "Are you serious? Want to take him now, for lunch hour? I'm supposed to go out with some of the sound guys and I'm gonna miss my ride if I don't go now."

"Uh, of course." She smiled, but she seemed surprised and a little flustered. I wondered what this exchange was about. Lucas put my leash into her hand and snaked away through the crowd, squeezing his way out the door. Her bracelets jangled as she lowered her hand, holding my leash.

She looked down at me, and I read a mix of things on her face: shock, amusement, irritation, chagrin. "I didn't really expect him to take me up on it *now*," she said. I wagged. She bent down. "I'm Pilar. It's nice to meet you, Apollo." More wagging from me. I wondered if she knew about her striking and unusual smell?

When we got out of the Wednesday meeting room, Pilar took me down a hall I'd never seen before. This one had a painted ceiling covering up the scary area where the pipes ran. Posters showing giant human faces lined the walls. The people who passed us said hello in cheery voices. A few even stopped to pat me on the head. I wanted to stop and sniff their pockets for mints or M&M's, but Pilar kept me walking.

She paused next to a door. "I just want to pop in here in minute. You don't mind, do you?" I wagged.

Her voice was so gentle, I loved hearing it. We entered the room, which smelled disgusting—of paint, plastic, chemicals, glue, and wood shavings. I wanted to haul Pilar out immediately, but she held onto my leash. And then, underneath all the scents, I detected something else. A wanting smell. Not exactly like Pilar's—this one was harsher, more intense, and not as well masked as hers was by the fake-vanilla perfume she wore.

Men of varying ages sat in this room, hunched over workbenches on high stools. They were each busy fiddling with something. Pilar took us up to the youngest man in the room.

"Hi A.J." Her voice grew even warmer, as if what I'd heard before had been her arctic winter voice. "I have Apollo with me. I thought he might like to see the props he'll be using this week."

A.J., who'd been watching us cross the room, stood up suddenly from his workbench and nearly toppled his stool over. An older man looked at him and rolled his eyes. A.J.'s face turned pink. He came around the bench, close to Pilar, stuffing his hands into his pockets.

"Sure, that's a great idea. Let me grab 'em. We can take 'em over to the prop table."

His tone sounded cooperative, but I could tell he was nervous. Sweating. He wore a sweatshirt, and I wondered if he would take it off to cool down, but he didn't. He didn't take off his baseball hat either, just grabbed three things off his workbench and followed us out the door.

"So," he said as we moved down the hall, "how'd you get Apollo?"

Pilar began to talk, but I stopped listening. Tone of voice offered me no clues with these two. They were far better at masking their voices than Lucas was. No, with these people scent was everything, and their scents were so fascinating, I was happy to keep my focus there. A.J.'s reminded me of some wet coffee grounds I'd found in a parking lot once. Pilar's made me think of the way my fur smelled when I'd fallen asleep in the sunshine. Together, they made a heady combination. No wonder they'd kept looking at each other during the Tuesday meeting when they should have been listening to Mason.

When we reached my practice area next to the stage, A.J. put the things on the table and then we all played a silly game in which they offered me the things, one by one, to sniff or bite. I pretended to, but this clearly wasn't a work activity. It was never my job to just examine a thing. Things were for taking and putting, or nosing, or pawing. Or occasionally eating. But only if someone brought me a treat—say a cookie or a piece of bacon—but these two hadn't. Their pockets were empty. I was relieved when they finally finished, but as they did, I noticed a strange uptick in tension. A.J.'s scent became almost overwhelmingly sharp, nearly sour. And Pilar's ran with a new, cold note.

"Well, I guess I should be getting back," A.J. said. He sounded reluctant, as if he was going to leave but didn't want to.

"Yeah, I guess I should, too. I have to eat lunch," said Pilar with the same tone of unwillingness.

I sat down. These two clearly needed my help. Sending thoughts to people is difficult, and it doesn't always work. Sending thoughts to two people at the same time is much, much harder. At least in this case, A.J. and Pilar seemed like they would be fairly receptive. Still, there was no denying the challenge.

I breathed in deeply through my mouth, then out through my nose. Letting my mouth pop open so I wouldn't get overheated, I focused all my energy on sending them this thought. *Ask*.

Ask. Ask. Ask.

I kept it up until I started to feel faint, then I shifted on my paws. A.J. and Pilar were looking at each other, each fiddling with a different thing from the prop table. Suddenly, they opened their mouths at the same time.

"Do you—"

"Would you like—"

They laughed and both turned pink. They had to look away from each other to the props in their hands. Pilar's bracelets slid down to her wrist. Then, with a burst of coffee-ground smell, A.J. set his thing on the table with a thud. "Hey, would you like to go out sometime? Maybe this Friday?"

Instantly, Pilar's scent bloomed with sweetness. She smiled, and I wagged furiously. "I'd love to. Thanks."

I let out my breath in a snort. At last! At last that sickly, tense smell was gone, siphoned off by the air ducts and doorways. Their new smell was heady and wonderful, salty and sweet at the same time, like kibble mixed with carrots. I felt dizzy. And proud. This was love, this was the smell and taste and look of true love, and I had helped. I wasn't just sending my own love out to others—I'd helped them come together and create more of it. More for the world to share. I was so giddy I thought I might fall over my own paws.

When Lucas came back to claim me, smelling of yeasty sugars and acting sharp and cold, I barely noticed. Long after A.J. and Pilar had gone, the memory of that smell stayed locked in my brain, like a treasure. I opened that treasure four times during the afternoon, and that night, as I lay with my rope after sending my love out into the world, I unlocked it again and let its goodness wash over me.

⌨ *Samantha*

At 8:50 on Monday morning, I paused in front of the heavy double doors, wiping my palms on my skirt. Somewhere in this cave of a building, I would find Mason Hall, and I was dreading that moment more than my next dentist appointment.

I stepped through the door into a rush of climate-controlled air. The lobby was sterile, with terra-cotta tiled floors and generic corporate paintings on the walls. The man at the check-in desk gave me service with a smile. When I told him I was meeting with Mason Hall, he whipped out a photocopied map and drew a thick red line on it connecting the lobby with Mason's office.

"I'll call and let him know you're on your way."

Oh, please don't, I couldn't help thinking. But I swallowed that thought and smiled instead. I was here to get a job, get the dirt, and get the truth. I couldn't wimp out. Thousands—no, millions—of women's lives would be changed for the better if I could see this through. Not to mention my own.

Map in hand, I headed through one set of double doors, then another, following a maze of tiled hallways, many of which featured framed posters of past reality shows. I spotted a number of old "friends," shows I'd trashed in my blog—*Call Me Cupid, Date of a Lifetime*, and one of my favorites, *Extreme Dating*, which was still running on cable. Even for a jaded viewer like me, there was something funny about watching people try to woo each other while dangling from a bungee cord.

As I walked down this gauntlet of falsified romance, I passed several clusters of chatty people wearing headsets and casual clothes. For once I felt sufficiently chic in the outfit Valerie had chosen for me—an apple-green twinset, black skirt, and the black boots from my legal uniform. I'd even managed to do my own makeup while Valerie's voice rang in my head, saying "Blend—really blend it all in. Come on, use your hands and get in there—don't be shy. It's *your* face!"

At the end of the hall, I slowed down, knowing from my map that I was nearing Mason's office. I could hear voices coming from inside, and as I got closer, I looked through the glass walls and saw five people leaning over a large desk, gesticulating about something. After a few minutes, someone behind the desk said something dictatorial-sounding that ended the conversation. Everyone gathered his things and left, filing out in front of me. *Great, I was about to interview with little Napoleon. Or big Napoleon,* I corrected myself, remembering that Mason was always the tallest man on the show. Unless he cast a whole lot of short people to make himself look tall? I was about to find out.

With my heart in my throat, I raised my fist and

knocked on the door. I could see Mason through the glass—I'd have known him anywhere. He waved me in.

I'd never met anyone as famous as Mason before. Sure, I'd run into a few actors who'd had small parts on a few shows, but no one with a regular gig like Mason. I'd looked him up on IMDB—from the time he hit Hollywood five years ago, he'd been working steadily, first as the host on the short-lived *Spin Doctor*, a show about radio DJs, then on *Race of a Lifetime*. His bio said he'd gotten his start with a radio show in college, and moved up to hosting pledge drives for his local PBS station. *The Love Dog* was the first project he'd produced. I guessed it was pretty special to him.

"Hi," he said as I slipped through the door, his eyes still on the paperwork in front of him. "You're Valerie's friend? Sabrina?"

"Samantha," I corrected, striding forward to shake his hand. Mason lifted his head, and I found myself pinned by a bright blue gaze. His eyes weren't this blue on television. I gulped, then took a breath. If there was one thing my years as a paralegal had taught me, it was how to act cool even when I was sweating.

I offered one hand, but he caught it in both of his and held it for a second. I felt a trill of panic. Was this some New Agey thing? Was he about to read my life line or check my chakras or something? I took a hasty glance around for meditation pillows and incense holders, but everything looked normal. Corporate. I didn't even see as much as a gong.

Once he let my hand go, I started to fish my résumé out of my bag. Mason watched me, then gestured to the couch and chairs in the far corner of the room. "Let's sit down over here for a minute," he said, aiming for a corduroy armchair. As he settled into his seat, I took the opportunity to get a really good look at him. He was one of the handsomest men on television, after all, and Cassie would kill me if she knew I'd gotten this close without admiring him.

Mason looked different than he did on camera. More . . . real, which struck me as a dumb thing to think, because of course this was real life and TV was TV. But still. In person he had laugh-crinkles around his eyes and a shaving scratch on his chin. His hair, which on camera was always gelled and worked in fifty subtle, artistic directions, just looked clean and flat in person, as if he were a normal man who washed his hair in the morning and nothing more. I was surprised.

I sat down on the middle of the couch opposite him and instantly regretted my seating choice. That couch must have been sat on, slept on, and jumped on by a few thousand angry gorillas—the center cushions gave away like a beanbag, leaving me feeling very short and very stuck.

"So, Valerie had a lot of great things to say about you," Mason said. He crossed his legs in that spread-out way men do, ankle over knee. "You made quite an impression on her."

"Well, she's really terrific," I said. Whew, I'd never felt so warm in my entire life. Why had Valerie thought a sweater set was a good thing to wear to an interview? I debated taking off the cardigan, but decided I would feel weirdly naked in the shell. "She's been so supportive. And she knew I really wanted to work here."

"Right, so she said." Mason smiled, a handsome quirky smile, and I felt all my defenses go up. Of all the types of men in the world, handsome ones were the worst. Somehow a good-looking face made women confuse hormones for love at about three hundred times the usual rate. Well, I was tougher than that. I gave him a cool look and dug in for my first big lie.

"I just love what this show does for people. It gives them such hope. And Apollo is amazing, the way he pulls people back together, as if it's a natural instinct for him."

"Well." Mason's smile faded by a few watts. "The show is more scripted than it probably looks on TV."

No kidding. There, Sam, I thought. *You've only been here five minutes and you've just found your first nugget of truth.* "Well, he clearly has a lot of love in his heart. It's obvious from the way he looks into the camera."

I was hoping another truth nugget would fall from Mason's lips, but it didn't. Instead he said, "Apollo's a very special dog. He's more than just a cast member. That's why I need the right person—a trustworthy, caring person—to take care of him. His health and well-being are extremely important."

"Right, to the show," I said, sure that was his point. With this corporate office and staff to boss around, Mason probably had his eyes firmly on the bottom line. That's what reality shows were, right? Cash cows.

"Not just to the show," he said. "To everyone. You'll understand better when you meet him. Apollo's one of a kind. He means a lot to me personally, and I won't let just anyone be his handler. That's why I wanted to do these interviews myself." I dropped my eyes and stared at my hands, hoping my real motives weren't obvious. Mason went on. "Apollo's an amazing dog.

Lucas, his trainer, owns him, but I like to think that we're all here to take care of him. We're his village, if you know what I mean. And you'd be taking care of him more than anyone. Your job would be to give Lucas a little more free time, and give Apollo more one-on-one time."

I looked up at Mason and caught him looking right back at me. As I swallowed and looked away, I squirreled away another nugget of truth. Mason liked Apollo. And he didn't just like him—he cared about him. That would make an interesting tidbit for the *Telltale*. Maybe this wasn't going to be as hard as I'd thought.

I was relieved when Mason took his eyes off me and got down to regular interview business. The résumé I'd sent him played up every dog-sitting job I'd ever had, making them sound more like dog-nanny positions than weekends I'd spent on a friend's couch, rubbing her golden retriever's tummy. I'd highlighted the time I spent volunteering for the Glendale Humane Society, walking dogs and brushing cats. And I'd crafted a personal statement that I thought was a masterpiece of gibberish. *My life's goal is to improve animals' lives and well-being by providing care, comfort, mental stimulation, and healthy activity. I'm seeking a job where I can make a difference to my coworkers and employer, and leave the world a better place in the process.*

"That's a noble goal," Mason said as he lowered the sheet of bond paper.

"And by working here, I can accomplish all of it at once," I said, trying to look starry-eyed. "I can enrich Apollo's life and help people at the same time by helping the show. The better able Apollo is to do his job, the more love he'll be able to spread in the world. And that's what it's all about, right?"

Right. I smiled broadly after I delivered this coup de grâce. If Mason didn't think I was a nut, he'd decide I was perfect. I waited for him to say as much, but instead he bounced up out of his chair. "Let's take a tour," he said, moving to the door as I struggled to pull my rear out of the vacuum-vortex that was his couch.

In the hall, I had to walk fast to keep up. "So," Mason said as we sailed down the hall, "do you have a dog?"

"No," I said, hoping this wouldn't disqualify me. "A cat, but no dog. But I did have a dog growing up."

"Yeah?" He gave me an encouraging look.

"Norah. A German shepherd. She was the best dog I've ever known. She and I grew up together, really, and she—well, she was there for me through my parents' divorce. I don't think I would have made it to adulthood without her." I stopped talking, my voice already thick. I couldn't go on without starting to cry. What choked me up wasn't the fact that she had died—that had happened a lot of years ago. It was the magnitude of what she'd done for me. She'd been there for me, day after day, ready to listen to my problems. Or she would romp around, helping me forget them. I never thought about her without feeling grateful.

Mason glanced at me and seemed to understand, because he didn't push for more. In fact, he kindly changed the subject, giving me a rundown of the position's wages and benefits. I listened and tried to take it all in, but my mind was filled with visions of Norah's graceful nose and her sweet amber eyes.

Mason talked as we speed-walked down the halls.

"*The Love Dog* came in as a midseason replacement. The network canceled *Operation Bridezilla* over the winter hiatus, and we're taking their spring slots. It's a big opportunity—ten episodes to get a foothold."

"It must be going pretty well," I said, working to keep up with him. "The show has decent ratings, doesn't it?"

Mason nodded. "It does at the moment, but that can change in a heartbeat. We need to keep doing this well or better. Better would be ideal, of course. Television is all about the ads, and we need viewers to get that revenue. That's why these last four shows are so important." He looked at me as we rounded a corner. "We'll need Apollo in top form every single day."

I swallowed wrong and had to cough. "Wait, there are only four more shows?"

"Yup. Three here in L.A., then the season finale in Madrona, Washington. That's my hometown."

Mason kept talking, but I wasn't listening. I was too busy panicking. Only four more shows! I had to get enough material for all of my articles in just four weeks—that was ludicrous. It meant turning in an article almost every week, beginning with this Friday. If I got the job.

Absolutely insane.

Mason led me to a door, opened it, and we stuck our heads into a long, tiered room filled with black metal desks, computers, and screens. A crew of bleary-eyed people sat eating doughnuts and clicking mouses.

"This is *The Love Dog*'s brain stem," Mason said. He was holding the door open, and I had to stand close to him to look in. I thought how light-headed and giggly it would make Cassie to be this near him, and praised myself for being levelheaded enough to not even notice the heat coming off his shirt or the way he dipped his head toward mine and spoke in a low voice. "It's the control room, where every cut and take is put together to make a show that's exactly twenty-two minutes long. These guys head up everything, from the credits and theme music to deciding which camera to use for a shot. They're the best in the business."

I looked in at the best in the business, thinking Mason might have been saying that in front of them as a way of buttering up his crew, but no one else seemed to have heard him. All the people in the brain stem were staring deep into their computer screens.

Next, he led me down a flight of industrial-looking stairs into a cavernous, dark room that was bigger than my high school's auditorium. "So," he said, "if that was the brain stem, then this is the heart." He waved his arm around proudly, and I tried to look suitably impressed by the hodgepodge of cameras and chairs, rows of banked movie-theater seats, and towering lights on metal stands. People milled around in every corner of the room, carrying things, speaking into headsets, looking at clipboards.

"See that woman down there, the one in the white shirt?" I spotted a woman with blond hair that was turning gray, cut into a sharp bob. She was surrounded by nodding people in headsets. "That's Imogen Blakely. She's the field producer, the most important person here."

I looked at him with surprise. Surely, as executive producer and lead actor, he was the most important person here?

"You've seen reality TV," he said. "You know the interviews they do with the guests where they get to share what they were thinking or feeling? Imogen's the one asking the questions that gets that footage. She's with the guests every minute, especially when they're on location, filming with Apollo. She watches it all and tells us what to focus on, what to cut, what's missing. Imogen's been doing reality TV from the start. There's no one better. I'd introduce you, but she barely has time to eat, let alone meet people."

Hmm, interesting. A considerate boss. Well, there wasn't any dirt for the *Telltale* there, unless Imogen had a heroin habit. "There sure are a lot of people down there," I said, nodding at the scene below us. After the silence of my apartment, the crush of humanity had me feeling a little claustrophobic.

"Nearly ninety people work on this show, and most of them pass through this room at least once during the day. Up there we have the stage set," Mason continued, pointing to a dark area in the center with a parquet floor and cozy chairs. I recognized it from the show, but like Mason it looked different in person—surprisingly three dimensional. "This back here," he said, gesturing to the empty theater seats, "is where the crew and studio folks can watch the taping. We don't have a live audience—that's almost impossible on an animal show—but we do always have an audience. It's just made up of our own people. Apollo loves it." Mason grinned. "And there to the left—stage right—is the place where Apollo practices the skills he uses in each show."

Skills. Very nice. That sounded so much more authentic than "tricks." I looked around the room with a sinking heart. If I had my way and outed *The Love Dog* as a sham, its ratings would sink. Some of these people would lose their jobs. Could I really be responsible for that? I knew how it was to be out of work; I understood the paralyzing terror of an unknown future.

"Would I be called upon to teach him skills?" I asked.

"No, no, his owner will do that. Lucas—you'll meet him soon. Lucas is the trainer. He's responsible for getting Apollo to act and behave the way we need. You'd just be Apollo's handler, caring for him before Lucas arrives and after he leaves, bringing Apollo to the stage, that sort of thing. Of course it would help if you sat in on the training, so you were familiar with the techniques Lucas uses. He won't be here every day, and it would be nice if someone was around to give Apollo a quick refresher if he needed it."

"Sure," I said, "I'd be happy to."

"Good." Mason gave me another charming smile, which I deflected by looking as superior as possible.

"I'm happy to do anything that helps Apollo," I said. "I can't wait to meet him."

The words were barely out of my mouth before we were interrupted by a petite woman with dark, curly hair and a headset, who sidled up close to Mason. Quite close. I wondered how he felt about this invasion of his personal space.

"Rebecca, what's up?"

Rebecca pointed at her clipboard and started rattling off names and technical terms that sounded as foreign to me as Gaelic, but without the lyric beauty. When she'd finished, Mason turned to me.

"Sorry, I'd better get on this. Rebecca, can you find a PA to take Samantha to meet Apollo? Oh, and Rebecca, meet Sam. She's going to be Apollo's new handler."

I nearly choked. "Really?" Had Mason Hall just said I was Apollo's new handler?

He turned to me, a full-force charming smile on his face. "Really."

I had the job? A tremor slid over my skin, and I wondered if I was scared, excited, nervous, or a combination of the three. Would I survive in this strange land full of cameras and key grips? And what about Mason—would it be weird to see him here at work, knowing I was supposed to uncover his druggie past, assuming he had one? My head was spinning.

It wasn't until afterward, after Mason had shaken my hand and welcomed me aboard, after I noted the warmth of his hand and the way his eyes held mine, that I realized what a dark look Rebecca had shot me as she spoke into her headset.

A minute later, a pretty young woman named Pilar led me down a gloomy hall full of old noisy pipes that smelled like garbage. Pilar described herself as a production assistant. "In my case, that means I follow the guests around and make sure they get places on time. And I keep them from getting lost. The studio's a big place."

"This reminds me of the basement in the house I grew up in," I said, looking up and down the hall. "I thought aliens lived down there."

Pilar laughed. Her pretty bangles danced on her wrist. "Yeah, totally. And you should be careful in these back halls—it's easy to get lost. Who knows how many people have gotten trapped back here, never to be heard from again."

I was about to ask her how she liked her job when a noise buzzed in her headset. Pilar pressed the earpiece in closer and started rattling off a series of acronyms, names, and abbreviations that sounded like ancient Martian. I followed behind her, letting my eyes wander over the drab walls and stained linoleum floors.

"Sorry about that," she said, her attention suddenly back on me. "I have to dash back, but we're almost there. It's just through these doors."

She put her shoulder against two heavy double doors and shoved. The second we passed through, I heard a voice coming under a door on the right-hand side of the hall. I couldn't make out the words, but the voice sounded angry. Condescending. And cold.

"Um, that's the door," Pilar said. She could hear the ranting as well as I could, and it was obvious she didn't envy me having to open the door and go in.

"Who is that in there?" I whispered to her.

"It's Lucas. Apollo's trainer. He's just like that." She shrugged, implying that Lucas was Lucas in the way that lemurs were lemurs and Sherman tanks were Sherman tanks.

Great. Just great. Pilar was clearly anxious to go, so I waved good-bye to her and turned to face the door. I could hear the words better now, and they didn't make me any more eager to turn the knob.

"If I don't get a break from this horseshit soon, I'm gonna explode. It's total crap that he's locking us into that contract. When we signed, this show was nothing but a dream, but now it looks like it could run for years. Years! Like I have years to spend babysitting you? I have other clients, other jobs to do. I used to have a life. What do I have now? A half-hour lunch break and ten-hour days. It's bullshit. Total bullshit. Where's that handler he promised to hire? I needed them here a week ago."

Double great. Well, at least he knew I was here to lighten his load. I squared my shoulders and reached for the doorknob. It would be better to get this over with, and maybe coming in during the rant would give me a little bit of an edge with Lucas. Besides, I was here to free him, right? My presence would help him get his life back. I was doing him a favor—there was nothing to be afraid of.

I pushed the door open. A glare of fluorescent lights made me blink, but in a few seconds I made out a small white room that was bare of furniture except for a metal table and a large crate pushed against the far wall. And something large and furry, sitting in front of the crate with its head bowed so low, its chin touched its paws.

It was Apollo.

Apollo

I heard footsteps coming down the hall long before they reached us. Two people—two small people—had come through the heavy doors and were standing outside ours. Lucas didn't notice. He was too busy being loud and full of his metallic smell to notice anything. I tried to make myself small—when he was upset, it was best to disappear. If he saw my face, it would only make things worse.

Then the door opened, and I held my breath, thinking maybe I *was* invisible. I wanted to be. It was always bad when someone interrupted Lucas. Mason had once, and afterward Lucas smelled more like iron than he had in all the time I'd known him. Except for that one time, of course.

A small-size person stood in the doorway, and I wanted to look, but invisible dogs don't do that, so I held absolutely still. And I waited to see what would happen.

"Hi there." It was a woman's voice, not too old. I wanted to wag, but I didn't. I like women. They're much less likely to have a metallic smell than men. Also, they're smaller, which feels friendly. "I'm Samantha Novack." The woman's voice was tight and tense. "Mason Hall sent me down here to meet Apollo. It looks like he might hire me as a handler . . . assuming you approve."

Lucas snorted and set down the leash he'd been holding. I couldn't see him because I wasn't moving my eyes, but I could feel the change in his posture, the way he turned toward the woman and leaned against the table. That was a good sign. Something about her made him welcoming.

"Of course I approve—I've been after him for weeks to hire a handler. So are you full time? Can you start tomorrow? Early? Like six?"

She paused, but only for an instant. "Absolutely. If that's when you need me, I'll be here."

I had a sense that she was looking at me. My tail wanted to wag again, but I held it still and tried not to breathe. She might have cheese in her pocket. Or a mini pizza. I wanted to check, but I didn't. Lucas had accepted her so far, but I didn't want to push my luck and ruin things, not after the mood he'd been in tonight.

"Great. Show up here, right here, at six tomorrow morning and I'll show you what to do. You can shadow me for the day, then after that you can take care of his morning routine and the times when he's off camera. I'm Lucas, by the way." I heard him push himself off the table and walk toward her. My belly clenched, but I stayed still.

"Hi, Lucas, it's nice to meet you. Um, should I meet Apollo—to see if we get along?"

"Oh, no, he likes everyone. Just be here at six. And bring a lunch. It's a long day."

There was a pause, and no one spoke. I felt that she was looking at me again, maybe trying to see me inside my crate. I held my breath and tried not to move.

"Right, okay. Thank you. See you then." I heard her shuffle out of the room and close the door behind her. That was it. She'd come and gone, and I hadn't gotten to check her pockets for mini pizzas. I would just have to wait and see if she came back. And maybe that night I would send her my love, just in case.

–8–

🦴 Apollo

The next morning, I hid my rope and lay at the front of my crate, listening for cars and movement. The garbage cart went by, a happy sound this time since it was Tuesday, still early in the week. I felt a twinge of excitement as the building slowly woke and got ready for a new day. A man's footsteps went down the hall and through the heavy doors. Then, a few minutes later, the doors pushed open again and a woman's footsteps came through. They came down the hall to my door. They stopped.

I wagged softly, with caution, since I didn't know who it was. The person didn't move. I could almost smell her through the crack in the door, but not quite. We both held still on opposite sides, waiting.

At last I heard Lucas burst through the doors.

"Oh, you're here." He sounded gruff, like he always did in the mornings, as if he needed to clear his lungs.

"I thought I'd just wait for you here," the woman said. The same woman who came yesterday—she was back! I let my tail thumping accelerate slightly. It was rare for a new person to visit two days in a row. They usually just came once, like Pilar. I heard the woman talking with Lucas some more as he opened the door, then they stepped in and turned on the light.

I stayed where I was—Lucas didn't like me to jump up and get in his way first thing—and watched them. She looked at me, then at Lucas, then at me again as if she were trying to understand something complicated. Lucas called her over to the table.

"These are the leashes I use in the morning—one for walking through the studio and one for the tread-mill. You'll need to pack a bag with brushes, combs, and a towel. Sometimes he gets poop on his ass, which is a real joy to clean off."

She watched and nodded, like she was a dog learn-ing to do a trick. "How do you get him to perform the skills? Does he get biscuits?"

Lucas's eyes got round. "He never, ever gets biscuits. No cookies, *no* people food. We can't have him pork-ing up. All of his food is measured, and if I ever hear of you giving him extra, you'll be out on your ear. The rules for handling him are simple. No treats. No days off. No field trips. Got it?"

She nodded. I wondered what they were talking about. Lucas seemed calm enough—she was helping, I could tell, by listening quietly. I didn't know what to make of her. From this distance, she seemed to smell all right, but I was perplexed by this attention she paid to Lucas. Of course I was grateful that she was keeping him happy. But if she was this nice to him, did that mean she was going to be just like him? Were they friends?

After more minutes of talking, Lucas handed her the leash and waved in my direction. She came close and crouched down in front of me. I wagged like crazy—even if she was just like Lucas, I still couldn't keep myself from getting excited. Her breath smelled sweet, not like Lucas's cigarettes and coffee, and her hands moved in a predictable, gentle way. I sniffed the air around her, but she didn't seem to have any food in her pockets. Just a general scent of peanut butter. She clipped the leash on my collar, touching me softly at the neck. Then she stood and looked at Lucas.

Together, the three of us marched down the clanky hallway to my outdoor area. Lucas said more words to her—he seemed to be enjoying his work this morning, telling her what was what. He was like one of those dogs that enjoys correcting the younger dogs and keeping them in line. Maybe this was all he'd ever needed to be happy, another human to boss around.

We went through my usual routine while Lucas barked his orders. Eventually we reached the studio and settled into our work area. She stood off to the side while Lucas had me practice the things I'd learned the day before. I wanted to show off for her, so I did it all perfectly, hitting my marks and panting at the camera. I couldn't tell what she thought. She kept looking around the set, her eyes wary, a nervous smell coming off her skin and clothes. Her nervousness started to make me anxious, which made me bungle my last two skills. Lucas got angry, but he kept his jaw clenched as he corrected me. Maybe he was showing off for her, too.

We had just finished practice when Mason appeared, his clipboard in one hand. I wagged furiously.

"Morning," he said—his tone was always bright and clean. "I just wanted to see how Sam's fitting in. All good?"

In that second, the brew of scents took a sudden change. She started sweating—not the nice-smelling sweat that comes from exercise, but a sour, chemical sweat. A burst of metallic odor flooded off Lucas. They both turned to Mason, grimaced like nervous dogs, and said, "We're just fine!"

I looked from face to face, trying to understand. What had Mason done to upset them like this? Lucas often turned nasty when Mason came, but why was *she* so upset? Couldn't she see how wonderful Mason was?

Samantha

Lucas let me take a coffee break at 10 A.M., and I wandered away from the set like a zombie. I'd been working for four hours, and my head felt as full as if I'd just been through a two-year crash course in neuroscience. Leashes, pills, brushes, and props swam in my mind. My ears were full of terms I didn't understand—gaffer and Foley mixer and transcoding operator. The one great relief was that Lucas didn't expect me to help with training Apollo. I could barely keep "stage up-left center" straight from "stage down-right"—I could never be clear enough in my own understanding to convey directions to Apollo.

Feeling blurry eyed and a little woozy, I wandered in the direction of the food service area I'd seen when Mason showed me around the day before. My brain screamed for caffeine. I heard the spit and sizzle of a milk steamer and shambled in that direction, getting in line behind two men in headsets and a tiny, elegantly dressed woman in four-inch heels.

My phone played a chord from "Blackbird"—I had an incoming text. It was from Vern at the *Telltale*. RESEARCH OK? HOPE U JOIN US, it read. Thanks for not pressuring me, Vern. I put my phone away. *A few deep breaths, here in line, and you'll start feeling human again,* I told myself. *In and out. In and out. Easy does it, Sam. Just breathe.*

"Hey, how's it going?"

I nearly jumped out of my first-day-of-work clothes. Mason's voice was unmistakable, and I started sweating before I turned to face him. The pressure of trying to get dirt on him was wearing me down, and I hadn't even started yet.

Vaguely, I realized that he'd asked me a question and was waiting for a response. "Um, fine," I said, "just fine. How are you?"

He seemed to find that question funny for some reason. Maybe asking the producer how he was doing wasn't done on a reality show set. He did crinkle his brow for a minute and consider before answering. "I'm good. Thank you. Things are mostly on track this week, which is a relief. How do you like Apollo?"

"He seems great," I said. "I can't believe he can keep all those different skills straight, and for no reward at all."

"Yeah, he's really disciplined. But how about when he's not working? Are you two getting along?"

I opened my mouth and closed it again, unsure what to say. How could I describe the scene when I'd entered the room that morning, with Lucas listing off tools and items while Apollo lay at the door of his crate, seemingly frozen? No dog I'd ever known lay still like that when a new person came into the room. His discipline was so strong it was a stifling presence.

I was in awe of it and disturbed by it at the same time. He hadn't even sniffed me when I put his leash on, just held perfectly still as if he was afraid of offending me. And what about Lucas? This was his owner, his guardian, yet Lucas never said one word of greeting, never offered a single pat or hand for sniffing. I hadn't seen them touch once through the entire morning. Lucas handed off props, he directed and clicked his clicker, but he never touched. It creeped me out.

"I don't think Lucas really wants me to buddy up with him," I finally said. "I thought I might wait and try that tomorrow, when I'm on my own."

Mason peered at me intently. "I want Apollo to be happy here," he said quietly. "I don't think he's had a lot of joy in his life, but he'll need it if he's going to keep on with the show. He's the Love Dog—he has to be happy, right?"

"Of course." Ahead of me in line, one of the guys snapped open a newspaper. In a jolt, I remembered my primary mission, to get the goods on Mason Hall and the show. Ugh. Playing spy wasn't my ideal role. I took a deep breath, remembering my dreams of writing for a living. It was very close now—if I signed with Vern and gave him a great first piece, I'd be on my way. The line moved forward, and I scooted ahead a step before blurting my question.

"The show is pretty scripted, though, isn't it? I mean, it's not like Apollo has a lot of leeway in how he interacts with the guests."

Mason made a considering face and rocked his head from side to side. "Scripted, yes, to a certain extent. But Apollo has a subtle effect on every part of the show. You may not be able to see it, but his energy is what makes *The Love Dog* special. That's why he needs to be happy. His enthusiasm underscores everything we do. Most of us only see him when he's on set. We don't know what he and Lucas do when he's not performing. I know he loves being on stage. It's the rest of the time I'm worried about."

Well, I thought, *that served me right.* I'd tried to engage Mason in a conversation about how canned the show was, and he turned it back to Apollo and why he needed to be happy. Score one for you, Mason Hall.

I stepped up to the counter to order my large Earl Grey tea. Before I was finished, Mason was at my side, asking for his usual. I skirted the counter to wait for my order and again he appeared at my elbow. What was going on—was he spying on me, too? I gave him a nervous smile and tried to think of another probing question, but my brain was glue. I was too tired, too overwhelmed. And, in the next instant, too startled by the sudden presence of Rebecca, the compact, curly haired person I'd met the day before. She appeared out of nowhere between us like a will-o'-the-wisp, her face glowing as she looked up at Mason.

"Coffee break? Want to go over the storyboards while you drink it?"

"Ah, hi, Rebecca. You remember Sam?" We gave each other a perfunctory nod and smile. I wished my tea would arrive so I could escape the awkward tension she'd created. "We were just talking about Apollo," Mason said. "I was explaining that we only see him on stage—we don't know what his downtime is like. I think he might need a little more fun. Don't you think?"

The blank look on Rebecca's face made it plain that she'd never considered Apollo's life at all, joyless or otherwise. "Sure! Of course! We have to take care of our number-one star. And you sure don't have time to go checking on him, Mason. Now about those storyboards—they're done, but just the first draft. They're down in the writing room. I thought we could go over them, maybe brainstorm some changes?"

"Um, okay, but not now. I've got to go over budgets with the network guys. Have to keep the big dogs at the network happy if we want to get picked up for another season." He smiled at both of us, letting us know that he bore the suits no ill will. *Which,* I thought, *was probably a lie.* What executive producer didn't bump heads with the network from time to time? Though, I considered, good ratings probably went a long way to smooth over any potholes in the road. And *The Love Dog's* ratings were pretty decent.

The barista put my tea up on the counter, and I exhaled a relieved breath. Time to escape. Maybe I could find a quiet corner where I could sit alone and sip for a few minutes before I had to get back to Lucas and Apollo. The hubbub of this place was giving me a headache.

"The Earl Grey appears at last," Mason said. He smiled at me, his eyes intensely blue. I stood there, transfixed. It wasn't every day that I stood next to someone who was this damned attractive. "See you around, Sam. And good luck with Apollo. And Lucas."

He said this last with a look that met me right in the eye. The look caught and held me, thick with meaning, as if we shared a secret that no one else was in on. An odd feeling tickled my throat. Were he and I in cahoots suddenly? Somehow? Did he suspect what I did, that Lucas didn't give a hoot about Apollo?

As I walked away, I tried to clear my head and figure out what I'd learned from this little interaction. Was there anything I could use for my first article?

Rebecca clearly had a crush on Mason. Whether he returned her feelings was a question for the universe to answer. That was hardly news. I thought back to the ranting and shouting I'd heard out of Apollo's room the day before. If Mason knew Lucas was acting that way toward his star, he'd be shocked. Or . . . did he know? Was that why I was here, to be the buffer between Lucas and Apollo?

I gave my head a shake and sipped my tea, which was really not cool enough to drink. This place was too confusing for words. I'd be lucky if I ever figured out how to get through the day, let alone put together an exposé article.

*T*hat afternoon, Apollo was called away to the photo room for a shoot. "I'll take care of this one," Lucas said, making it clear that this particular job was too important for the likes of me. "I'll have to make him sit on a mark and face different directions. You can hang out until we get back—it'll probably be an hour or so."

Excellent—a break! I headed back toward the café and ducked into the first quiet corner I could find. Before I could lose my nerve, I pulled out my cell phone and called Vern at the *Telltale*.

"Okay," I told him, "I'll take the job. You can consider me under contract. But I need the pieces to be anonymous. No byline, okay? If anyone here found out I was writing them, they'd murder me. And there's something else you should know."

"What's that?" I could hear him typing in the background and guessed that he was multitasking.

"The season only has four more shows. They're tap-

ing three more here, this week's show and the next
two, and then doing a season finale on location in
Washington state."

"Oh, yeah," Vern said breezily. "Everyone's season
is wrapping up."

"But that only gives me three weeks to get material!" Rebecca walked past, and I ducked deeper into
the shadows. I dropped my voice to a whisper. "What
if I can't do it?"

"You will." Vern was typing again. "I'm cutting that
check today. I know you'll work it out."

I hung up, my mind racing. How was I going to learn
what I needed to know in such a short time? I watched
people moving up and down the hallway. I needed a
friend. Someone I could pump for information. A friend
or two. Or maybe three.

Moving on autopilot, I headed into the café, got a
ginger snap cookie, and looked around. There was only
one face I recognized.

"Hi there," I said to Pilar, the PA. "I'm Sam. We met
yesterday?" I gave her a massively eager smile. Pilar
nodded. "Could I ask a favor? I wonder if you could
explain to me a little about how the show works?"

"Sure," she said, motioning to the chair opposite
her, which I slid into. "What do you want to know?"

"When do they tape in that big auditorium?"

Pilar laughed. "Waiting to see some actual TV-
making happen? That won't be till Wednesday. Mondays and Tuesdays are for blocking and lighting.
Imogen and her crew will take the guests out to film
on location on those days—sometimes with Apollo,
sometimes not. Wednesdays and Thursdays are for
shooting Mason's intros and outros and for anything
they want to do with Mason, Apollo, and the guests in

the studio. That's the part in the auditorium that you're waiting for. You know how the show often ends with Apollo taking something out to the guests? That happens here, on the set. Then on Fridays we do pickups, tidying up anything we missed during the week."

I nodded, pretending I'd followed all that.

"And of course promo gets squeezed in between, wherever it fits," she went on. "Like right now. Next week's guests are doing a photo shoot with Apollo, so I have a break. You, too, I'm guessing. They'll call us when it's wrapping up. The woman, Honey, was pretty excited to meet Apollo."

"Honey? Her name is Honey?"

Pilar laughed and tucked her pretty dark hair behind her ear, her bracelets jangling. "Well, you know. She's an actress."

Ah! I leaned toward her. "Are they all actors, the guests who come on?"

She nodded. "Pretty much." Pilar didn't seem as disturbed by this as I thought she should be, but my heart rate picked up. A real scoop at last!

"But the world believes they're real people. Doesn't it bug you that they aren't? That they're acting?"

"Hey, this is Hollywood! What do they expect?"

A group of people came into the café, and Pilar turned to scan the crowd. She was so intent about it, I finally asked, "Are you looking for someone in particular?"

Her blush was fierce. "Oh, no. Well. Okay, kind of. There's this guy. We were supposed to go on a date last Friday, but he called at the last minute and said he had to cancel."

"Did he say why?" I broke off a piece of my cookie.

Exposé or no exposé, this was just interesting. Maybe Pilar needed to start reading *Unvarnished*.

"No, he didn't. And I haven't seen him yet this week. Weird, isn't it?" Her face told me she found it far more troubling than weird. "I don't know—maybe he just wasn't as interested as I thought he was."

"Or," I said, venturing further than I probably should have, "maybe you seemed more interested than he wanted?"

She gave me a sharp look, and for a minute I regretted what I'd said. But then I didn't. This was a classic mistake women made. They sailed into new relationships with their brains leaping forward by weeks, months, years. Before a first date they had visions of poufed white dresses and family vacations. All their questions—is he The One? Will he commit? What color will my bridesmaids wear?—ruined the chance to just go on a date and get to know someone. Couldn't a date be a date and nothing more? Women needed to stop investing so much emotion into what ought to be a simple opportunity to talk with a man and see if they had things in common. It was a date, for Pete's sake, not a lifelong commitment.

"Maaaybe," Pilar answered slowly. "I might have. But I really like him—I think we could hit it off in a big way, you know?"

I shrugged. "Maybe a date's just a date," I said. "No need to go thinking ahead to things that might or might not happen. It's just a date."

"Right," she murmured into her latte. "It's just a date." Suddenly, her thoughtful mood broke and her smile popped out. "Maybe I should just forget him and find myself a date with someone else." She laughed, clearly embarrassed, and reached into her pocket for a folded square of paper. Slowly she smoothed out the paper on the table in front of her. "I had maybe a little too much wine last night," she said. "I wrote him this note." She spun the paper around so I could read it.

"*Dear A.J., Why couldn't you tell me the truth? If you don't want to go out with me, just say so. Thanks, asshole.*"

"Well, it's very direct," I said, grinning.

Pilar folded the note back up again and put it into her pocket. "Direct, sure. But I'm not going to give it to him. He can suffer with the silent treatment."

-9-

Apollo

The next morning, an amazing thing happened. I was awake, as usual, with my rope hidden under my blanket, waiting for the sound of Lucas's footsteps. But they never came. Instead, hers came, tapping lightly on the floor. She opened the door to my room, turned on the lights, and stood there, looking at me. I stayed absolutely still.

"It's so weird," she said softly. Even though I couldn't tell what she was saying, it seemed that she was trying to calm me. "I've never seen a dog that acts the way you do. Don't you want to come over and say hello?"

She came toward me and crouched down, then extended a hand near my nose. I gratefully sniffed it all over, front and back, and then—since she didn't seem to mind—I smelled her sleeve and her jacket. And the leg of her jeans. Then I sniffed her shoes and her other hand. It was incredible. I don't know when I'd had such leisure to smell a person. And she smelled so nice, like cars and wool and some kind of strange, sweet lemony lotion. I thought she might have had toast for breakfast. With peanut butter *and* honey.

When I had finished, she stood up and got my leash, then we headed out to my area. Unlike Lucas, she was full of things to say to me. Kind, chipper-sounding things like, "You must have to pee so bad!" and "I guess you don't mind the early wake-up call, do you?" I grinned when she talked, but I still tried to stay professional. She worked with Lucas, after all. Her standards and his were probably the same.

I did my morning peeing (the best pee of the day), then we went indoors where I ate my fish pill, had breakfast, and walked on my treadmill. Lucas usually sat down for this and drank coffee, but she did something bizarre. She stood beside the treadmill and marched in place. "I might as well get some cardio in, too, right?" she said, pumping her arms. It was companionable, almost like we were out walking together. It was nice.

After breakfast, we left the room and headed out into the halls. When people passed, I did my usual lunge-and-smell—and she surprised me again. Instead of marching on the way Lucas did, pulling my leash in closer, she stopped. She actually stopped walking and let my leash go slack. The first time it happened, I was so shocked I didn't know what to do—I just looked up at her and tried to read her face. But the next time, I took full advantage. I went right up to a man in overalls and sniffed his incredible-smelling work boots. He must have stepped in *jam,* their odor was that good. And he had a dog at home—some kind of tiny toy breed. He scratched my neck under the collar, which was heaven. I couldn't believe the day I was having.

Eventually we arrived at our work space near the

set. She asked me to sit, which I did, then she sat on a folding chair. After about five minutes, I realized that we were waiting, probably for Lucas, so I went ahead and lay down. I thought I could feel her eyes on me, so every so often I shifted my eyebrows and glanced up at her. She wasn't moving, but she was looking down at me. I didn't know what to make of it. I pretended not to notice.

"I'd like to pet you, you know," she said quietly. This sounded like more soothing talk, so I rested my chin on my paws and let her voice flow over me. "I'd really like to treat you like a normal dog. But I'm afraid that if I do, I'll never be able to bring myself to debunk the show. I mean, you're its star! How can I be buddy-buddy with you and then out you as nothing more than a performing dog? The dissonance would kill me. And it wouldn't be right to you. Not that you'd read my article or anything, but still. I'll only know you for about three weeks. I won't be back next season— there's no way. It wouldn't be right to make you care about me. It just wouldn't."

She said this sadly, as if she was explaining why I couldn't go for a car ride. My ears drooped. I wagged my tail slowly in hopes of getting her talking again, but it didn't work. So I sighed and went back to waiting.

Eventually I heard footsteps and sat up, wagging because I could tell it wasn't Lucas coming, it was three people. One of them was my friend Pilar! I had sent Pilar and A.J. love the past two nights—I wondered if she knew.

Pilar brought two strong-smelling people with her. One was very small, but wore dangerous pointy shoes, the kind that could hurt a paw badly if she stepped wrong. After Pilar said hi to me, she introduced this woman as "Honey." Honey bent down and kissed me on the top of the head, which I liked on the one hand because it was gentle, but I also didn't like because she had something gooey on her lips that I could feel in my fur afterward. And her sweet flower smell stuck to me, making my belly feel woozy.

The other person was a man called Chad. Pilar stood behind the two of them, put a hand on each of their shoulders, and said, "These two are our happy couple for next week. Isn't that sweet?"

Honey and Chad looked at each other with lowered eyes, careful not to touch. My heart jumped—these two had a history. They didn't like each other, that was obvious. But there was something running deeper between them than simple dislike—a deep, subtle smell, like burning wood, hid underneath their icy cold feelings. There had been love here once. These two were a project!

There had to be something I could do—I needed some free time to think. If only Lucas would quit making me train with that silly glass shoe—I didn't want to carry it onto the set and set it on a velvet pillow. Not now. I needed to think. Needed to plan. I had to sort this out. The Love Dog had a mission.

Samantha

The night of my first day at work, I'd lain awake until one in the morning thinking about how sunk I was. I'd never find any dirt on that show. Never. I wasn't brave enough, for one thing—I didn't have the guts to schmooze with people just so I could backstab them later. And for another, everyone seemed so darned happy. How could I find a disgruntled employee if they all liked their jobs?

But the very next day, a glimmer of opportunity presented itself. I was sitting with Apollo, waiting for Lucas to arrive, fearing that a lot of my work life was going to be spent sitting and waiting, when Pilar brought over the new couple, Honey and Chad. Chad looked cold and distant, as if he wanted to be anywhere but standing with me, Apollo, Pilar, and Honey. Honey looked like her skin was on fire. Uneasy feelings were burning inside her. She was able to set it aside, though, to display her undisguised love for Apollo. She wrapped him in a hug and kissed him on the head, even though she then had to spend the next five minutes pulling his hair off her lip gloss.

I watched her eyes—something was troubling her. *There,* I thought. *That was my in.* I just needed to befriend Honey and I'd learn something. If I didn't learn some dirt about the show, maybe I would at least pick up something about her life that I could use as leverage. Somehow. That always worked in the movies, right?

Besides, maybe I'd get lucky. Maybe whatever had her upset *was* about the show. Then I'd be golden. And because Honey didn't work here, I didn't need to worry about feeling guilty when I saw her after the article came out. By the time it came out, she'd be long gone, off making a soap commercial or auditioning for a pilot. Honey was the perfect target.

When Lucas took his lunch break, I walked Apollo to the café and bought a Diet Coke. Then I led him up and down the halls in search of Honey. I had no idea where the guest stars were stored until the show needed them, and I kicked myself for not having asked Pilar that question. Eventually, though, I caught a break. I saw Tyshawn, one of this week's guests, coming up a set of stairs I'd never been down. Holding my breath, I dashed down the stairs with Apollo at my heels.

A hall lined with doors stretched out in front of us. I started down it, smiling at everyone I passed as if I belonged there, as if I weren't an interloper who was set on destroying the show. Finally I found one with a whiteboard attached to the front on which someone had written "Chad Arlington" in curly letters. The next one said "Honey Manns." Pay dirt.

I stood outside her door for two full minutes, waiting for my heart to quit jumping around. When it didn't, I gave up and knocked on the door. I had no plan, no idea what I was going to say. But I was here, and I told myself that had to count for something. Surely the right words would just come to me.

Honey opened the door, and I stood there, mute.

"Oh, hi," she said sweetly. Her perfume was so strong, I could feel it soaking into my clothes. "You're, um . . . ?" She gave me a charming, puzzled look. Then she saw Apollo. "Apollo! Hi!"

He wagged his tail like a superstar. When she came forward to pet him, he sat automatically. Because he was just that good. "I'm Sam," I said. "We met yesterday. I noticed that you liked Apollo and thought you might want to see him again. He's such a great stress reliever."

"Thank you so much!" She bent down and rubbed his head, but didn't kiss it this time. When she straightened up, she held her dressing-room door open. "Want to come in? I could use a little stress relief."

I headed in, leading Apollo. Honey's dressing room was far nicer than I'd expected. She had a white couch, a mahogany desk with a Tiffany lamp, a minifridge, and a glass-topped coffee table. In the corner near the door, a costume rack held about thirty different outfits, presumably things Honey would wear on Friday for taping.

Apollo sat down on the floor and looked at us both expectantly. I held out the Diet Coke, the gift I'd brought Honey, feeling lame. She probably had Cristal and Perrier in her fridge. And brie flown in from the Île-de-France.

I sat on her white couch while Honey rubbed Apollo's chest. He looked as blissed out as I'd ever seen him, panting with his eyes closed. The poor guy got so little affection. Lucas never let him go outside or run around like ordinary dogs. I wished I could give him more, but I didn't have a yard for him to run around in. I didn't even have my own house. All I had was a mountain of bills and a dirt-filled article to write.

As I pondered this, Apollo did a lovely thing. Ever so gently, he pressed his nose to Honey's cheek, then he laid his head against her arm and sighed heavily. It was so tender, my heart melted, and I wasn't surprised to see tears in Honey's pretty brown eyes. This was my opportunity.

"Are you okay?" I said, trying to keep my voice hushed. "Is anything the matter?"

Honey sniffled. I saw a box of tissues on the desk and passed it over to her. "Thanks." She continued stroking Apollo's silky head. "I know I should be more professional than this. I should be tough like he is, right?"

"Right." I nodded. "He who?"

Honey leaned in close. "Chad."

"Oh. Chad. The other guest. So, uh, do you know him outside the show?"

"Yeah." She laughed in a weak way and dabbed her eyes again. "Ironic, isn't it? Chad and I actually are the real deal. We're a couple with problems. Serious problems. So serious, we've already broken up."

"Wait, you used to go out? But then what are you doing on the show together?"

Honey looked baffled by my question. "It's a job."

"Yeah, but if you broke up, surely it must be painful . . ."

"Of course it is," she said, looking down at Apollo, who panted languidly. "We auditioned for it while we were still going out. And we got the call—it's a huge break. Do you know how many people watch this show? Not just regular people, but talent scouts and agents and producers. I couldn't say no. Besides," she gave me an empty smile, "now we're authentic."

I stared at her and hardly knew what to think. Honey was one of the most beautiful women I'd ever seen, but her story was 100 percent typical. Should I scribble down the *Unvarnished* website address for her? Pat her on the back and go on my way? *Wait*, I told myself, *you're here for dirt on the show. Honey's an insider—a vulnerable insider. You'll never find a more perfect source.*

"Listen," I said, "I'm new on the show. I'm still trying to learn my way around and get my bearings. Can you tell me a little about how it all works?"

"What do you mean?" She ran her hand down Apollo's blond head.

"I mean, are you and Chad going to be yourselves

on the show? Are you going to talk about your real problems?"

Honey glanced at the half-open door to her dressing room. "I'm not supposed to say. Everything about next week's show is strictly confidential."

I pretended to laugh this off. "Oh, but you can tell me. I work here!"

"No," she said, shaking her head, "seriously, I can't. My contract has a clause in it that says if I tell anyone anything about the show I've taped, they can fine me one and a half million dollars. Million! And it's not just now—that goes for after the taping, too. I can't say a thing, not even a peep."

Ah. So that's how it was. Well that explained why I'd never found a disgruntled ex-employee or former guest who wanted to dish about *The Love Dog*. They probably all had to sign secrecy contracts. And who was going to squeal with more than a million dollars on the line?

I knew when I was beaten. I was just about to gather Apollo's leash and quit the field of battle when a dark curly head popped in the door.

"Honey, I didn't want you to forget about that fitting in costume." Rebecca spotted me, and I swear her nose wrinkled like she smelled something bad. "What are you doing here?"

I tried to look innocent, though I was sure my skin was turning green from guilt. "I just brought Apollo down to see Honey. They really hit it off and—"

"Only certain designated staff members are allowed near the guests. And that doesn't include you. Or Apollo." Rebecca held the door open, a stern look on her face. I stood slowly. As soon as he saw me move, Apollo stood and came to a perfect heel.

"It was nice meeting you, Honey. I think Apollo really appreciated the attention."

Honey smiled, I smiled, and Rebecca looked severe. Then we left, and that was the end of that.

Apollo

Samantha had me confused. She seemed so nice, with her soft voice and gentle manner. She let me do all kinds of things Lucas would never allow. But whenever Lucas appeared, she acted like a beta dog, letting him prance around with his loud voice and bristliness. If she was second to him, then Lucas must be in charge. And if she was following Lucas, then I couldn't really trust her, could I?

Still, she led me to new places. With her, I'd been to the very bottom of the studio building. We'd walked into the cafeteria, where *fourteen* different people stopped to pet me. And today we were exploring a new part of the set, down hallways I'd never sniffed. Samantha seemed nervous, peering in doors and looking up and down the hall. Her anxiety made me pant. My paws felt slick on the tile floors. I followed her, glad to be going somewhere new, but wondering what had her worried. Was Lucas down here? I couldn't smell him, but I stayed alert for a whiff of metallic anger odor.

At last she stopped at a door, looked up and down the hall, and then pulled me in behind her. I held my breath, waiting to see what terrible monster lurked inside. But the room was empty. All it held was white tables and plastic chairs, like the big meeting room upstairs. I sniffed dry-erase ink and carpet, plus spilled soda. Near the corner, I was pretty sure someone had ground Doritos into the carpet, but I couldn't find any crumbs. Just a lingering scent of fake sour cream.

Samantha was busy examining the whiteboards and colorful markings that lined the walls of this room, so I decided to lie down on top of the Doritos spot. My head felt full this week. I was facing a professional dilemma, and I couldn't figure out what to do.

Honey and Chad had the saddest hearts I'd ever encountered. Honey couldn't even look at Chad without a shuddering breath that was so quiet I didn't think anyone could hear it but me. And Chad acted full of bluster, but he always turned a shade pinker when Honey was around. There had been love there once, I was sure of it, but something had broken it. Something was stuck. They were like two dogs who wanted the same toy and were ready to fight over it—completely forgetting that they were normally best friends.

I had some ideas about ways to help, but the only time I saw them was on the set. And when I was on the set, I was performing the skills Lucas had taught me, like nudging Honey in the backs of the knees with my nose or taking Chad a tug-of-war rope. None of that gave me time to send thoughts to either of them.

I was lying there, sniffing Doritos and thinking about love, when I heard a familiar squeaking sound down the hall. It sounded like shoes, the same shoes that had surprised us when Samantha and I visited Honey in her perfumey room. They belonged to the little woman who wore the headset, and the last time she spoke to us, Samantha had been nervous. Fearful.

The squeaking shoes were coming nearer. I stood up, panting hard, and went closer to Samantha—still being careful not to touch her. Lucas hated it when I brushed against him. She looked down at me, smiled, and said something, but then she went back to looking at the whiteboards on the walls. Disaster! The shoes were closer than ever. Soon they would turn down the hall our room was on, and we'd be caught. I felt sure Samantha didn't want that.

There was only one thing to do. I stood very still, lowered my head, and concentrated. *Leave now. We should go.* I aimed the thought directly at Samantha. *Leave now. NOW.*

Samantha swung away from the whiteboards.

"I think we should go," she whispered, picking up the end of my leash. In five steps, she was at the door with me on her heels. I was panting so hard I could barely hear the squeaky shoes. It had worked! She'd heard me! Lucas never heard my thoughts, even the ones that were meant to help him. Most people didn't hear me. But she had—she was different!

We stepped into the hall and turned left. Before we'd passed the threshold, the little woman in the headset rounded the corner ahead of us. I felt Samantha's grip tighten on my leash. Traces of the fearful smell waved off her skin. We kept on walking.

"What are you doing down here?" Little headset woman seemed irritated with us.

Samantha straightened her shoulders. "Lost again! This place is a real maze. I wonder if the studio's thought about posting better signs?"

Little headset woman gave her a hard look. "Generally, the people who come down here all know where they're going." Her words had a pointed sharpness to them that made me think of the metal prongs in a corrective collar. If she'd been a dog, she'd have bared her teeth at us. "You really need to stick to the upstairs hallways."

"I would, but they're so crowded," Samantha said. She had a smile on her face, but I could tell she felt anxious inside. Like she wanted to put her tail between her legs. "And Apollo needs a walk between training sessions. It helps him calm down." She looked down at me. "Doesn't it, boy?"

I wasn't sure what she was saying, but her tone was chipper, so I wagged. The little headset woman was frowning at us, her arms crossed. She looked like she wasn't going to let us leave, as if Samantha and I were in big trouble. I could only think of one way to help. I moved closer to the wall and lifted my leg, as if I was about to pee.

"Hey," Samantha said, drawing me away, "see that? We'd better run!"

We zipped away, moving as fast as we could. As soon as we were out of the woman's sight, Samantha started to laugh. "Oh, Apollo, you are just the best, do you know that?"

My tail kept wagging. Samantha had actually heard me! That was the most exciting thing that had happened since the day Mason gave me my rope.

It made me wonder new and wild things. If I sent her thoughts about rubbing my belly, would she do it? My tail wagged harder, imagining. I couldn't think of the last time someone had rubbed my stomach. It had probably been Kim, or Lucas before he turned cold to me. My belly was the best part of me, more important even than my feet. All of my love came from my belly. And my best ideas.

We climbed the stairs and wove through the halls

until we reached the set. There we stood together in the wings. I shifted from foot to foot, unsure if I should try to send her the message. It would be a simple one. And because I wanted it so badly, I knew I could send it clearly.

Just then, Lucas came in, shuffling and smelling of cigarettes and fried fish. "You can't leave his leashes in a heap," he grumped. "That's what the peg is for."

"Right, yes, of course," she said, instantly subservient. She jumped up and started moving my leashes while Lucas stood with his hands on his hips, watching. As the power of the room circled around him, my wonderful idea toppled to the floor. I didn't fight to get it back. There was no point in sending the message to Samantha. Even if she heard it, she wouldn't do the rubbing. Lucas was her alpha; she was the beta. She would never do it. She'd never know I had helped her downstairs, saving her from the little headset woman. I was the only one who would ever know.

—10—

💻 Samantha

I drove home that night with my mind spinning over what I'd seen in the writer's room. The show was more than scripted—it was blueprinted, micromanaged, and orchestrated down to the last second. Those storyboards had the whole thing sketched out. I'd seen every last minute of the Honey and Chad episode, including acting notes for each of them. Honey was supposed to soften and wipe away a tear when Apollo brought her a purple rose, a reminder of her first date with Chad. Chad was to reach out and hug her after she told him she knew he needed time with his buddies. It was as fake as press-on nails.

I was ecstatic.

The storyboards also showed Apollo's tasks throughout the show. I'd seen when he was supposed to bound onstage, bursting through a wooden flap that had *Mender of Heartaches* printed on it. I knew now why we'd been practicing with the plastic rose, why he'd spent time sitting with Chad and Honey on the set couch, and why he had to trot around with that ring box in his mouth.

As I'd stood there, looking at the boards, I could hear Apollo breathing behind me. I knew I was acting standoffish with him. I couldn't help it—considering that I was there to out the show, being kind to him felt smarmy. But as I looked over those boards, I felt a new emotion welling up. Sympathy.

Poor Apollo. He really was a talented dog—he could handle all manner of skills and tricks. And look what they were doing to him, making him trot around with ring boxes and roses. I felt a little silly even thinking the thought, but wasn't his time worth more than that?

I'd only had my new job a few days, but already I was growing used to the shock I felt when I entered the silent world of my apartment after all the hubbub of the studio. Zephyr ran to greet me, and I let her sniff my hands and clothes as long as she wanted. She seemed to find Apollo's scent fascinating. I found two new rejection letters in the mailbox, as well as a warning notice from the credit card company. Vern's check was going to come just in time.

My mom had invited herself over for dinner (which she was bringing), so I took a shower and prepped my taste buds for organic mushrooms and sprouted bulgur. Sure enough, when Mom arrived, she plated up bowls of quinoa stir-fry that mounded over with straw mushrooms. "I've been making my own sprouts," she told me. "These are lima bean. What do you think?"

I munched along, avoiding the question, complimenting Mom instead on the bright orange scarf that held back her long, gray hair. It was a batik, she told me, made by a friend of hers at the artist's co-op. The patterns were designed by women in villages in Indonesia.

I figured I was in for another long talk about the importance of microlending to help the rural women of third world countries, but Mom made some uncharacteristically vague remarks about the weather, and then fell silent. I raised an eyebrow at her.

"Is something up?" I asked. "Is it Cassie? This new guy of hers?"

Mom tried to look blank. "Cassie's fine, I think," she said, fishing out a lima bean sprout with her chopsticks. She'd challenged herself to eat with chopsticks for an entire year—she never went anywhere without a pair. "She and Lulu came over to plant zinnias and sweet peas the other day. They seemed great."

More silence filled my little living room as Mom chomped on bok choy and I piled quinoa onto my fork. I gave her one more curious look, and she cracked.

"I wasn't sure if I should tell you this or not," she said, lowering her bowl. "Louise Ordway called me."

Louise Ordway—Richard's mom? The mushrooms in my mouth suddenly seemed huge and disturbingly chewy. When I finally got them down my throat, I took a drink of water. "What did she want?" I asked, trying to sound normal. Levelheaded. Cool as cool could be.

"Just to talk about Richard and find out how you are. See what you're up to. She said—well, maybe you don't want to hear."

"What?"

Mom looked uncomfortable, like an unwilling messenger. "She said Richard's been trying to get in touch with you."

"Why?"

"She didn't say. Maybe he's lonely?"

Richard, lonely? I almost laughed. He was the one who'd always complained that I forced him to be too social. That I made him go to too many dinners with other couples. *We always have people over,* he'd said. *Why can't we just be quiet at home?* This, I must add, was like telling a hermit that she threw too many parties. I mean, I'm hardly Ms. Social. I like quiet nights with my cat more than most people. It was just that, compared with Richard, I looked like the queen bee of socializing.

"Well, he deserves it if he is," I said.

"So he does," Mom agreed. "I implied as much to Louise, but she was pretty cagey about what he wanted. Just said she hoped you would pick up the phone if he called. I hope I haven't upset you, sweetie. I just thought you should know."

I squeezed my nails into my palms, surprised by the angry heat that rushed to my brain at the mention of Richard's name. I remembered a time early in our relationship, maybe at about the three-month mark, when I was over at his apartment. Richard was working on one of his never-ending research projects, staring at his laptop screen with his glasses pushed up on the top of his head. I had my guitar with me, and was trying to master the opening to Heart's "Crazy on You." From time to time, as I paused between attempts, I'd look up at him and try to decide if he looked adorable—in a nerdy, sweet kind of a way—or utterly burned out. He'd reached that point where his eyes were turning red, and I knew that all this staring at the screen would result in his spending all the next day complaining about eye twitches.

I'd decided that he was adorable, if slightly nerdy looking. I tried the opening riff again, getting caught up in the undulating rhythm that drew me like a traveler on a mysterious road. The bluesy sound reached deep into me and stirred me from the core up. I looked at Richard again. He was rubbing his eyes. The poor man needed a break. And I was just the woman to give it to him.

I set my Gretsch aside, walked slowly over, and stood behind him, rubbing his shoulders and chest in slow, purposeful movements. I slid a hand up through his hair and let my nails trickle down his scalp. Then I bent down and kissed his neck.

"Um, Samantha?"

"Mm-hmm."

He shifted to the side, turning to look at me. "What are you doing?"

I smiled slyly. "You looked like you could use a break," I said.

Richard's glasses tumbled off his head, onto the floor. He bent down to get them, breaking contact with my hands. When he came back up, his face was pink—whether from being upside down or being aroused, I couldn't tell. "Now's just not the best time," he said. He nodded at the screen. "I'm really pretty deep into this." I stepped away. He turned and caught my wrist. "But, maybe later?"

"Sure." I nodded, knowing my face was flaming. I went back to my guitar and bent over my songbook. I played a few halfhearted songs while Richard sank back into his data. Half an hour later, I mumbled something about feeding Zephyr and slipped out the door. We never talked about that incident again. But on my way home, I vowed to let Richard set the tempo when it came to sex. I wouldn't put myself out there like that again. I just couldn't.

So it was gratifying to hear that he was lonely. That should be exactly what you get when you dump your fiancée at the altar. When she's the one who has to march to the front of the church, alone, and tell everyone they have to go back home because the groom won't be coming after all. I could still feel the ice in my stomach as I made that long walk. I could hear the starchy sound my wedding dress made as everyone turned to look at me, wondering *what happened*? *Why isn't the music playing*?

I'd thought Richard loved me, and that our love would last forever. Seeing it crumble was so painful that I'd fallen into a sensory coma for months after it happened. When I woke up, I was faced with a completely different realization. I hadn't just been hurt. I hadn't just been mortified. I had been stupid. Plain old stupid. And that hurt worst of all.

After dinner, Mom served us fruit salad and loaded up my fridge with tofu, tempeh, and two huge bags of spinach from the garden. "I can't keep up with it," she said. "I've frozen two batches of spinach soup already, and the freezer's getting full. Can you take it to work?"

What, and hand it out as a door prize? I could just imagine how popular that would be at the studio. *Spinach, spinach, get your free spinach!*

"Sure," I said. "I'm sure I can find something to do with it."

Mom closed the refrigerator door and turned back to me, smiling. "Do you remember that garden we had when we lived in San Antonio Heights? Where Norah used to eat the cherry tomatoes right off the bush?"

I laughed. The three of us—Mom, Cassie, and I— had huddled inside the kitchen window, watching as our big German shepherd crept up to the tomato bush, looked around to make sure no one was watching, and daintily bit off a little red fruit. She ate five of them while we cracked up inside the house. "Yeah, we kept wondering where they all went."

"And then we knew!" Mom's eyes were shining with the memory. "You and Norah were so close. It makes me happy that you have this new job, working with Apollo. I always wished you'd get another dog."

I felt a tightening behind my eyes, so I turned around and pretended to be busy putting the dishes in the sink.

"She was like your lifeline, I think," Mom said, "when your dad and I were getting divorced. I remember you spent every spare minute with her. And she was just devoted to you."

I nodded. We'd been devoted to each other. I remembered the way she would let me kiss her good night, planting one soft kiss right above her nose, then leaning my forehead against hers while I rubbed her neck. At first I'd been afraid I was imposing myself on her, putting my face up against hers like that. But it wasn't long before she started lifting her face to mine, raising her nose to be kissed and then leaning her head toward mine. It was our own version of the Vulcan mind meld. As long as we were like that, it seemed like we were one creature instead of two. It was the safest feeling I'd ever had.

🦴 Apollo

I stood in the wings with Lucas, waiting for his cue. He was nervous—the sweat on his shirt smelled sour and sharp. But I wasn't. This was a studio day, and on these days I spent more time with Mason than with any other.

Yesterday Mason and I went the beach with the crew, then to a gravelly place where Chad and Honey ate ice cream cones. Today, in the studio, Mason was sitting on the couch with me at his feet. He was speaking seriously to Honey and Chad in a tone that I understood completely. I figured he was telling them to get their relationship in order, that their unhappiness was causing heartache for everyone around them. He was acting as an alpha dog should, helping the others get in line for the good of the pack. Chad and Honey didn't have to be best friends and share a dog bed or clean each other's ears, but they had to drop the ugly feelings that bubbled up whenever they were near each other. *We can all sense those feelings,* I imagined him saying. *You have to let them go.*

To support Mason's case, I lay on the ground and fixed them, one at a time, with my most convincing stare. At last, here, I had time to send them my thoughts. *Listen to him.* I beamed my thoughts at Honey first, then at Chad. *You'll be happier if you do.*

That was a joyous moment, and when Mason was finished talking, he set his hand on my back and I felt filled with light. We'd been working as a team, a perfect partnership! I felt I'd been a real help to him, and that gave me more pleasure than anything.

The director called, "Cut," and Mason stood up, so I stood, too, sure that our work was done. But almost immediately, Chad and Honey started whispering to each other, their faces red. Honey said two words to Chad, then swung back to face the audience, her legs crossed, arms folded over her middle. Chad was spread out, knees apart, arms resting on the back of the couch.

But he wasn't relaxed. A muscle in his jaw twitched every few seconds, and he drummed his fingers on the couch fabric.

I felt like jumping on both of them and licking their faces until they laughed, or at least smiled. Honestly, why couldn't they just have a quick fight and get over it? Dogs would have settled this long ago. A few snarls, a bite or two, and they'd know how things stood. Then they could go back to important things, like enjoying being onstage with Mason.

But when I looked for him, Mason was gone. That wasn't strange—I often worked on the stage with people other than him—but I did like to keep tabs on him. At last I spotted him up in the audience seats, where he never went. He was sidling in, moving past people from the prop department and the writers' room. He seemed to be moving toward one person in particular. I had to strain my eyes against the lights to see—it was Sam.

My heart swelled with pride as he sat down next to her. Sam was one of my people— she spent more time with me than anyone in this room. If Mason had a dog's nose, he'd have known that she smelled of me. Sam might even rub my belly one day. And Mason had chosen to sit next to *her*. I felt as warm as if his hand were still on my head. I sighed with pleasure. Seeing this made up for the fact that I had to go work with Lucas again. It almost—almost—let me ignore the nasty emotions that simmered off Honey and Chad. I just had to keep my eyes fixed on the good things. That was the way to build love in the world.

Samantha

When Mason appeared beside me, I was so startled I almost dropped my tea.

"Mind if I sit here?" he asked, smiling my way. It was a boyish smile—sweet and unassuming. I suddenly felt bad for the thoughts I'd had about him weeks ago, sitting in front of my TV screen. Because he was so handsome, I'd automatically dubbed him as the kind of arrogant jerk who used women and threw them away. But maybe I was wrong. Maybe he didn't know how much the female world drooled over him. Or maybe he truly didn't care.

Regardless, why was he sitting next to me? And why did he keep looking at me in that way that made my skin feel sunburned?

"How does it look?" he asked, watching me resettle my tea, uncross my legs, and cross them again.

"How does what look?" I asked.

"The show. The episode." He waved at the stage. "Apollo was great, as usual."

Was he fishing for a compliment? I looked over at

him. His eyes were shining, and he was leaning toward the stage as if he couldn't wait to see what would happen next—even though he must have seen the storyboards. He looked as if he was about to leap out of his seat in excitement.

"It's great," I said. "It's going really well."

"You're not just saying that?" His face was serious now.

I gave a little laugh. "You don't need me to tell you that people love this show, right?"

"Sure," he said, nodding thoughtfully, "but that doesn't mean it's as good as it can be. I don't want us to be complacent, putting out a show that's just okay. I want *The Love Dog* to be great."

We both watched the action on the set for a minute, then Mason gave a quiet snort. "Apollo's brilliant. I don't know how he understands what people want him to do, but he really gets it. The first time I met him, on the *Race of a Lifetime* set, it was like he read my mind."

I thought back to what Valerie had told me. "That was the season finale?"

"Yeah." Mason was grinning, chuckling to himself. "The winning team was so pissed at each other they couldn't even talk about the amazing victory they'd just had. I'd been working with Apollo for a couple of days by then and I saw how well he responded to direction. So finally, after I'd tried everything—and I mean everything—to get these two people to warm up, I brought Apollo in. And I went around behind the winning team with a couple of cheese crackers—you know the ones that come in the little packets? I held the crackers up between them, where Apollo could see but no one else could. Then I dropped them and left.

I think they landed on the people's shoulders. Apollo was on them in about half a second. He licked the heck out of those people, and it totally saved the day. That was when I knew he could be the star of a show like this. Even without food, he'll do anything he's told to do. His instincts are amazing. Plus, he looks the part, doesn't he?"

I looked up at Apollo, sitting on the set, and wondered if I should tell him I thought the dog's talents were wasted on a scripted show like this. That he seemed capable of so much more. *No*, I thought. *That would seem crazy*. Instead, I decided to dig a little, to see just how much Mason knew about the Love Dog's fakery. "Well, this was my first time really watching him work, but I thought he was terrific. You all did an awesome job, especially considering how Honey and Chad feel about each other."

He glanced at me. "What do you mean? How do they feel?"

I shrugged, trying to give the impression that it was common knowledge. "Well, they were a couple back when they signed on to the show. And now they're not. Haven't you seen the nasty looks they give each other?"

"Nooo," he said slowly, "I sure haven't."

After that he was quiet for a long while, and I kicked myself for ruining my own chance to keep him talking. We watched Apollo trot around on stage with a rose in his mouth, pretending to take it from Chad to Honey. Mason pulled a headset from his pocket and said a few cryptic things to Imogen Blakely, then sat back in his seat, his arms crossed. A minute later, Honey said she needed a bathroom break and the director told everyone to take five.

"I had a thought about Apollo," I said. In the tiers

of seats above and below us, I sensed members of the crew listening, but pretending not to. I kept my voice low and my face angled toward Mason. "It's his room."

That got his attention. I swallowed hard, hoping I'd be able to hold his interest.

"What about it?" He leaned closer to me, sucking half the air out of the room.

"Have you seen it?" He must not have, or he would've known what I was talking about. "Well, it's pretty awful. It's just a cinder-block room. Hardly homey. I know he spends most of his time in his kennel, but even so, that room has to have an effect on his morale."

"What do you mean? I thought he lived at Lucas's house."

I gave him a quizzical look. "I think Lucas lives somewhere north of Santa Clarita. Wherever it is, it's pretty far away. No, Apollo stays here at night. He sleeps in a kennel in that nasty little room way down deep in the bowels of the building. It's completely industrial—all noisy pipes and bare walls. Hardly star accommodations."

Mason looked down at his shoes. Again I had the feeling that I'd just blown a little boy's belief in Santa Claus. "Wow, I had no idea. I thought he went home with Lucas every night. Will you show me where he stays? If it's as bad as you say, I'm sure I can do something to make it better."

I resisted the urge to put my hand on his sleeve, to smooth the fabric and try to unrumple him. I hadn't meant to depress him, just distract him.

"Thanks for telling me," Mason added, fixing me with his bright blue eyes. "It's hard to know everything that's going on in this place. I need people like you to let me know when things aren't right, especially with

Apollo. He spends so much time here, I want to make sure his life is as good as it can possibly be. A studio is really no place for a dog."

I couldn't have agreed more. And I realized, as I glanced over the handsome angles of his face and saw the way his auburn hair tumbled across his forehead, that I was developing far too much sympathy for Mason Hall. I needed to be a barracuda. Dirt, that was what I was here for, not to help Mason turn the studio into a fun zone for Apollo. I needed to pry, and pry hard. But first I just needed to get him talking.

"Did you have a dog growing up?" I asked, feeling sure that he must have.

Mason got a distant look in his eyes, as if he were remembering something cloudy and very far away. Then he nodded. "Wonderful dogs. We had three when I was growing up—all border collies. I spent hours throwing tennis balls for them in the park by our house. I wish we had room for that here—I'd love to play ball with Apollo."

Hmm, border collies. Now we were getting somewhere. "Where did you live?"

"Madrona, in Washington state, the town where we'll be filming the last show. You've probably never heard of it, have you?"

I shook my head. Mason nodded, seeming unsurprised. "It was a great place to grow up. As a kid, I could ride my bike all over town with one of the dogs trailing behind me. The town is a lot bigger now, but it's still pretty cool. They have this big dog festival every year called Woofinstock. People come from all over, but it's really a festival for dogs. The people are secondary. Apollo would love it."

"Doesn't it rain all the time in Washington?" I knew

I was supposed to be digging for dirt, but this conversation felt so easy, I didn't have the heart to alter its course.

"Yeah, yeah, that's what everyone in here says," he said with a grin. "But the rain keeps it green, so it's all good. Though there is that old joke, that we only have two seasons, rain and August. We just say that, though, to keep the Californians from moving in."

"Fair enough. And I bet people there aren't sad to skip out on our big Los Angeles fires."

Mason shook his head. "No, those things are brutal. Problems in the Northwest are more along the lines of slugs and mildew."

I sat back and took a sip of my tea. I really, really sucked at this. Here I was, on a mission to dig up dirt about this guy, and all I could do was chat with him about the rain in Washington. As much as I enjoyed hearing about his family dogs, there wasn't going to be anything there that I could print in the *Telltale*. No one picked up the scandal mag for news about someone's childhood pet. I needed to find a little misery, a tiny speck at least. "So, your family . . . ?"

He shrugged. "It's pretty Norman Rockwell, to be honest. A mom and a dad, and an annoying little brother." He turned to look down at the stage, where Lucas was leading Apollo back and forth on his lead. Was I imagining things, or had a shadow fallen across Mason's face? My every instinct told me to leave a sensitive subject alone, but I kept on pushing.

"Yeah, I have an annoying big sister. It's amazing how much chaos she can stir up."

"Mm-hmm." His eyes were fixed on the stage, but his mind seemed to be a thousand miles away. Maybe a thousand miles north on Interstate 5.

Mason's eyes shifted toward me in a questioning way, as if he were trying to read me, to get a sense of who I was. I tried to look as trustworthy as possible, not an easy feat when I felt like such a traitor, as if the word *spy* was about to break out on my forehead. In the end, I hid my face behind my paper cup and pretended to sip my tea.

He tipped his head closer to mine, his eyes downcast. "I shouldn't have called him annoying. Annoying is more than an understatement. It's missing the mark altogether. Zach is . . . troubled. He has problems. Drug problems."

I froze. Or, to be more accurate, my limbs froze—and my mind along with them—but my heart pummeled against my rib cage. This was unbelievable. Had he really just dropped a plum piece of information right in my lap? Seriously, a druggie brother? My hands suddenly felt very cold in spite of my hot teacup.

"Wow," I breathed, unsure what to say. I still couldn't believe my . . . what? Luck? Was it really luck when a spy uncovered secrets she never really wanted to know about? "That must have been rough. For your whole family."

Mason nodded. "It's worse for my parents," he said. It might have been my imagination, but I thought he looked faintly relieved. I, on the other hand, had never felt more agitated in my life. "But it's changed my relationship with him forever. Every conversation is loaded now. It's impossible to talk about something simple, like even baseball, without Zach feeling like I'm making some kind of value judgment."

He ran a hand across the back of his neck. I couldn't help thinking that it was a move that would play well on television. As if he didn't have enough female fol-

lowers already—that one little neck rub was enough
to arouse half the population. "That was how I knew
Apollo was special in the first place," he said. "When I
first met him, on the *Race of a Lifetime* finale, I had
my brother with me. During breaks and whenever we
had a free moment, Apollo would go sit by Zach. He
sought him out—it made Zach feel special, I could tell.
They spent hours together with Zach just petting
him and petting him. And during those days, I don't
know—I felt Zach change a little. Perk up. Smile a little
more. Then, the day the shooting wrapped, he told
me he was ready to try rehab." Mason sighed softly.
"He only stayed for five days, but still. It was the first
time he'd gone voluntarily. And it was all Apollo's
doing. This might sound crazy, but I know Apollo
changed him, put his mind in a better space. I've always been grateful for that."

Suddenly the Earl Grey wasn't sitting right in my
stomach. I didn't want to hear any more about Mason's
brother, or his family, or any of his secrets. I didn't even
want to hear why he was so grateful to Apollo. But he
kept talking.

"The truth is, I need to visit home more. It would be
better if I did."

I squirmed in my seat. "I'm sure the show must keep
you pretty busy."

Mason shrugged. "Sure, but that's really just an excuse. I could visit more if I tried. In fact"—he glanced
up at me, his eyes bright—"that's part of why I want
the show to go on the road in Madrona. To see if we
could film there, if we get picked up for another season. I'd love to move the whole show, if we can make
it work with the weather. It's almost as cheap as filming in Canada."

I sat there, dry mouthed, while Mason moved his attention to the stage. The break was over, and Chad and Honey had resumed their seats. I could see Pilar wearing her headset, clipboard in hand, running around, ducking under the sound booms. Apollo, I knew, was waiting in the wings for his entrance. My phone buzzed in my pocket and I pulled it out. Vern had texted: LOOKING FORWARD TO UR FIRST ARTICLE. I stared at the screen, my heart thumping. Then I deleted the message and slid the phone back into my pocket, wishing I could slip away along with it.

Apollo

I sat in front of the swinging wooden door, my whole body wriggling. I was excited—Mason was watching, Sam was watching, and Honey and Chad were waiting for me on the other side. I'd had some time to think and I was ready. I had a plan.

Lucas bent down and held out the rose, and I clamped it between my teeth. Then I dropped my head and—before I could think too much about it—burst onto the stage. Honey looked surprised when I trotted out and dropped the rose into her lap. She glanced at Chad, her eyes narrowed into slits. He pretended to smile back and gestured at the rose as if it were something exciting, like a bone or a piece of rope, but he couldn't hide his real feelings, not from me. When he looked at Honey, he was irritated and ashamed, and somehow that shame made him even more irritated. He looked like a dog who's done something wrong and is waiting to be punished.

Well, this time I had a surprise for him. I knew the

next thing I was supposed to do was to wait offstage while Chad and Honey sat on the couch together, but I paused for a moment before I took my mark. At the moment, only the three of us were on set. Everyone else was either in the wings or up in the seats, watching. Lucas would never know; Mason wouldn't know. Only Honey and Chad would be able to see and hear me. I leaned in close to Honey and put my muzzle right near her hand.

Then I growled. Ferociously. With my teeth bared.

Honey jumped. Chad started and leaned in. "Hey!" he said, edging his shoulder toward Honey. "What do you think you're doing?" He had one eye on the cameras, one eye on me. I dropped my head and slunk back, pretending to be chastised. As I backed away, I saw Chad's hand cover Honey's. Her face was a mixture of worry and relief. I felt bad for scaring her, but it was all worth it when I saw her turn her body toward Chad's, dipping her face toward his shoulder. He sat tall, legs spread, making himself as large as possible. Perfect. He might not be able to talk to Honey, or to give her roses himself, but if he would move like this to protect her, then there was still love between them.

I loped off the stage, feeling light and frothy like a cloud. I'd spent a lot of time watching clouds during my weekends at Lucas's place. When you're locked up in a kennel for days at a time, there isn't much more to do than watch the sun trace its line across the sky and look for clouds. I loved clouds—they brought shade and sometimes rain. Clouds were full of love, and right then I felt full of clouds.

The air around the stage was a note warmer now, and the sharp, tangy smell was gone. I didn't detect any love—not yet—but a spring wind had blown the bad feelings away.

When I left the stage and returned to Lucas, I felt a twinge of regret. If he knew what I'd done—that I'd growled at a guest—he would probably lock me in a kennel for the rest of my life. I hadn't thought about that when I made my plan. I would have to be more careful while Lucas was around. And with Sam, I would just have to wait and see.

I sat down next to Lucas's feet, prepared to be the world's most obedient dog to make up for that growl. He seemed agitated, moving his hands in and out of his pockets, looking from the stage to the steps that led to the seating area. "Where is she?" he muttered gruffly. His right hand reached for his shirt pocket, then dropped down.

Just then I heard the jangle of metal bracelets behind us. Lucas and I both turned to see Pilar, her clipboard on her hip. Lucas's face lit up. "Hey, do me a favor?"

Pilar looked wary. She lifted her eyebrows in a questioning way.

"I get a cigarette break at ten. Sam's gone AWOL. Can you keep an eye on him for a second?" Lucas tilted his head toward me, and I shifted from paw to paw. I hoped his agitation had nothing to do with me. I hoped no one had told him about the growl.

Pilar bent her face to look at her watch. "Sure, if you're quick about it. I have to get Honey and Chad ready in fifteen." She stepped close to me, and Lucas strode away, reaching into his shirt pocket as he went for a pack of cigarettes. Pilar looked down at me. "You sure had an effect on Honey and Chad out there," she said. "That was the first time I've seen her look at him without seeming like she's about to cry. They don't call you the Love Dog for nothing, eh?"

I sensed a compliment, so I wagged my tail. Pilar had such a gentleness about her. She also had a scone in her hand. Blueberry. With icing. I wanted to be kind to her—not just because of the scone, but because she'd always been nice to me. And who knew, maybe I'd get a fat wedge of scone.

I saw Pilar looking across at the props table, the place where they kept the purple rose when I wasn't taking it out onstage. Behind it stood A.J., the same guy Pilar and I visited in the room that smelled like chemicals and plastic. He had his face down, pretending to be busy, as if he didn't want to look at us. Which was silly, of course. I'd smelled the odor he gave off when he was near Pilar—I knew about his passion for her. And I knew she felt the same, although today her scent was spicy with hesitation, sharp notes overlaying the brown-sugar smell of her.

Ordinarily, I would have kept still. My desire to obey Lucas would have kept my butt planted on the floor. But Lucas wasn't there. And I had just achieved great things on the stage—I could feel the love at the tip of my nose, on the bridge of my belly, and the pads of my feet. And those feet itched for action.

I dashed away from Pilar and ran around the back of the props table. As I'd hoped, Pilar looked up when she saw that I had gone. "Hey, Apollo! Come on back— I'm supposed to be watching you."

I hid underneath the props table, watching A.J.'s shoes shuffle back and forth. A second later, Pilar's suede clogs appeared not far from A.J. This was my moment. I slipped out from under the table, scooting behind A.J. Putting all my energy into my shoulder, I bumped into the back of A.J.'s knees, knocking him into Pilar.

They would have fallen, but as he crashed forward, A.J. grasped Pilar around the waist and caught his other hand against the props table. She hung there in midspace, her hands clutching his shoulders. They hovered for a second, while a soupy mix of scents crackled through the air. My tail zipped back and forth.

A.J. pulled them both up to standing. His face was red; Pilar's a rosy pink.

"Apollo, man, what did you do that for?" Even though he used my name, he was looking at Pilar.

She took a step back. "Apollo, come on. We're in the way back here." Pilar turned away, beckoning for me to follow her. Instantly, I was up on all fours, ready for action. I'd had so much success—their scents had blended, and the mix was so strong it made me feel light-headed. I couldn't let them break apart now.

As Pilar walked away from the table, I ran up behind her and butted the back of her knee with my head. These two were acting the way people did sometimes, each pretending the other didn't exist. I'd seen this before—people could sit next to each other and not even exchange a look. I needed to shake them up, knock things loose. When Pilar crouched down, thinking I needed something, I used my teeth to grab the piece of paper that was sticking out of her back pocket. I remembered this paper, remembered the smell that clung to it—a mix of anger and self-righteousness, a smell I'd noticed on Lucas a thousand times.

When Pilar saw what I had done, her face turned white, but it was too late. I was already on my way to A.J., halfway through pressing the paper into his hand. It crinkled as he unfolded it. Then he flushed deeply.

"Uh, Pilar, I can explain . . ."

She swung toward him, one hand on her hip, her small body throwing off anger. "Okay. Go ahead then."

A.J. looked at his shoes. "Um, well, it's kind of complicated."

Pilar raised an eyebrow. "I'm kind of complicated, too," she said. "Come on, Apollo. We have things to do."

I followed her with heavy paws. What had happened? I'd done everything right, I was sure, but now they were further apart than they had been before. Touching hadn't helped. Sharing anger and secret feelings hadn't helped. What was I missing? Why did humans find love so difficult?

—12—

⌨ Samantha

That day's taping seemed to take an eternity. I stayed in my seat in the audience, while my mind fidgeted over what Mason had told me. A druggie brother—why would he have told me that? *I'm a virtual stranger. What was he thinking? Doesn't he know I could snitch to a tabloid, some smear magazine that's desperate to get its hands on a story like this? What in the world made him trust me with his family's darkest secret?*

The more I hashed it over, the more I blamed him. He worked in Hollywood—he should know better. I mean, really, why had he told me? It was the last thing I wanted to know. If he'd told me that he sold black market chimpanzees, or had shot someone, or secretly owned a telemarketing firm that purposefully called people at six o'clock every evening, I would have known what to do. I'd have ratted him out the way he deserved. But this was different.

I sat through the taping with a scowl on my face. The second it ended, I jumped up and pushed my way through the crowd down to the bottom of the stairs. When I caught up with Apollo and Lucas on the side of the stage, I couldn't speak quickly enough. "Lucas, I can manage Apollo for the rest of the day. Why don't you take off? I know you have to be in Culver City for your next taping. If you slip out now, you'll miss the worst of the traffic."

Lucas looked surprised, startled even, as if no one had ever done anything nice for him before. I smiled to show him I meant it. Within three minutes, he was gone.

I patted my leg, and Apollo followed me at a close heel as we speedwalked all the way to his room. I stuck my head inside, grabbed the longest leash I could find, and closed the door. Apollo sat at my feet, his ears perched in a quizzical way.

"I need some air," I said, "and I'm guessing you do, too. This place isn't a convent, you know. You have a right to step outside." I knew I was saying this more to myself than to him. Lucas had told me not to take Apollo out—other than to his pee area—but what dog lived his entire life inside a building?

Together we walked briskly back to the main studio. Apollo's golden tail fluttered behind him like a banner, and I felt for a second like a medieval knight with Apollo as my squire, displaying our colors for everyone to see.

When Apollo and I reached the heavy double doors that led from the studio to the parking lot, I bent down and snapped his leash to his collar. He panted with excitement. I heaved the doors open, and we stepped out into the dry heat and smoldering smell of over-cooked asphalt. I turned us to the left, where we could keep out of the sun—I didn't want Apollo's paws to roast on the hot pavement. We slipped from shady spot to shady spot, sometimes using the shade of SUVs and pickup trucks as a bridge between overhangs. Apollo's ears were lifted, his tail high. His nose scoured the air, picking up invisible scents.

After we'd walked for five minutes, we finally reached a scrubby patch of dirt and vegetation. I let Apollo's leash go slack, allowing him to explore at will. As he nosed around a dried-up sprig of oleander, I pondered my dilemma.

"He is a public figure, after all," I said. "He has to expect that people will talk about him. I mean, when he does all that stuff the movie and TV stars do—go out to dinner with supermodels and hit the red carpet at movie premieres—he has to expect that the tabloids are going to chatter about him. They'll dissect what he wears and how much his date weighs. That's what they do, right?"

I sighed and sat down on a broken piece of curb. Apollo, who'd sniffed every square millimeter of open ground, came to sit beside me. I looked at his golden face, admiring the way the hairs swirled around his eyes and nose. "You sure are nonjudgmental," I said. With cautious fingers, I reached out and smoothed the fur at his neck. He had the longest eyelashes I'd ever seen on a dog. "I'm sorry I haven't given you more affection. It's just that I'm a traitor. You don't want a traitor petting you, do you?" He shuffled a little closer. "Are you sure? I mean, I don't even believe that you're a love dog—that's how far I am from believing in this show. I'm here to undermine it, that's the truth. If I found out something awful about you, like you snort doggy cocaine, I'd write about it. I'd tell everyone. That's how bad I am."

Apollo blinked his big brown eyes, lifted one paw off the ground, and set it back down. He edged a tiny bit closer. I moved my hand down to his chest, and he closed his eyes. Then he sighed softly through his nose.

As I watched, Apollo slowly lowered himself to the ground. He moved gingerly, as if he had pain in his hips, though the way he glanced up at me made me think his hesitation had more to do with not wanting to scare me away than with arthritis or stiffness. He eased down onto his belly, looked up at me for a long moment, then rolled very slightly onto his left side. He held his right paw up off the ground, like an open invitation. I may have had my reservations, but I wasn't cruel. I crouched down and began to rub his belly.

A quiet shudder ran through Apollo's body. He looked up at me, blinking rapidly. I saw a thousand emotions in the sheen of his eyes—gratitude, appreciation, comfort. And yes, love. Though he had no reason to love me at this stage in our relationship, that was the message he was sending. I swallowed hard and focused on moving my hands across his fur. Love. The last dog that had looked at me this way was Norah—wonderful, brilliant, sensitive Norah. The most incredible dog I had ever known. I blinked away a few tears and stared at the silky hairs on Apollo's paws.

"You're right," I said, feeling his golden energy wrap around my heart. "I'm not a mean person. I just want to write. And if I'm a writer, surely I can find plenty to say about the show without having to dig into someone's personal life. I'm not here to destroy anyone. I'll write about the show, but I won't say anything about Mason's family. That's a bridge I won't cross."

Apollo reached out his left paw and set it on my

forearm. It was odd—here I was, the world's biggest
skeptic. And yet, this moment with Apollo had filled
me with more love than I'd felt in years. Love seemed
to be in my veins, like champagne bubbles. I hadn't
even felt like this when Richard and I were planning
our wedding, or when he asked me to marry him.
Strange. Very strange.

The following night, I sat in front of my computer
screen and typed my first exposé. "*Love Dog Secrets
Revealed*," I typed. That seemed like an appropriate
tabloid headline. I stretched my arms overhead and
got to work.

> *Around the world, hundreds of thousands of people
> tune in every week to watch Apollo the golden re-
> triever mend Hollywood's broken hearts. But would
> those viewers feel differently if they knew they were
> watching paid actors read scripted lines? What if
> they knew that Apollo's every move was carefully
> planned and practiced before each show? Or that,
> as often happens, the couple in question doesn't even
> know each other until they meet on set?*

My fingers scurried across the keyboard. Earlier that
evening, as I'd sat in traffic, I'd made a mental list. In
this article I would cover the storyboards, the actors,
and Apollo's training. Without naming names, I would
let the world know about the confidentiality agreement Honey had told me about and the $1.5 million
penalty for leaking secrets. I would say nothing about
Mason. Or Apollo. Maybe for the next piece I could
find out whom Mason was dating and do a little re-

search on her. Anything else I found out this week could go into the piece I filed from Madrona, Mason's hometown. It sounded like a nice place. The people of Los Angeles would probably enjoy reading about a town that wasn't overpaved, overgroomed, and overly filled with cars.

Still, when I e-mailed my article, I had some doubts. Vern wanted dirt on Mason Hall, and I was the dump truck that was supposed to deliver that dirt by the yard. Was this dirty enough for him? Without some dishy details, Vern might not pass my name up the ladder.

I jumped up, restless. Before I knew it, I was scrubbing the bathroom sink while Zephyr sat on the edge of the tub, her tail swishing. "I did the right thing, didn't I?" I asked her. "Not writing about Zach? Even if I get to know Mason Hall better and he turns out to be the world's biggest slimeball, I don't want to be the one who rats out little brothers in the press. It wouldn't matter if he found out it was me or not—I'd have to live with knowing I'd done it. No," I said, feeling more sure as I polished the chrome faucet, "I did the right thing. And my decision has nothing to do with Mason as a person. I'd do the same for anyone—it's just about being decent. Not about his being cute and having nice blue eyes and being the kind of person who brings somebody a cup of Earl Grey because they happen to remember that's what they drink."

I rinsed out the sink and was about to tackle the toilet when the phone rang. Even though it was nine o'clock, my first thought was that Vern had gotten my article and was calling to say how disappointed he was. I ran to the kitchen, feeling my heart bounce up and down in my throat.

"Hello?" I grabbed the receiver so quickly I was

slightly out of breath. Zephyr padded into the kitchen, looking curious.

"Hi."

It took me a full minute to realize that the voice on the other end of the line wasn't Vern's. It was Richard's.

"Oh. Richard. Hi." Dammit! He was the last person I wanted to talk to. Why hadn't I recognized his number? He must have changed it. "What is it? Why are you calling?"

"Well, I, uh, I just wanted to talk to you, Samantha." I pictured him sitting at the desk in his apartment, his computer screen glowing in front of him. Richard was never far from some kind of screen. I wondered if he was remembering to take his allergy medicine and to look away from his laptop every twenty minutes, the way his eye doctor told him to. Then I gave myself a mental kick in the pants. I didn't need to worry about Richard anymore—he'd relieved me of that job.

"Uh-huh." I paced to the window, looked out at the darkness, and walked back to the wall, waiting for Richard to say something more. Was Mom right? Was he lonely? If so, it was his own fault. The pig.

"There's something I need to tell you."

"Oh? What's that?"

"I, uh . . ." Long silence followed. I took a deep breath.

"Yes?"

Richard was quiet on the other end of the line. A sick feeling curled in the base of my stomach. This wasn't about his being lonely. Goose bumps popped out on my skin.

"I'm engaged," he said. "I'm getting married."

I stood completely still in my silent kitchen, surrounded by my silent apartment. Richard. Getting married. To someone other than me.

"I wanted you to know," he was saying. "I didn't want you to find out from someone else."

I could barely hear him. All my senses seemed to have quit working. I saw nothing, heard nothing. I swallowed down a thick throat, amazed that my feet were still on the floor, that I was still upright.

"Right. Of course. Thanks for telling me."

"Are you—you're not—"

"What?"

"Are you upset?"

Was I upset? Was it upsetting when the floor fell out from under you? When a roof crashed down over your head? Should I tell him the truth, that I felt like I'd been stabbed in the guts? Richard was getting married. He'd run away from our marriage, and now he was marrying someone else. Someone he actually thought he could live with. Someone better.

"Who is it?" I asked. Then I blurted, "No, no. I don't want to know. I don't. I hope you actually show up at the church this time. Or maybe I hope you don't. It doesn't matter." Humiliation was creeping up my legs, threatening to swallow me whole.

"You might have thought you loved me, Samantha, but I don't think you did. Not really. When you fall in love for real, it'll feel like so much more . . ."

What bullshit. That was pretty rich, coming from the guy who asked me to marry him and then bailed on our wedding. I'd been the one sitting at the church in a big white dress, wondering why no one could find the groom. I was the one who had to tell everyone our wedding was off because the guy who'd asked me to marry him didn't have the decency to show up. *I* didn't know what love was? Really? *I think I know pretty well, actually. Love is a four-letter word that you say to someone right before you walk away forever.*

"Oh, Richard," I said. "Go fuck yourself."

−13−

🦴 Apollo

What a week this was. Every day when I woke up, I had a full day of happiness to look forward to. First I would chew on my rope. Then Sam would arrive and we chatted while she got my leashes and things ready. We'd head to my area for peeing and marking, then I'd walk on the treadmill while she did lunges and knee raises. After that, I had my fish oil pill and my breakfast, then Sam brushed me with strokes so light my fur felt like feathers.

After that we did different things. Some days I had training with Lucas and time on the set. Other days we all rode in a bus and went somewhere fun with the guests. Lucas used to drive me on these outings with me riding in a crate in his truck. Now that Sam was with me, though, we took the bus and I got to look out the window while I sat on a plush bench. I liked to move from seat to seat, smudging the windows with my nose as I looked for other dogs. Sometimes Sam talked to me. Other times she sang.

Then, on Thursday, something miraculous happened.

When Sam was walking me through the cafeteria (where *six* people stopped to pet me), Mason came up to us. He rested his hand lightly on my head while he spoke with Sam. Then she turned, and he turned, and we all three walked down the hall toward my room.

Nothing like this had ever happened before! I was so excited I trotted out ahead of Sam as far as my leash would let me go. My tail fanned the air behind me. Sam and Mason were speaking to each other, but I could barely concentrate on their tone. I was too excited just to be walking down the hall with my two favorite people.

When we arrived at the door to my room, I hesitated, one paw raised. Were they sending me to my kennel? It was still afternoon, far too early for me to go to bed. But this was clearly an unusual day, since Mason was with us. Maybe I had to leave for Lucas's ranch right now. When Sam spoke, I perked up my ears and tried to gather what I could from her posture and the sound of her voice.

"This is his room," she said. "Whenever he isn't on set or somewhere in the studio with me, this is where he is."

She pushed open the door and held it while Mason walked in. He looked around, shaking his head. I took a few steps toward my crate, waiting to see if one of them would put me in it, but neither of them moved. They just kept looking around the room.

"It's miserable," Mason said at last. "Really depressing. Why didn't Lucas ever tell me his room was this bad?"

Sam shrugged. I had heard the word *Lucas*, so I listened hard. Whatever they were discussing, I hoped it wasn't about sending me to Lucas's place early. I wanted to stay right here with the two of them.

"I'm not sure it's high on Lucas's list of priorities," Sam said. Just then, the pipes went *clang, clang, clang,* and I flinched. "See?" she said, gesturing to me. "That noise freaks him out. And he has to sleep in here all alone."

Mason nodded as if he were thinking. I wondered how it would be, as the alpha, to have so many under-lings to keep in line. I was glad to see that Sam was more than just one of his many pack members—she had clearly risen to a higher status. That, of course, re-flected well on both of us.

"Well, no more," Mason said. His tone was firm. Decisive. I gave a quick wag in support. "We'll move him right away. The office next to mine has been empty ever since the studio took their accounting in-house. He can go in there. It'll feel like an office, not a home, but it's a damn sight better than this." He turned to Sam. "Do you have any spare time this afternoon? When Lucas is working with him? I'd like to have him all set up in his new place by Monday."

"Wow, sure," she said. They turned toward the door and I sat down, ears drooping, sure they were going to leave me here. Sam's "Come on, Apollo," surprised me so much I ran for the door and almost got tangled up with her legs. "Desperate to get out of here, eh, boy?" she said. As we turned down the hall, she smiled at Mason. "Thank you so much for doing this. I really didn't expect you'd have time to come see his room today, much less be able to move him."

Mason grinned down at his shoes as they walked. "It's nice to be the guy in charge sometimes. Especially when you can take care of something that needs fixing."

He glanced over at Sam at the same moment she looked at him. That's when I saw it. And the second after I saw it, I *felt* it. Felt it everywhere—in the air, under my feet, deep in my lungs. He liked her. It wasn't love—not yet. But it was the first hints of it, like shoots of grass springing up in the dirt. Mason, Chief Mason, our great leader, liked Sam! Sam, who fed me my fish oil pill and walked me on my treadmill! Sam who rubbed my belly! I was so pleased I almost tripped over my own feet.

Sam looked down. "Easy there, buddy. We can't have you getting injured, you know."

She and Mason both laughed in that light, soft way of theirs. Of course, why hadn't I noticed it before? Budding love, right here in front of me. I'd never had a project so close to home. And I'd certainly never had one that mattered so much. Any project that involved Mason was serious—serious enough to drop everything else for. And for Sam to be involved . . .

I looked up at Sam. So far, I'd only gotten a sense of how Mason felt. Surely Sam saw what Mason was— our leader, our alpha, the one who spoke in the Tuesday meeting and made everyone else sit and listen. Mason was the ideal mate. He was perfect—powerful, yet gentle, decisive, yet kind. I'd never met a man I admired so much.

Sam was hard to read, though. I'd been trying to understand her for a full week now and I still felt puzzled. If Mason liked her, why did she feel subservient to Lucas? And why was she avoiding Mason's gaze? She was like a dog who was so insecure she didn't want to sniff noses with anyone. She had that air of reluctance right now. But why would she try to resist Mason? Why would anyone?

🖳 Samantha

Mason surprised me. I didn't think he'd follow up on my comment about Apollo's room. I didn't even think he'd remember. But when Apollo and I hit the studio Thursday morning, after I'd been at work a little over a week, he came our way, taking his usual long strides. As soon as I saw him, an attack of guilt made me blush all over. Even though I hadn't written about his druggie brother for the *Telltale,* I had slammed his beloved TV show to a million readers. If he found out, he would still hate me. *When* he found out, I corrected. There was no way I could keep this secret forever. I could never forget that my days on the set of *The Love Dog* were numbered.

Last weekend I'd deposited Vern's check and sent a big one of my own to my credit card company. I should have been feeling relieved, getting that massive debt off my back. Instead, for some reason, I just felt trapped.

"Samantha, morning," Mason said, cutting his way through the crowd of PAs in headsets, sound guys in sweatpants, and strung-out-looking writers. Mason wore a V-neck sweater that looked like it might be cashmere, brown corduroys, and Doc Martens. Thanks to Valerie, I didn't feel like my usual shlumpy self. I wore knee-high boots, a short skirt and tights, and a top with a swirly orange print that I never would have attempted two months ago. Did I imagine the look of approval on Mason's face when he saw me? That seemed impossible—he must be used to women who wore Vera Wang and Valentino. "I can't break away right now," he said, "but later I was hoping you'd show me Apollo's room. The place you told me about?"

I was stunned then, and I continued to be stunned two hours later when he actually appeared, ready to explore the bowels of the building with me. And that level of stunned was nothing—it was bargain-basement stuff—compared with how I felt when he offered Apollo the office next to his. Absolutely remarkable. I was so glad I'd decided to keep his family secrets to myself.

On our return, after we reached the main part of the building, people swarmed us, showering Mason with questions. They wanted to know what to do about a broken light, whether the assistant director's mother could watch the taping, and was Apollo going to pose with a Seminal phone, in a nod to our top sponsor? A five-foot-tall woman with hoop earrings the size of my fist squeezed in beside him.

"Sorry—Mason, can I have Apollo for just fifteen minutes today? Twenty, tops?"

I looked at Mason with my eyebrows raised.

"Isabella, this is Sam, Apollo's handler." Isabella smiled at me enthusiastically. Mason turned my way. "Isabella's in promo. She wants to do a photo shoot of Apollo so she can have pictures to send out to his fans."

Isabella leaned toward me, her breath smelling like cinnamon gum. "I answer his fan mail," she said. "A photo with Apollo's paw print on it would make my packet super cool."

Just like that, Apollo and I had a date with Isabella's photo crew. *Fan mail. Unbelievable. Who writes fan letters to a dog?* Ordinarily, I'd have dismissed such letter writers as freaks with nothing better to do, but I couldn't do that, not in light of the conversation I'd had with my own sister that very morning. Cassie had called me on my way in to work.

"So?" she'd asked, sounding breathless. I could hear *PBS Kids* on TV in the background. She must have been getting her daughter, Lulu, ready for school. "What's Apollo like? Do you get a serious love vibe off him? Is everyone on the set wildly happy in love or what?"

I'd laughed. "Ha-ha, very funny. Good one, Cass."

"No, I'm serious. He's the Love Dog—there must be some serious romance floating around that place. Or does he save it all for the couples on the show?"

"Cass, he's just a dog."

She snorted. "Just a dog, my big behind. Sam, he's the Love Dog! I know you weren't a believer before, but I thought you'd be converted by now after seeing him at work. Besides, you know dogs can sense all kinds of things we can't—cancer and seizures and panic attacks. It isn't crazy to think Apollo has extragood senses when it comes to love." She gasped, suddenly overcome by a great notion. "Oh my God, Sam, do you think I could meet him? Could I bring Liam to meet him? If he could see us together, I bet he could straighten things out in a heartbeat . . ."

And that's when I realized the glaring truth. My sister—my very own sister, the woman who shared more of my DNA than possibly any other person on the planet—was never going to believe that Apollo was just a dog. A dog like Norah, like Benji, like Lassie, like thousands of other dogs. It didn't matter how many articles I wrote explaining that the show was staged and scripted. She would still think Apollo had some magical love power. She'd think it because she *wanted* to. Desperately. And no amount of ink from me would ever change that.

Plus, Cassie would never be swayed by one of my articles because Cassie didn't read the *Telltale*.

Only one thing would convince her, and that would be seeing the truth with her own eyes. If once, just once, the show threw its script away and let Apollo trot around doing his own doggy thing, the women of the world could see that nothing could fix a relationship that was already broken. The 2 percent who'd found genuine love had their own brand of magic or luck or whatever you wanted to call it. The rest of us were just doomed to break up.

When Mason was done fielding the barrage of questions, he invited me to see the office that would become Apollo's new room. As we walked together, he turned to me. "So," he said, "do you think he'll be happier now? Is there anything else he needs?"

"Well," I said, and then hesitated. I'd had a thought and I was about to blurt it out, but I hadn't taken any time to weigh whether it helped my cause or even if it was a good idea. In fact, it was probably a very bad idea. The thought had popped into my head when I was talking with Cassie and now I found myself about to air it—half-baked—with Mason. Mason, my boss. Who wasn't my real boss. Sometimes I made myself crazy.

"Well," I said again, "I think there is one thing that frustrates him." *Samantha Novak, you are a total idiot. Shut up, shut up, shut up!*

"Yeah, what's that?"

I tried to hold the words back, but they slid right

out. "He doesn't actually get to be the Love Dog. On the show. It's all scripted for him, and all he does is carry roses around and take walks on the beach. He does what Lucas teaches him to do and nothing more—he has no freedom whatsoever." I took a deep breath and channeled Cassie. "He never gets to use his love power."

To his credit, Mason didn't laugh too loudly. "His love power?"

I smiled, hoping he saw that I, too, knew I was spewing crazy talk. "You know—he's the Love Dog. But he doesn't really get to spread any love. He doesn't get to mend any broken hearts. It kills him. You can see it on his face."

Mason looked down at Apollo, who at that second looked wildly happy and not the least bit like a frustrated Cupid. "Huh. You really think he has love powers?"

I tried to make my face look blank, knowing how stupid I sounded. If only Cassie were here. Cassie or any of the thousands of women like her who were dying to believe Apollo had a special gift. "Sure," I said, fighting to not choke on the words. "That's why you hired him, right? It's the reason he's the star of the show. I saw what he did for Jonathan and Keisha. I've heard about the *Race of a Lifetime* finale. And you can't tell me you haven't noticed all the happy couples here on the set."

Mason's eyes darted around, then he looked me straight in the eye. I gulped.

"Look," I said, "I know it sounds dumb. But seriously, haven't you felt a tremendous amount of love coming off him? I don't mean to go all woo-woo on you, but I think he really has something. If you turned him loose during taping and let him do his own thing, I think he would surprise you."

"Hmm. Interesting."

Great. I probably should have just run the stuff about his brother, I thought. Mason was going to avoid me now anyway. This was what I got for getting greedy. I should have been happy with stripping the façade off the show for the *Telltale*'s readers. That should have been plenty. I'd debunked this silly Valentines-and-hearts show and gotten myself started on a writing career—that should have been enough for anyone. But no. No, I had to talk to my sister that morning and decide I would change her mind, too. I had to push the show's producer to do something he never, ever would do, something that would jeopardize the entire season—and all of these people's jobs, his included. I had to open my big mouth and suggest that Apollo be turned loose to "work his magic" on the show. Yeah. Right. Smooth move, Novak.

"Do you know why I hired you, Sam?"

Mason's voice startled me—I almost dropped Apollo's leash on my own foot. "Um, no."

His eyes drifted down to the tips of my boots, then back up to my face. "It was because of the way you talked about the dog you had when you were a kid. What was her name?"

"Norah."

"Yeah. Norah. When you talked about her, I could see how deep your bond was with her. I wanted Apollo to have a relationship like that. A real relationship." He dropped his voice and tipped his head toward mine. "I don't think he gets that with Lucas. Do you?"

Uh, was he serious? "No. No, I don't. Not even close."

Mason nodded. "I don't get to spend a lot of time with Apollo, so I don't always know what's going on, but that's the vibe I've gotten. When we set out to hire a handler, I wanted someone who would be his advocate, who'd get him what he needs." His eyes met mine, and for a second I felt flooded in blue. "Thanks for being that for him." He gave me the kind of smile you get from the cool boy in high school, the one who can afford to be nice to everyone, even the nerdy girl he sits next to in biology. Mason crouched down and tousled Apollo's head, then he turned away and was instantly consumed by a fresh crowd of staff members with burning questions.

My head felt ready to crack apart. How many messes was I going to make here? I'd already squealed about the show in the *Telltale*. I'd sneaked into places I wasn't supposed to go, spying on plans for future shows, getting information I was never supposed to have. And now I'd actually tried to convince Mason to turn the show over to a dog? Don't get me wrong— I liked Apollo. But still. No one really expected him to morph into a cross between Dr. Phil and Dr. Ruth. Mason must have thought I was the valedictorian of idiot school.

−14−

Apollo

I couldn't believe the day I was having. Not only had Mason walked all the way down my hallway *and* stepped into my room, but then afterward, with half the studio waiting to see him, he'd stood and talked with Sam and me for wonderful minute after wonderful minute. I had sat at his feet, soaking in his smell, feeling his confidence flow through the air and attach itself to my fur, my paws, my nose.

Mason stood near me, gesticulating as he talked with Sam, sometimes frowning or nodding as she spoke. I watched him closely, absorbing every clue. He did feel something for her—now I was absolutely sure of it. And she felt . . . nervous around him. Tense in a sage and vinegar kind of way. Was that attraction? Or just a pack-member's anxiety in the face of the alpha dog? It was hard to be sure.

I knew about the many forms of love. I knew there was a vast difference between the type of dedicated love I felt for Mason and the soft, assured love a puppy feels for its mother. I understood that there was love between dogs, love between friends, and the begrudging, I-put-up-with-you-because-I-have-no-choice love between colleagues and siblings. And I also knew about desire. I could smell the heat and the nervous tension floating off people's skin when they were drawn to someone else, someone they couldn't stop looking at.

So I knew what to look for when I gazed up at Mason and Sam. I knew what Pilar and A.J. both wanted, even if I didn't understand the strange human issues that were keeping them apart. Thanks to my early years on the ranch, I knew that things could go wrong between human mates, the way they had with Honey and Chad. That was why my work was so important. Without help, human bonds could break forever. I'd seen it happen.

By the time Mason patted my head and turned away from Sam and me, I felt as cheery as a cheese sandwich. I pranced around behind Sam, my paws bouncing off the floor. My ears were up, tail was up, everything up, up, up. I was happy, and so was Sam.

Which was why I was surprised to feel the change in the air when the little woman in the headset appeared, her face tight and pinched. Lucas was right behind her, and when I saw the set of his shoulders, my tail drooped. I didn't need to sniff his skin to sense his metallic anger. I ducked my head and prepared for the worst.

"I know what you've done," he said, striding up to us. "Don't pretend you didn't do it. There's no point. Rebecca told me."

I opened one eye, surprised that his words hadn't been directed at me. His voice was tight and louder than usual, but his face, his tone, and his posture were all aimed at Sam. She was the one in trouble, not me. Sam was already doing the human version of the bad-dog skulk. I'd never seen a face look so guilty.

"She did?" Sam gulped so loudly, I could hear her swallow. A film of sweat appeared on her forehead. "I, uh, I didn't think it'd be out already." She took a step backward, her eyes shifting around the studio. "Who else knows?"

Rebecca bent closer, her clipboard clutched to her chest. "No one yet. But we have to tell Mason." She glanced up at Lucas. "I think we should all go. Right now."

Sam looked like she wanted to bolt. Or melt. Or cry. "Okay," she said faintly.

Rebecca turned, ready to march away, but Lucas stayed where he was.

"I don't give a shit about telling Mason," he said. "I don't need him to play Daddy for me and keep my dog handler in line. You broke my rules. It's bullshit."

Sam looked confused. "*Your* rules?"

"Yeah. My rules. You know, the ones I trained you on, your first day?" A sarcastic sneer drew his mouth out to one side. "No treats. No days off. No field trips. Or was that too complicated to remember?"

Strange expressions were scooting across Sam's face. I could hear Rebecca breathing behind me, the air shooting hard out her nose. I half expected her to growl. "But Lucas, I really think we should tell Mason. I mean, she took him *outside*—she went against your direct instructions. Mason's her supervisor—he's the one who should discipline her."

Sam, who had been standing rigid, suddenly drooped into her usual curves. "Outside. Right." She turned to Lucas. "Yes, I did take him out last week. We stayed in the shade and we didn't go far—we stuck to studio property. That doesn't really count as a field trip, does it?"

Lucas's eyes narrowed. "Yes, it does. Of course it does. Apollo doesn't leave this building."

Suddenly, Sam wasn't the dog in trouble anymore. Now her tone was questioning, light, and incredulous. "You mean he doesn't get to go outside? Ever?"

"Only with me," Lucas answered. But his tone was less brash than it had been. Power swung between them like a slack leash.

"Well that hardly seems right, does it?" Sam looked at Rebecca. "Does it seem right to you? Do you really think Mason will object to Apollo's taking a short trek across the parking lot so he can pee on actual plants, in actual dirt?"

"I wouldn't presume to guess what Mason thinks," Rebecca said. Her voice was higher than usual, and her dark eyes had an intensity that I'd only ever seen when Mason was nearby. As Sam turned back to Lucas, I saw Rebecca slip away from us, clutching her headset with white knuckles.

Sam didn't notice—she was intent on Lucas. "Can you give me a good reason why he can't go out? He was on a leash. There was no danger at all."

Lucas folded his arms. "Apollo is a very valuable property. *My* property. I have a right to protect my investment in any way I see fit. I don't like him leaving when I'm not here. Someone could steal him."

"Steal him? Wait—your investment? But he's not a thing—he's a dog." She looked down at me. My tail flapped against the floor. "A dog who needs to act like a dog sometimes. Not just like property."

"But he is property." Lucas's voice had a sharp edge.

"And he belongs to me. Not to you. Not to Mason Hall. Not to this TV show. To me. If you can't follow my rules, I'll give you the boot and find someone who can. Is that clear enough for you?"

Sam's eyebrows hunched together. She was about to say something when Rebecca returned with Mason trailing behind her.

Mason looked at the other humans, gave me a quick glance, and said, "What's up?"

Everyone's posture changed. It was as if they were dogs at a dog park who'd just established their hierarchy when a hundred-pound German shepherd came through the gate. Lucas looked stiff, his face dark and displeased. Sam looked guilty. And Rebecca looked pleased with herself.

"Your new dog handler has been breaking the rules," she said. She spoke quickly, as if she was afraid she wouldn't have a chance to get it all out. "She took Apollo outside last week. Into the parking lot. Lucas had no idea."

Mason raised his eyebrows at Sam, who swallowed. She licked her lips. Then she nodded. "That's right. I took him out into the parking lot so he could pee on actual bushes."

My great leader shifted his gaze to Lucas. "And this is against your rules?"

"Yeah, sure." Lucas was trying to make his voice casual, but I could tell how uptight he felt. He put his hands into his pockets, then took them out again. "But I don't need you to get in the middle of this. I can handle it. Samantha won't do it again. Will you?" He fixed Sam with a hard glare.

She crossed her arms in front of her chest. Rebecca, standing across from her, looked as if she was bouncing inside like a Jack Russell with a tennis ball. "Mason has enough to worry about," Rebecca said, "without a dog handler putting the star at risk. What if something had happened to Apollo? We can't put a show on the air without the Love Dog."

Sam looked as if she'd been squeezed into a corner. I knew how she felt—it was like when Lucas came into my cage at the ranch, a loop-leash in his hand. I'd finally learned that there was no escaping. Lucas would catch me—he always did. But Sam didn't seem to have learned that lesson yet. She looked up at Mason, her jaw stiff, like she didn't agree with whatever the people were saying. Like she was trying to decide whether to fight or to tuck her tail between her legs.

"Sam," Mason said, "I'll have to ask you to follow Lucas's rules, okay? He's the trainer, and Apollo's owner. He has the right to decide how Apollo will be cared for. And that includes where he can go and with whom."

A quiet moment followed. It was so quiet, I could hear Sam breathing. Lucas's breath was coming hard through his nose. I shifted my weight back and forth between my paws, wishing someone would say something. I knew I wasn't in trouble, but it didn't matter— I just wanted the horrible tension to be over. I licked my nose again and again, sending a silent message to Sam.

It's okay, I thought as hard as I could. *Mason knows what to do. Follow his lead. He's our alpha—just follow him.*

She blinked a few times, as if she was trying to shake something out of her eyes. Then she looked down at me, her gaze locked into mine. I couldn't tell what she was thinking, but she seemed to be communicating some secret thought with me. "Okay," she said at last. Her voice was rough. "Sure. I'll follow the rules. I won't take him outside anymore."

Her voice had an edge, as if she wasn't sure why she was saying the words.

"Good," said Lucas.

"Fine," said Sam. I opened my mouth and exhaled the hot air from my lungs. She'd done it. Again. Once again, she'd heard what I said. And acted on it. Amazing!

Lucas shoved his hands back into his pockets. "I think we're all good here, then." He turned to Mason. The look on his face was hardly friendly. "I don't think there's any more need for you to stick around. Sorry we troubled you for nothing."

"It's no problem," Mason said. "And while we're on the subject of Apollo, I've decided to move his room. I'm giving him the office next door to mine. It'll be quieter and nicer for all of you. You can make the switch this afternoon if you have time."

Lucas nodded slowly. "The office next to yours, huh? Real star status."

Sam and Mason exchanged a silent look. "I think you'll all enjoy being closer to the set," Mason said. "There's no need to be off in the hinterlands if there's something closer, right?"

That made Lucas pleased. "Absolutely. Apollo deserves an upgrade. Sam, take care of moving his stuff into the new space this afternoon, will you? You can set it all up the same way. I'll check it out before I leave for the day." Lucas nodded to Mason as if they'd reached a level of mutual respect. Then he turned away and strode lazily to the snack bar.

Sam and Mason stood across from each other, with Rebecca bobbing at Mason's right hand like a little dog waiting to be noticed. Mason gave her a flash of a smile. "Thanks, Rebecca." He was about to say something more, but she leaned in, resting her hand on his sleeve.

"You're so welcome. I know you need to know what's going on. You can't be everywhere at once, can you? And nothing's more important than our big star." She looked pointedly down at me, which was strange since she'd never paid me any attention at all before that moment. I wondered if she remembered the way I pretended to pee on the wall the other day. "We can't have him getting hurt. Where would the show be then?"

Mason nodded, but he wasn't paying attention to Rebecca. His eyes were on Sam. "Absolutely. Now, if you don't mind, Rebecca, I need to talk to Sam for a minute."

"Oh." Rebecca pulled her hand off his sleeve and stepped back. "Right. Of course." She gave him a sympathetic look. "Being the boss is a thankless job, isn't it?"

With a pitying smile at Sam and nothing for me, she scurried away. As she passed me, her perfume fell on me like a mist, tickling my nose.

Once she was gone, Sam wrapped the end of my leash around her hand and looked up at Mason. "So, am I in big trouble?"

He lifted his eyebrows. "For letting Apollo get some fresh air? Nah. Not with me. I did mean what I said— you can't break Lucas's rules. He is, ultimately, in control of Apollo. But that doesn't mean I think his rules are good ones."

"Well, okay then."

"And I know that was awkward about the new room. I just had the sense that Lucas might not appreciate knowing you had brought it up with me. Seems like he might have taken umbrage."

I started to pant. Here they were, my number-one project pair, standing face to face. I looked up at Mason and my heart filled with hope—his eyes were warm, like the sky over the ocean on a hot day. His body was angled toward Sam in a way I found very encouraging. His shoulders curled in her direction, elbows out at his sides, making him look bigger, more impressive. Even his head was cocked forward a little, as if he was eager to hear what she might have to say. Most important, a soft smell like baking bread and hot pine needles flowed into the air around him.

But then I looked at Sam. She looked as ruffled as I did when Lucas came in smelling of metal. Something had her worried, even though there was no one here but Mason and me. Was she unsure how to behave near the alpha? Did it make her nervous that our great leader had chosen her as a possible mate? I could understand that. Maybe she thought she would have to become the alpha female and put women like Rebecca in their place.

I would have to work hard with her. Maybe if I gave her a present, like my piece of rope or some cheese crackers, she'd have more confidence. Enough confidence to keep her chin up and see herself as a mate for Mason. It wouldn't be an easy job—cheese crackers might not do the trick. It might require a whole pizza.

* * *

🖥 Samantha

Sometimes I think there's something wrong with me. I mean deep-down wrong, like a messed-up twist in the genes or something. After getting fired from Camp and Donahue, you'd think I'd have learned to temper the truth with a little common sense about when to shut up. But no. No, that would be asking way too much.

There I stood in front of my two bosses and that snitchy little twerp Rebecca, and all I could do was push back against the rules. I, the traitor, the one who was taking a sledgehammer to the show's reputation, couldn't just nod and apologize. Nooo. I had to stand there with my jaw out, looking like an angry teenager, letting them know that their rules were stupid. That I'd play along because Lucas was the boss, not because I was a team player.

Of course, nothing changed the fact that Lucas's rules were stupid. Or that poor Apollo had to spend every day under fluorescent lights, feeling nothing but tile and linoleum beneath his paws. What kind of life was that for a dog? And he wasn't just a dog—he was a star. He deserved to have more freedom and more time having fun, not less.

For the fiftieth time that week, I wondered what Lucas's place was like. What did Apollo do when he went there? It didn't seem likely that he had much fun. I doubted that Lucas took him out for walks on the beach or let him lounge on the couch while the two of them watched a Dodgers game. Apollo seemed way too nervous around Lucas for anything like that.

And now that I'd finally apologized, here was Mason Hall, agreeing with me. Unbelievable. Just last week,

I'd shot the legs out from under this guy by sending in my piece to the *Telltale*. If he had any idea what I was up to, he'd feed my guts to sharks. But instead, he was commiserating with me, saying he thought Lucas's rules were mean. *I am an absolute toad.*

I couldn't look him in the eye, so I kept my gaze fixed on the top of Apollo's golden head. I licked my lips. "What do you know about Lucas?" I asked. I was hunting for a neutral topic, and this seemed as good as any. It was a million times better than "How do you think I've screwed you over?" or "How low can your ratings get before this show is canceled?"

"Not too much. I suppose I saw his résumé, back when we hired Apollo, but I don't remember it. We hired Apollo based on his screen work on *Race of a Lifetime,* not because of Lucas. Why do you ask?"

"I just wonder how he got into this work. I wouldn't say he seems like a guy who loves dogs."

Mason nodded slowly. "No, I'd agree with you there. I always had the sense that he inherited the business."

"And Apollo? Do you think he inherited him, too?" I could feel Mason looking at me and it made me so flustered I couldn't take it. I knelt down beside Apollo and buried my hands in his fur. That felt safe, until Mason crouched on his other side and started petting Apollo, too.

"Beats me," he said. "I don't know how someone like Lucas gets lucky enough to land Apollo. I really don't."

I swallowed hard. This was torture, absolute torture. It was almost as though Mason knew I was a spy and was keeping me close as punishment. Or to keep an eye on me. But he couldn't possibly know. Not yet. Could he?

Deep in Apollo's fur, my fingers brushed the side of Mason's hand and I flinched away. His hand was warm and awake feeling, as if all the energy, charm, and enthusiasm that I saw here at work was an organic part of him—part of his nature. No wonder Rebecca was smitten.

Studiously keeping my hands on my own side of Apollo's body, I braved a glance at Mason. Shadows had fallen across half his face, but I could see the serious line of his nose and the light-brown lashes that framed those bright blue eyes. We were close enough for me to spot the place he'd missed shaving that morning, a tiny patch of auburn hair at the base of his jaw.

I tried to swallow again, but my throat was too dry. I wasn't cut out for this cloak-and-dagger stuff.

—15—

🖥 Samantha

The next day, on Friday, the *Telltale* hit the news-stands. I bought a copy after I got off the bus coming home. Not that I needed to purchase one to know that they'd run my story—not when it was blazoned across the front page. "Love Dog Secrets Revealed! Is This Hit Show a Doggone Scam?" The front-page photo was a clip from the last episode, a blurry picture of Honey, Chad, and Apollo. It had clearly been taken with a wide-angle lens. Even Apollo looked like he'd gained twenty pounds.

I walked home with the tabloid hidden in my bag, feeling as if everyone could tell I was the one who'd written that story. My name was nowhere on it, but even so, I was sure my guilt had me lit up like a Christmas tree.

Minutes after I got home, Vern called. "It was a great piece," he told me. "Just what we wanted. Have you looked at it yet?"

"No," I said, pulling it out of my bag.

"Well, you should know that I made a few changes."

I flipped open the tabloid to a massive spread that featured photos of Apollo, of Mason in a baseball hat and sunglasses, and of Honey on the set of her last commercial. I scanned the article. "Looks like you just cut things," I said, relieved. "The stuff about the storyboards—was that no good?"

"Are you kidding—it was terrific! I trimmed it because I'm saving it. For next week. So there, kid, you've got one in print and one in the can."

"Oh," I said, feeling overwhelmed. "Thanks. That's great, I guess. But, um, I'm pretty sure they'll know it's me, on the set. They'll probably fire me on Monday."

"Nah, they won't clue in that fast. Almost a hundred people work for that show—any of them could have written this. Do you know what you're going to write about next? Something about Mason Hall?"

"Oh . . . I don't know. I, uh, I haven't found out anything about him yet."

"Well, get on it. That's what'll really sell papers—and get your name noticed among the inside ranks here. Mason Hall. He's the one the public wants to read about. Everything else is sideshow material. Keep your eyes on Mason Hall."

Saturday night, I got some much-needed cheerleading from Livy and Essence during one of our rare live chat moments. They'd seen my article—Essence had scanned it and sent it to Livy—and they thought I was doing great work.

It's bloody brilliant, Livy wrote. *The women of your country need a wake-up call, that's for sure. Imagine believing that a dog can fix your bollixed relationship—how dense can you be? We need women*

*to stop thinking they have to be in a relationship at all.
That they need men or this thing called "love." That's
the real issue.* Livy liked to call herself a love agnostic.

Essence chimed in to say half of her campus was
buzzing about *The Love Dog. I don't know why, but
people really believed he was magic or some shit,* she
typed. *They're moaning like they just heard the Easter
Bunny is a made-up thing. Everyone keeps saying they
saw him fix a relationship on* Race of a Lifetime.
*Dumbasses. Like anything on TV actually happens the
way it's presented? Talk about naïve.*

I appreciated their support, and it buoyed me all the
way through Sunday. But once I got ready for bed, all
my worries came racing back. When would it all hit
the fan? Who would be the first to accuse me? Would
it be Rebecca? Lucas? Or some stranger from the editing room? Would they go straight to Mason? Or out
me in front of everyone? I spent a fitful night punching
my pillow, then dragged myself into work on Monday
with my teeth on edge.

I slipped into the studio and hurried to Apollo's
new room, suddenly hating the fact that he'd moved
to the office next to Mason's. Why oh why had I
orchestrated that? The last thing I wanted was to see
Mason today, and now I was almost sure to. Honestly,
I was the worst spy in history. If I were James Bond's
partner, he'd shoot me himself.

At least Apollo was glad to see me. He pushed his
nose into my hand and wagged his tail like a feathery
plume.

"I'm sorry, buddy," I whispered as I clipped on his
leash. "I've done a bad thing, something that could
hurt this show you work for. I hope you won't mind

losing your job. At least you'll get to leave this building then, right?"

Yeah, right.

I rushed Apollo down the hall to his little outdoor
pee zone, then into the room where he worked out
on his treadmill. Even though the whole studio was
air-conditioned to arctic levels, I was sweating in my
short-sleeved sweater. The urge to flee the building—or
disguise myself, or hide under the espresso machine—
was overwhelming.

Twenty minutes later, Apollo and I were walking
toward the set, avoiding eye contact with everyone,
when a hand grabbed my arm. I flinched, sure I was
about to be locked in a dark room for occasional caning.

"Hey, Samantha, I've been looking for you."

It was Valerie Martz, the woman I'd defended when I
lost my paralegal job, looking camera-ready in a sheath
dress and three-inch heels. I braced myself. There was
only one reason she could have been looking for me.
The caning was about to begin.

"I heard you got the job—congratulations!"

I blushed and realized I was close to blowing my
own cover. I couldn't go assuming that everyone knew
my secret—my guilty face alone would get me caught.
Come on, Mata Hari. Try for suave.

With quite a bit of effort, I pulled together a stiff
smile for Valerie. "Hi there! Valerie, it's so nice to see
you. And thank you again for giving Mason my name.
This is a great job. I just love working with Apollo." I
looked down at his golden head and tried to let his
calm flow through me.

"Not a problem," Valerie was saying. "I was happy

to do it. And I never got to tell you—my mediation finally wrapped up, and I think what you said had an effect on the judge. He awarded me a lot more than Gene Camp thought he would."

I gave her a genuine smile this time and tried to breathe. Maybe I was making far too big a deal of this. No one had mentioned the *Telltale* yet—maybe my article wouldn't affect the ratings after all. Maybe tabloids didn't matter. My heart made a hopeful jump. If I could keep writing my articles and not harm the show, that was the best of all worlds, wasn't it?

"Oh, hey," Valerie said, dropping her voice and looking up and down the hall. "Did you hear?"

My blood stopped flowing. "Hear what?"

"There's going to be a big meeting. Everyone has to go. Something big is going on."

"What?" I asked weakly, wrapping Apollo's leash around my hand.

Valerie shrugged. "Beats me. Probably some change in the management structure. Nothing that's likely to affect us."

She turned and Apollo and I followed, since we had no excuse not to. Together, we joined what I now saw was a stream of people headed for the conference room. It was all I could do to keep my eyes fixed on Apollo and my feet moving forward.

As we slipped into the crowded conference room, I almost balked. *I could run away right now,* I thought. *Run away and never look back. I could find a job at a coffee shop or a car wash and leave behind this silly dream of becoming a writer.* That would be the safe, smart thing to do. That would save me from the angry mob this collection of people would turn into once my secret was revealed. There were only two things holding me back: Apollo and my blogging responsibilities. I owed it to Apollo to stay and do whatever I could to make his life better while I was here. And I owed Livy and Essence another article that might enlighten the women of the world.

Every seat in the room was taken, so Valerie and I stood against the back wall. Apollo sat at my feet and eased in until his warm body rested against my legs. I leaned on the wall, he leaned on me, and, in the front of the room, Mason began to speak.

"Thanks for coming everyone," he said, quieting the crowd. He was wearing a button-down blue shirt— what I'd come to recognize as formal attire for him. I wondered if he had meetings with the network bigwigs later. "I know this is an unexpected meeting, but something unexpected has happened."

When Mason reached into his back pocket and pulled out a rolled-up copy of the *Telltale,* I thought my heart would break out of my chest and go tearing down the Golden State Freeway. He slapped the tabloid onto the table in front of him.

"Someone has been leaking secrets about this show to the press." He looked around the room, his voice level and steady. "Someone told the *Telltale* about the casting process, about how we choose our guests. They talked about our confidentiality agreement. These are privileged secrets. We all know that good entertainment is built on keeping secrets a secret. The audience doesn't want to see behind the curtain. No one wants to know how the sausage is made. Viewers want to see a polished, organized, finished product. That's what makes a good show. None of it can be done without a high level of trust among the people who work behind the scenes. If we don't have that, our show is doomed."

Again, he looked around the room. His blue eyes were suddenly piercing, and when they landed on me, I thought my skin would curl up and fall off. *I'm so sorry, Mason. I didn't want to tell the show's secrets. But I had to. I just had to. The bills were terrifying— and I really, really want to write!*

"Someone here has broken that sacred trust. Obviously, this is a serious offense. This article"—he slapped his open palm against the *Telltale*—"could kill our ratings. It could cost us tens of thousands of viewers. Loss of viewers means loss of jobs. So, since all of your jobs are at stake, I assume that anyone who has any information about this will come and tell me. Right away. If you did it, confess. If we act right away, we may be able to control the damage." His voice became tight as he reached down and crushed the tabloid in his left hand. "I'll try to overlook the fact that you've undercut me—undercut us all. It makes me sick to think of a spy here. We're supposed to be a family. We work on a show about love, for chrissakes."

My legs were shaking. Mason said a few more words, but I didn't hear them. I couldn't—my heart was booming too loudly. I couldn't stop thinking about the next article, the one that was coming out in a week. If the fallout from the first one was this bad, how would things be next Friday?

Around me, people rose and filed out the double doors. I stood where I was, sure that if I left the safety of the wall, I would faint. Apollo leaned harder against my legs, buttressing me.

"Wow, how about that?"

I jumped an inch. It was Pilar, standing at my elbow. Her hair was in a high ponytail and, as she swept a few loose strands back, her bracelets jangled. "Can you believe someone actually did that? Sold out the show for a little tabloid money? What an asshole. I bet it was one of the sound crew. Those guys are always disgruntled."

I nodded. Even if I'd known what to say in the face of all this, I couldn't trust my voice. All I could do was watch Mason as he moved toward the door, stopping to talk with Imogen Blakely and the head story editor. He looked like a zombie. As he shambled past us, I noticed dark half-moons hanging under his eyes.

Rebecca bobbed beside him, her curls bouncing. "I went over the records," she said. "There are twenty-three employees of the show who haven't signed confidentiality agreements. I think we should start with them." She handed Mason a list, which he shoved into his pocket. As they walked past us, he gave me a sad little smile. Rebecca gave me a smirk that let me know my name was at the top of that list.

I've never spent a more miserable day. It wasn't just the terror of being caught—it was the knowledge that I deserved to be caught. And punished, publicly shamed, and whipped. Everywhere I went, people whispered about the article, making the hairs on my arms prickle. By noon, I was ready to run out on the stage and scream, "It was me! I'm the spy, I'm the one, just kill me now!"

But I didn't do it. I didn't do it because I was afraid, and my urge for self-preservation proved mighty strong. And because I didn't want to leave Apollo. Not yet. Not now. If I left him, he'd be back to working with

Lucas all day long—an angry Lucas, because he'd have to do all of his work and mine, like before. I hated to think what that would be like for Apollo.

And because my psyche really couldn't take the level of guilt I was feeling, I employed a time-honored avoidance technique—I turned my attention to something else and ignored the massive bomb that was about to go off at my feet.

Oddly, it was Lucas who distracted me. Lucas, who trotted into the studio like the most important man in L.A., Lucas who snapped at Apollo for seeming distracted, Lucas who smelled like whisky right after lunch. Once again, I wondered what his place was like. I didn't believe for a second that Apollo enjoyed going there on the weekends. In fact, if I trusted my instinct, I would guess that he dreaded it. *Beautiful, wonderful Apollo should never feel dread,* I told myself staunchly. He deserved my help, if I could figure out how to give it. I might be a slimy, rotten, no-good traitor who was ruining some people's favorite show, but if I could help Apollo, I could still feel okay about myself.

Of course, there wasn't much I could do about the situation at Lucas's place. I had no control over what happened there. I didn't even know where *there* was. But here, at the studio, I did have a tiny amount of leverage, for the moment, anyway. I could make sure his life here was what it should be—even when I wasn't around.

But how?

I was voicing all this to Pilar during my afternoon break when she surprised me with a solution. "No problem," she said. "A nanny cam, that's what you need. My brother has three of them. He was so positive his nanny was stealing cash out of their bedroom dresser. Turned out it was his own wife, sneaking money to buy cigarettes. She'd told him she had quit." Pilar shook her head. "What a moron. They never use the nanny cams now. I'll bring you one and you can spy to your heart's content." Her choice of words made me blush. Spy, thy name is Sam. Fortunately, Pilar's attention was caught by a fresh idea of her own. "Hey, maybe I should use one to spy on A.J. and see where he goes on the weekends. I wonder how I could plant a stuffed bear in his Jeep?"

Apollo

Something was very, very wrong. From the first moment Sam let me out of my crate in the morning, I knew she was upset. She couldn't stand still—she kept picking things up and putting them down, rearranging my leashes and combs. I wanted to send her some messages like I had last night to tell her how much I liked my new room. When Lucas dropped me off that morning, I thought I was in the wrong place. But then he put me in my crate and I found my rope hidden in the back where I always kept it, and realized that my things had moved here when I wasn't looking. The new room smelled like coffee and printer ink. The only sound here was the steady hum of the air-conditioning coming out of the vents. Outside my crate, musty carpet reached from wall to wall. I loved it.

But Sam was agitated. At first I thought it might have had something to do with the new room. Maybe it was too quiet for her? Maybe she didn't like carpet? I changed my mind, though, when we set out for my pee area. As we sped down the hall, she couldn't keep her eyes faced forward like she usually did. She kept peering around, looking up and down halls as we walked, darting looks at people's faces, their hands, their shoes. She was like a dog that senses a fight coming and wants to stay out of it. A nervous dog. A dog that's been in the garbage and is hoping it won't get caught.

I concluded, then, that this was a people issue. I knew *I* wasn't angry at Sam, so it couldn't have anything to do with me. And the more I looked at her, the guiltier she seemed, skulking down the hall. When the woman in very high heels stopped to talk to us, Sam looked ready to piddle on the floor, she was that anxious.

Then came the meeting. At first it was fine, and I was pleased to see Mason in his usual place at the front of the room, the center of everyone's attention. But Mason didn't sound right. His voice was tight and low and louder than it needed to be since everyone was quiet and listening. His words had a bite to them.

As Mason talked, the air in the room changed. People started to sweat. Some of them looked indignant, some nervous. Feet twitched. Hands played with paper cups and pens. The people looked around at each other as if they were trying to detect who'd had sausages for breakfast. I felt my hackles rise, and I had to lean against Sam to keep from barking or chewing on my paws.

That was this morning, and things hadn't gotten any better. Sam and I tried to stick to the standard routine, but everything was out of step. She couldn't be calm. I tried to help her, but it only made things worse—she didn't like it when I pulled on the leash to help her walk it out, or chewed on my rump to ease the tension.

Only Lucas acted like his usual self. It was a relief when he snapped at me for not paying attention. And even better when I realized that he was right, that I needed to concentrate on my work to find a happy zone on this miserable day. I learned to drag a cloth bag out from under the coffee table on the stage, to grin with my teeth showing, and to bark after someone said, "Apollo thinks it's a good idea. Don't you Apollo?" When we finished, I felt exhausted and gloriously right with the world.

After Lucas was done training me, Sam returned, smelling like that tea she likes and the rose soap from the bathroom. She seemed slightly calmer—she didn't spend all of her time looking behind her, as if she was about to be tackled. Just some of the time. She took me away to brush my hair and clip my nails.

"Thank God we're finally alone," she said, holding my back paw. I hated having my nails trimmed, but I pretended I didn't mind. I stared at the crack under the door and tried to think about what French bread covered with sloppy joe sauce would taste like.

"This has been the worst day of my life. They know all about the article, but they don't seem to know it's me. I'm glad not to be caught, but I just keep waiting for it, you know? Like any second the cops are going to arrive and haul me away in handcuffs. And that look on Mason's face this morning—it was awful. I felt like I'd drowned his puppy. I was ready to bag the whole thing right then and there, but what can I do? I can't give the money back. I don't have it. And now he has the second one in the can already."

She looked at me as she set down the clippers. "What I'm trying to say is that I'm totally screwed. You see what I mean?"

I wagged my tail. Whatever she was saying, it was doing her good. I panted softly and looked at her eyes, and thought about cheese. I wondered which I liked better, cheese that came in squares or cheese that came in sticks?

She stroked my head. "You're such a great dog, Apollo. I mean, you're really something special. I haven't known a dog like you since Norah. It's like you can see inside me—like you know exactly what I'm feeling." She bent down and dropped a quick kiss on my forehead. I almost melted with happiness. "Always trying to make people feel better about themselves—that's you."

Sam stood up and got my special brush. I wagged harder, since I loved the feeling of being groomed. Especially the way Sam did it, teasing through the tangles gently, working upward from the ends. Being brushed while thinking about cheese—a perfect end to a long day.

"I'm going to do everything I can for you between now and whenever they find out about me," she said, combing my back and my left side. "To begin with, I'm going to watch and see how Lucas treats you when I'm not here. I have a feeling . . . Well, let's just say I have a feeling that it isn't good. Not that he abuses you or anything. I don't think he'd ever hurt his *property*. But I don't think he's as kind to you as he should be. My guess is that Mason's going to be surprised to learn how he really is."

She exhaled softly, like a sigh, and I wondered if she was thinking of Mason. *You deserve him.* I pushed the thought out toward her. *You should welcome him as a mate—don't be afraid. He likes you. That's all you need to know.*

Just when I thought I might be reaching her, when a tiny smile played on her lips and her eyes had a faraway, fantasy look, something buzzed in her pocket. She jumped, then stood so she could yank it out.

"Hello?"

I heard the rumbling vibration of a voice on the other end. Sam's pupils grew big and dark.

"How did you get this number?"

She sounded so irate that I stood up and hovered near her, my ears alert. More rumbling came through the phone.

"No, Richard, I don't want to talk. I don't care if you feel bad—I'm not about to up and forgive you for dumping me and marrying someone else. You're just going to have to live with the fact that you did a shitty, shitty thing. Now leave me alone, okay? Can't you have the decency to do that?"

She pulled the phone away from her ear and tapped a button. Then she stared at the phone as if she couldn't believe what it had done to her. For the first time, I detected a metallic anger seeping out of Sam's pores. It wasn't directed at me, the way it was with Lucas, but smelling it made me ache for Sam. Why should she have to feel angry?

After twenty long breaths, she noticed me standing at her feet and bent down to stroke my head. "It's okay, Apollo. Don't worry. That was Richard—my asshole ex-fiancé. You don't know him. You wouldn't. He doesn't even like dogs. He blames it on allergies, but there are hypoallergenic dogs, aren't there?" She exhaled through her nose. "I don't know how he got my cell number. The shithead. I'll have to have it changed."

She shoved the phone back into her pocket and sat

down on the floor with a huff. I sat beside her, holding still while she started to brush.

"Richard. God! I'm lucky to not have married him. If we were married, he probably would've fallen for this other woman anyway and we'd be divorced right now. Divorced like half the people in this country— like Mom and Dad, and Cassie. Richard did me a favor by dumping me at the altar. Seriously, love between people is trouble waiting to happen." She leaned in toward me. "We should all just love dogs and forget about men, right?"

Just then, I heard footsteps outside the door. My ears perked up, my tail swished the air uncertainly. Would the footsteps stop? Yes, they did! Was it—could it be— Mason? Yes, it was!

Mason came through the door, changing the energy in the room instantly. Sam's face broke out of its freeze. My tail beat back and forth, brushing the unloving thoughts away. *Thank you for coming,* I beamed to Mason. To Sam, I thought, *look, he sought you out. You're special to him. He's upset today and he came to you. Let him share his problems with you while you share yours. The two of you can help each other.*

Sam scrambled up off the floor when Mason entered. He gave her a little half smile, a smile of shared sympathy. Then he leaned against the table and looked down at me. "That looks like a nice project," he said. "Brushing Apollo."

She nodded. "It's a Zen exercise. Gives you plenty of time to think."

Mason laughed. "Well, that's the last thing I need. If I do much more thinking, I'll be rounding up a mob with pitchforks and torches." He grinned at her. "So I'm here to ask for help."

"Help from me?"

He nodded. "I was hoping you'd help me get out of my head for a little bit. By having dinner with me. There's a great little Thai place not far from here."

I thumped my tail against the floor. Whatever was happening, it seemed like a step in the right direction. Mason was presenting all the right signals—openness, charm, a soothing tone of voice. His pine needle smell was stronger now, and it wafted around the room making me think of deep forests. Mason was inviting Sam to move closer to him. If only she were in a better place. As it was, she'd never accept him without a little help. I took a deep breath.

Mason can help you. Open your heart to him. It'll all be okay.

Sam looked down at me, her eyes cloudy with conflicting thoughts.

You can trust him. He can help you.

Mason took a half step forward. "Apollo thinks it's a good idea. Don't you, Apollo?"

Ah. I knew this line from my training that morning. I let out my most boisterous bark. Then I barked again.

"All right," she said, laughing, looking from me to Mason. "Okay. Dinner it is."

16

💻 Samantha

Pilar is a wonderful, wonderful person. Just when I thought I was going to have to live with guilt piled on top of guilt as I rooted around for something more to write about, she offered me a beam of hope. We were taking a quick afternoon tea break. "We have a good half hour before we have to go back," she'd said. "Apollo's doing his promo shots, then a kid from the hospital's coming to visit. It'll take them awhile."

"What kid?"

Pilar shrugged and stirred her iced coffee. "I don't know—I can't keep track. Most days when Apollo's on set some kid or charity person comes and has their picture taken with him down in the photo studio. That's what the swag's about, too. It's photos and stuff that they send out for charities to use with their fund-raising. I bet the PR team sends a hundred a week."

I leaned forward a little. "That must be standard on shows like this, right? It's all part of promoting *The Love Dog*?"

She shook her head, frowning. "No, I don't think

so. It's Mason—he's really big on that kind of thing. Giving back. Or," she corrected with a grin, "having Apollo give back, more like it. Though they say Mason gives wads of cash to some spay and neuter program. You know, all these famous people have to have a pet charity."

"What charity is it?" I was almost panting, I was so excited. "The Humane Society? PETA? Best Friends?"

"I don't know, no one ever says. Might not even be true, you know?"

She was right, of course. It might not be true. But Vern had said I could write about positive things. If this *were* true, I might be able to write an article that didn't bind my stomach up in knots.

I found Mason standing outside his office. He looked exhausted, his blue shirt rumpled. There was something strangely endearing about the weary crinkles around his eyes. I yanked my gaze away.

The Thai restaurant was something of a dive. Mason drove us there, and when we arrived I saw that this was why he'd chosen it—because it wasn't the kind of place paparazzi expect a star to dine. Even so, he put on a beat-up Lakers baseball cap and sunglasses before getting out of the car, then walked briskly to the front door. Once we got inside, he relaxed, pulled off his sunglasses, and gave me an apologetic smile.

"They're like ants," he said. "One paparazzo spots you and second later you're covered in them."

The restaurant was a snug little eight-table place with a pair of carved wooden elephants guarding the front door. A portrait of the king and queen of Thailand hung on the wall near our table.

"They look happy," Mason commented as we sat down.

"Maybe they have their own version of a love dog in Thailand," I said. He looked at me intently, his eyes the blue of a desert sky. I blushed. Why did I say stupid things like that? I gave myself a little shake. I had Mason's undivided attention. I needed to find out more about this charity of his, so I balled up my courage and tossed out some questions.

"It's nice to see Apollo doing so much charity work," I said. "How do you choose what groups he works with?"

Mason shrugged. "There's a system," he said. He glanced at the window and took a sip of water.

I flailed around for another question. "Do you think he likes meeting with the hospital kids? That's where they're from, right?"

"He never seems to mind."

Mason hailed our waiter and engaged him in a short conversation about Thai beer. At last we were alone again. I made one last attempt.

"I was just surprised to hear about all the great work Apollo does with nonprofits. I would have thought you'd want people to know about it, that it would be good promotion. For the show."

He gave me a long, serious look. "But if we did it for our own benefit, it wouldn't really be charity, would it?"

I sat back in my seat. I had no comeback to that. This was clearly something Mason didn't want to talk about—and no prodding from me was going to make him. I would just have to talk to someone else. My mind flashed on a small woman with dark curls and a headset. Rebecca. Rebecca would tell me. She'd love to rave about Mason's philanthropic side.

Before I knew it, my mouth was blurting out the first notion my mind had linked with Rebecca. "You do know that Rebecca likes you, right?"

"What? Rebecca?" Apparently Mason's thoughts had been on the menu. "Nah."

"Oh, definitely. Come on, you must have noticed. You're not oblivious."

A faint pink flush on his cheeks told me that I was right. He did know, he was just modest enough to pretend otherwise. *Boy, Cassie would love this guy.*

But he hadn't been offended by my bringing up something so personal. That was encouraging.

"Maybe you should bring your girlfriend to visit the set," I said, "so Rebecca can see where things stand."

"My girlfriend?" A light smile played over Mason's lips.

I talked faster. "Sure, you know. You must have some beautiful, high-powered girlfriend waiting in the wings. Or at home. Or . . . wherever."

"Hmm. And what does it say about me if I don't? Will that make me a loser?"

"Oh, no. No, of course not." I eyed him carefully. *Could it be that he wasn't seeing anyone?* Wait—he was probably just teasing me. I grinned. "It would just make you between girlfriends, which is a very popular place to be here in L.A."

He gave a funny little snort. "Well, bully for me. I don't have a girlfriend—not at the moment, anyway."

I wasn't sure how to cover my surprise. An attractive guy like Mason? I knew he was in high demand. I'd assumed he had a glamour girl waiting in the wings—an actress or supermodel, or maybe a wildly successful fashion designer with her own boutique on

Rodeo Drive. It was a switch to picture him going home to an empty house.

Regardless, there went my dreams of writing a piece on the woman he was dating. "Well, don't worry," I said. "I'm sure you're a hot property among the famous and single set. Another ingénue is sure to come along any minute."

"Oh, not an ingénue. Ingénues are the worst!" Mason grinned, and I felt my heart lift, nudging my face into a smile. The server came by and engaged us in talk of pad Thai and tofu with green beans. He brought us white wine—Napa Valley chardonnay—in chilled glasses. When he moved away, Mason shifted his glass and looked up at me. "Have you ever dated anyone famous?"

"*Me?* Are you kidding?" I stopped chortling long enough to say, "No, I sure haven't."

"Then you don't know what real torture is. I've gone out with a few—two actresses and one wannabe actress. All disasters."

I laughed. This was the first time spying had actually seemed fun. Maybe he would dish about some actresses that I could write about. "Do tell. I want to know everything that's wrong with those flawless, picture-perfect women."

"Where do I start? I guess the root of the problem lies in just what you said—they're picture-perfect. And, seriously, that's all they think about. If you're out in public, they're always looking around to see who has a camera, who might be watching. It's like trying to have a conversation with a mom who always has half of her attention on her baby. You never get the full person—just what's left over when they realize no one cares that they're out at Melisse or wherever."

"I can see how that would get irritating after a while," I said, nodding. "Unless you were the same way?"

That earned me a deep chuckle. "The last thing I want is to have some photographer shoving his camera in my face while I'm trying to have dinner. That's how guys like me get arrested for assault and destruction of property. No, let me tell you, it gets to be a drag going out with someone who's more interested in other people than in you. Nothing—*nothing*—matters more than what *Entertainment Weekly* has to say about them. Or *Star*. Or even the *Telltale*." I squirmed at the mention of my own publisher and was grateful when the server appeared with hot plates and little bowls of superspicy condiments. "There's no higher authority than *Entertainment Tonight*," Mason went on, diving into his pad Thai. "Can you imagine not caring about anything except how famous you are?"

"Or how thin you looked in your last photos?"

He gave me a grim look. "Don't even get me started on the food issues. The first girlfriend I had in L.A. had a vicious eating disorder—it took over her whole life. Dating her was one of the worst experiences I've ever had. You know, I came from a small town. I didn't know how the Hollywood standard of a super skinny body could destroy a person. After Tina, I was scared to date for a long time. It got so that was the number-one thing I looked for on a first date—a woman who could eat normally."

Inside, I shuddered. My picture of his gorgeous model/actress/fashion designer girlfriend withered away, leaving me with a mental image of a gaunt, angry young woman with limp hair and dark hollows under her eyes. I didn't even have the heart to ask for

Tina's last name. Whoever she was, I couldn't write about her. "You make this place sound downright evil."

"I'm sorry. I know you grew up here. And it's not L.A., it's the Hollywood culture. Our whole country requires the women on TV to look a certain way. The actresses that look 'right' get rewarded with bigger box office revenue and, before you know it, the studios want every woman to look like Cameron Diaz. It's the free market at work."

"Yeah, but it's cruel," I said. "Don't get me wrong. I love L.A., but it is hard on women's self-image. I mean, look at all the plastic surgeries and Botox and tanning salons. Sometimes I feel like the women in this city fall into two camps—the ones who are striving to look the part and the ones who don't even try."

Mason nodded. I felt my shoulders relax as I realized that we both knew which camp I fell into. I wasn't starving myself to fit into size-two dresses. I wasn't likely to get my eyebrows professionally waxed, let alone have someone shoot collagen into my lips. It was strange, though. I didn't know why I found this conversation so reassuring. Maybe it was just nice to meet a man who saw what the quest for perfection did to people. And, I supposed, Mason's harangue against Hollywood's culture of beauty came with an unspoken approval of me—me with my regular-size body, wearing the face I'd been born with. It was a nice feeling. After all, Mason was one of the hottest guys on TV. Even if he only liked me as a friend, it still felt good.

"After the last actress and I broke up, I decided not to date any more Hollywood women," he said. His face was serious as he spooned three-alarm chili paste onto his plate. "No one on TV or in the movies. No one who *wants* to be on TV or in the movies. I've had it with conversations that begin and end with best-dressed lists. With women whose hobby is Googling their own name and posing in front of the mirror. There has to be more to life than appearances. The tabloids should never dictate how someone feels about themselves, right?"

Ugh. Tabloids. "Sure, right," I said brightly. Inside, the tofu and green beans started a war in my stomach. I felt the same way he did about tabloids—if I was perfectly honest with myself, I was embarrassed to be writing for one. I was just holding my nose, submitting my articles in hopes of moving on and leaving the *Telltale* far behind.

"Their reviews don't mean anything," I said. "I mean, how many people really care what a gossip mag says?"

Mason held up his hand. "Don't get me started on tabloids, not today. Did you read that article?" My cheeks flamed as I gave a centimeter-size nod. "What a pile of crap. As if every reality show doesn't do it the same way. They made us sound like the only show that's ever auditioned contestants. Like we could do a show with a dog star without scripting it?"

"Couldn't you?"

He sighed. "Not really. I know you have your idea of letting Apollo act without any training, but I don't see how it could work. I mean, he is a dog. I just don't think he'd create good TV, left on his own." Suddenly, the wrinkles were back at Mason's eyes. He had that faintly persecuted look of a man fighting a losing battle. "But it doesn't really matter if every reality show does what we do. The truth is that now that everyone knows we do, it's going to hurt our ratings."

"Oh, but maybe not," I said, leaning forward. "How many people can possibly read the *Telltale*?"

Mason looked at me levelly. "It isn't just in the *Telltale*," he said. "It's everywhere you look online. It's the top trending news story of the day after Jolie Jameson's overdose."

A cold shiver ran across my skin. I stabbed a few green beans, then let my fork fall against the side of my plate. "Everyone loves *The Love Dog*," I said lamely. "Nothing will change that."

"I appreciate your optimism," Mason said. "But I've seen this happen before. The *Telltale* killed *Race of a Lifetime* with that story about how the races were rigged. People stopped watching overnight and the show died. That's going to happen to us—I can feel it. We air tomorrow night and on Wednesday morning I'll find out how bad our share is. It won't be good. The network execs will flip and I'll have to spend two whole days calming them down, time I should spend trying to fix the show. Then the season will end, and we won't be picked up. That will be that."

Right, I thought, *and it's all my fault.* I'd known my article could hurt the show, of course. But I never really thought it would be copied online and spread all over the country—even though my original goal was to reach every woman in the U.S. I'd never *really* thought my writing could kill the show.

"I'm sorry for griping about this," Mason said, resting his chin in the palm of his hand. "I didn't mean for our first date to go this way."

My mouth dropped open and I had to force it shut. A date. He really had just said that. I tried to move past everything that was ridiculous about this—Mason Hall, TV star, dating Samantha Novak, regular person—

and focus on not bursting out laughing. *No need to look too shocked,* I told myself. *Someone cool would pretend this kind of thing happened to her every day.* Still, I was too flummoxed to think. Or eat. Or take nice, regular breaths.

"No problem." My voice came out somewhere between a squeak and a cough.

"It's just these damned tabloids," Mason went on. "All they do is scrounge around for dirt. It's a despicable industry." He pushed his plate aside. "Anyone who works for one should be shot."

I looked down at my plate, hyperventilating quietly to myself. It figured that on my first official date after being dumped by Richard I was across the table from a man who wanted to shoot me. A divinely cute, famous man who was nice to dogs. A man I was hurting badly with my undercover work. There had to be something I could do.

"What if you had a plan?" I asked.

"A plan for getting rid of tabloids?"

"No, for fixing the ratings. A preemptive plan. Something you could have ready, so if the share does shrink, you can tell the network execs exactly what you're going to do."

He arched one eyebrow. "I don't really see what I can do to fix the ratings. I can't make people watch the show."

"No, but you can be its mouthpiece. You're a famous man. You can get onto any talk show you want."

"Hmm, I suppose so. But what would my message be?"

I made my wineglass pirouette on the tablecloth. "If this week's episode loses a big chunk of the share—and that's an *if*—then presumably it would be because people read the article and didn't like the fact that you hire actors and script the show. So what you'd need to sell them is the opposite of that."

"An unscripted show?"

"An unscripted show. I know you're leery of letting Apollo run loose, but if the ratings are bad enough, wouldn't it seem like a reasonable thing to try?"

Mason shifted his jaw from side to side. "The share would have to be pretty terrible."

"Terrifyingly low," I agreed.

"Well, it's certainly an idea." His face brightened. "And, as you say, it's good to have a worst-case plan. If I rearranged the filming schedule, maybe it wouldn't be too bad. We'd have to film Apollo every day of the week, probably—it would mean a lot more work for him. And the editing crew would have to work like demons."

"They could do it," I said, nodding. "See? It's do-able, isn't it?" I sat back feeling great. I should have been miserable—I hadn't learned anything about Mason's love life that I could use for my next *Telltale* piece. But I had some other reasons to be pleased. The show now had a chance of running unscripted, which would surely have a good affect on viewers like my sister. Once they saw that Apollo was just a dog— which they would, of course, no matter how skilled the editing crew was—they'd drop their illusions. I'd also helped Apollo by bringing him one step closer to the freedom I felt sure he craved.

But none of these successes were what danced through my head as I sat there across from Mason, watching him deliberate over whether to have dessert. No, the only thing I could think about was how those worry lines around his eyes had softened. Everything about him seemed lighter, brighter than it had when we'd arrived. I'd helped him. I'd listened to his problems and actually helped him.

The restaurant had a little outdoor patio, flanked by red-orange calendula and cosmos, and we took our wine there after dinner. Sitting side by side on a bench, I told him more about Norah and my parents' divorce, and how she would stick next to me as Cassie and I moved from one household to the other.

"Looking back," I said, "I think I was grabbing hold of her like she was a life raft or something. She kept me afloat."

Mason turned to me, his face tipped down toward mine. The light was dim, but I could feel him, warm and solid, just inches away. His presence blocked out everything—there was no restaurant, no bench, no flowers. Beyond our little pocket of space there was no street, no city. We were the only two beings in the universe, and I had a strange feeling that this moment had been plotted in the stars long before I was born. I'd just spent my life waiting for it to happen.

My heart beat so loudly I thought surely Mason could hear it. But instead of asking if I needed a trip to the emergency room, he said, very softly, "I hate to think of you hurting that way." Then he tilted his head closer. Our fingers touched. Before my brain could register what was happening, my body had lifted toward his.

The kiss was soft, warm, and sweet, and it hummed in every part of me, from my fingertips to the soles of my feet. I felt lit from within, half on fire. We both moved closer, suddenly hungry. One kiss turned into two, then three, then there was no telling one from another.

It might have gone on forever. But a soft click-click-click made Mason start and pull away, his eyes fixed on something over my shoulder, off toward the parking lot.

"It's the paparazzi," he whispered. "Let's get out of here."

🦴 Apollo

I was relieved to see that Sam was in a fabulous mood the next day. Everywhere we went, she hummed little tunes, smiling at me for no reason at all. I romped around, glad that we were so happy together. I gloried in our routine as never before, thoroughly enjoying my fish oil pill and our walk on the treadmill.

After my morning training with Lucas, when he'd left with his smoky-smelling friends, Sam took me to my room. I thought we were there to pick up a leash or maybe take a nap—sometimes I napped while she read the newspaper—but instead we spent the whole time focused on a pink bag Sam had brought with her. She set the bag in one corner of the room, looked at me to see what I thought, then changed her mind and moved it onto the table. Sam stepped away, considered the pink thing, and moved it onto the desk.

I sat down to watch. Sometimes people put on a show like this. Back when Kim and Lucas were still together, she used to dance when a song she liked came on the radio. All the dogs would sit in their cages and watch. Nothing like that ever happened at Lucas's ranch now, so I appreciated the chance to watch Sam move the pink thing to every possible location in the room. It was like we were playing a game.

At last she found a spot she liked for the thing, pushed against the wall on the far side of the table that held my leashes. It was near the coatrack where she and Lucas hung their jackets in the morning. Sam slid up next to the table, ducking under coats and sleeves, and put her head behind the bag. She looked out at me.

"How about that?" she asked me. I wagged. "It has a good view of the room. Think it'll look too obvious?"

I wagged harder. Sam straightened up and reached into the bag, fiddling with something. "There! All set." She gave me a big grin.

Later, after Sam had gone home, Lucas brought me back to my room. As we entered the door, his phone rang. He held it up to his ear with one hand while he unhooked my leash with the other.

"Kim?" He switched the phone to his other ear. *Kim.* It was Kim calling. I wanted to wag and pant and run in circles, but I held myself back. That would only make Lucas angry. "What is it? The check was on time this month, I swear it."

Faint traces of Kim's fluty voice drifted through Lucas's phone. Hearing her made my heart twist. *Kim,* I thought. *I should have been sending my love to Kim.* Even if she did do what she did to Lucas. Even if she had taken away half the dogs at the ranch.

Every inch of Lucas bristled. He stared at the floor, his mouth clamped shut, listening. I heard Kim's voice again, then Lucas saying, "No. No, I didn't."

Silence followed. I could barely breathe.

"I don't think that's any of your business, do you?

You made it perfectly clear that you don't give a shit what I do with my life."

I opened my mouth to pant. Lucas pushed one palm against his forehead and turned toward the wall. "Look, I've told you before. If you want to buy me out, you can. You just have to meet my price."

He was quiet for a minute, then, "I don't care if you *never* have enough money to do it. You were the one who chose to split things up this way, remember? It wasn't what I wanted. It was never what I wanted. You pushed it down my throat and now you can live with it."

I took air in through my nose, meditating on the scents of the room—the heated iron smell of Lucas, the choking dust of the carpet. I used these smells to center myself. Then, with all four paws resting on the carpet, I beamed my thoughts to Lucas. *Try not to be angry with her,* I thought. *It won't help you. I can feel how the anger hurts your body. New friends are better for you than Kim. New friends are better than being angry. I'm your friend. I will always be your friend.*

Lucas pulled his phone away from his ear. Kim's voice was gone—the room was silent. Lucas gave his phone a hard look. "Bitch."

I licked my nose. Lucas looked up from his phone, his eyes set in a hard glare—a glare that landed on me. "What are you looking at? Get out of the way!" He flicked the air with his hand and I scurried into the corner. "No—over here!"

He grabbed my collar and pulled me to the center of the room, where he picked up my feet, examining my paws with brusque movements. He looked in each ear, flipping my ear flap back in place with an exasperated breath. I knew what was happening. I'd been through this before. Sometimes, when Lucas looked at me, what he actually saw was Kim. Even though I didn't mean to, I reminded him of those times with her. Some of the times had been good, some *glorious,* but it was the bad ones Lucas remembered when he saw me—it was hatred and pain that made his face hard, with cheekbones jutting and a tight jaw. His whole body crackled with anger.

"Sit still, dammit," he hissed at me. I lowered my head, bowing to the force of his dark memories. "Don't look like that. I'm not going to hit you. Shit."

I recognized the word sit, so I dropped my butt on the floor. I didn't know how to make him forget about Kim or those terrible days after she left. I've never worked as hard as I did in those days, trying to send enough love to Lucas to keep him alive. Did I help him? I'll never know.

I had lived on the ranch for a few years, doing special filming projects that involved eating dog food, running through meadows, and a lot of sitting and staying. I was fantastic at the sit-and-stay. Kim could give me a certain look from across the room—a room filled with cameras, legs, and smells from the food table—and I would plunk my butt onto the floor like it was magnetized. Sometimes I worked with Kim, sometimes with Kim and Lucas. All the work was fun, but my favorite was when we all went to the filming together. Lucas and Kim would chat in the front seat on the drive there and back, their voices light. Music came out of the speakers on the dash and sometimes they would both sing along. Lucas was happy in those days, so happy he smiled almost all the time.

At the ranch, it was Kim who trained us, but Lucas was the one to bring fresh food and water every day. I lived in an outside kennel that was part of a long row of cages, and nearly every one had a dog inside. The yellow Lab was close to the house, the terriers were near me, and the border collie was on the far end, close to the big field.

Days were happy times. There was work to be done, food to eat, and—sometimes—rides in the car. I got to go on more rides than any of the other dogs, and I spent more time in training, too. Lucas was often gone during the day, away in his truck, but Kim was there. And, more and more, so was Dr. Danmore. He was a young man with pale hair who checked our teeth and gave us shots. He would lean against the metal poles between the kennels and say things that made Kim laugh. The more he came, the more she bloomed. Her cheeks and lips flushed pink. The pupils of her eyes grew black and round as they followed the movements of his hands and his back. She started wearing lilac perfume that made me sneeze.

All this excitement affected the dogs. The terriers barked all day long, and the border collie pranced by the door of his kennel, sure he was about to be let out at any second.

After a few weeks, Dr. Danmore started joining Kim when she took me out of my kennel for trainings. This was always done in a fenced yard on the far side of the house, out of sight of the kennels and other dogs. I loved going there with Kim. She always carried treats in her pockets. When she led me away, I felt like the luckiest dog in the world.

At first I didn't care that Dr. Danmore went with us. He would stand on the edge of the fenced yard and watch as Kim taught me to crawl on my belly or sit with a biscuit on my nose. But after a while, things changed. Kim spent more of the time in the yard standing close to Dr. Danmore, kissing him or pushing her body against his. I would shift from paw to paw, staring at the trees on the edge of the property. Sometimes I thought I heard Lucas's truck pulling up, and I would bark or race to the side of the fence, eager to see him. Kim always told me to be quiet—she said it in a more snappish way than she ever had before— and went back to touching Dr. Danmore.

This went on for weeks—or maybe months. Often, after we worked for a while in the fenced yard, they would leave me there while they went into the house. Kim would return for me hours later, whistling soft little tunes. She was happier than we'd ever seen her. And Lucas seemed happy because Kim was happy. But I noticed that he never went for car rides with us anymore. His truck was always gone and he was tired when he came home at night, smelling of hamburgers and sweat.

One day I was in the yard with Kim and Dr. Danmore when I heard the rumble and roar of Lucas's truck—not a phantom sound this time, but the real thing. I barked and ran to the edge of the fence.

"Quiet, Apollo," Kim said absently. Her hand was on the back of Dr. Danmore's jeans. His mouth was on her neck. I heard the truck door slam and I barked again. "Apollo. Shh."

From one corner of the fenced yard, I could see the path that led up to the front of the house. I stood there, wagging for Lucas—he should see that someone was excited to welcome him home. On the other side of the house, the terriers barked in unison. Lucas saw me and veered around the house, probably thinking that if I was in the yard, Kim must be with me. When he saw her standing with Dr. Danmore, he stopped walking. He stood still as a tree in the woods. The air felt so thick I could hardly breathe.

Then the yelling started. Lucas barreled into the yard, shoving Dr. Danmore out the gate and away from the house. Lucas was like a dog in a fight, arms and legs tossing out so he seemed larger than usual, his voice like a snarl. Kim shouted in a strained, high voice. Dr. Danmore mumbled with a red face, the border collie howled, and I barked as I ran in circles around Lucas, showing him that in case we needed to fight Dr. Danmore I was on his side.

"Go—just *go*!" Kim screamed at Dr. Danmore. He backed away from the yard, his hands up. Kim sank onto the ground, crying with her face in her hands. Lucas ranted and growled. I started to whine.

"Shut up, Apollo!" Lucas hollered at me. "Just shut the hell up!" It was the first time he had yelled at me.

*L*ater that night, Lucas sat on the bed and cried. I'd been left in the yard, so I could see him through the windows. Kim drove away the next day—she didn't come back. Lucas forgot to feed us that night and the next morning he stumbled out at noon, his breath sharp and strong. He didn't look at me as he snapped the leash onto my collar to lead me out of the yard and back to my cage. He dumped food into my bowl and kicked it across the cement floor. Lucas hadn't smiled at me since.

17

🖋 Samantha

When I arrived at the studio Wednesday morning, I knew the ratings news was bad without having to be told. There were signs. I was usually one of the first to arrive, but when I pulled in that morning there were already a few strange Mercedes and BMWs in the parking lot. The halls were quiet as usual, but the lights were on in Mason's office. I crept close to the door and heard hushed voices and rustling paper. The smell of espresso made my nose twitch.

The thought of Mason getting bad news behind those doors made my heart sink. I felt like I'd swallowed a fist.

At least Apollo was happy to see me. I gave him our now-traditional morning pets, stopping to rub his belly, then we plunged into our morning routine. My thoughts skittered around in my head, jumping like fleas. *How bad was the share? What will Mason do? Does anyone suspect me yet? How horrible have I made life for him? Will writing good things about the show do anything to make up for the harm I've done?*

While Apollo walked on his treadmill, I got out my phone and called Vern.

"Yeah?"

"Vern," I said, "I've been thinking about that next article. The one about the storyboarding."

"What about it?"

"If it isn't too late, I'd like to substitute another piece for it. I thought we could not run one this week, and instead I'd give you something else by this Friday. I think the story I'm working on this week is much better—"

"Too late."

"It is?"

"Too late. That thing's all laid out and on its way to press right now. Sorry, kid. But I'm glad you're working on something good. Can't wait to see it."

After I hung up, I stood staring at the empty space in front of Apollo. He was loping gamely ahead, unbothered by the fact that he never got anywhere. I, on the other hand, had gone further than I'd wanted. I was deep in the rabbit hole now, and when the next piece came out, I'd sink even deeper.

I was so wrapped up in my own worries I didn't even remember the nanny cam until Apollo and I returned to his room. I rushed to the bag, anxious to view the video before Lucas arrived. I pulled the USB drive out of the bag's secret pocket, fired up my laptop, and opened the file. After I fast-forwarded past the initial test clip of me waving at the camera and footage of me saying bye to Apollo, I found what I was after. I watched the whole thing. Then I removed the USB drive and slipped it into my pocket.

"I'm sorry, Apollo," I said. "That was pretty much what I expected." Lucas hadn't been abusive in the traditional sense—he hadn't hit or kicked Apollo. But the recording had shown me enough shots of Apollo's anguished face to know that he might as well have. "You're too sensitive a dog to be treated that way," I told him. "Mason will definitely want to see this."

Apollo and I stood outside Mason's office for five minutes, waffling. The meeting with the Mercedes and BMW owners was still going on. With every minute that passed I came closer to talking myself out of seeing Mason.

"He has a lot on his mind," I told Apollo. "This is probably the last thing he has time for today." What I really meant was that *I* was probably the last thing he had time for. But I felt sure he would always make time for Apollo, even if the fate of the show hung in the balance. Apollo, after all, was the show.

To be honest, I also felt funny seeing him after our kiss Monday night. I could still feel the tiny starbursts that had tingled through my body when his lips touched mine—but what if he'd spent the last thirty-six hours regretting it? I didn't want to look needy, standing here outside his office.

When the door opened, I led Apollo to the opposite side of the hall, out of the way of the men and women who streamed out of Mason's office. They all wore expensive-looking suits. These, I assumed, were the network bigwigs. There wasn't a smiling face among them.

I had just changed my mind and was steering Apollo down the hall when Mason called out to us. "Sam! Were you here to see me?"

I turned, but hovered where I was. "I was, yeah, but

if you're busy . . . You're busy, aren't you? I'll come back another time." The memory of our kiss came rushing back, making me blush.

"Come on," he told me, extending an arm toward his office door. "Come in. I'm glad you're here."

Apollo and I crossed the threshold into Mason's office, a place I hadn't entered since that day a million years ago when he interviewed me. He put his hand on my shoulder as he led me in, then let it slide down to the middle of my back. After he moved his hand away I could still feel a superheated spot where each of his fingers had touched me. This time, I avoided the butt-sucking couch and chose a bent-wood chair. Apollo busied himself with sniffing the corners of the room.

"So?" I asked. "The share—how was it?"

Mason grinned. "Shit city. Almost as bad as it could possibly be."

"And you're smiling because?"

"Because I was prepared for it, thanks to you. Because I just got through a meeting with the network without getting fired. And because I'm happy to see you."

I gulped. *Happy to see me.* How I wished I hadn't written that article. Those articles. If I hadn't been drawn in by dreams of writing and visions of paid-off credit card bills . . . But I did do those things. I had laid this trap for myself—I had no one else to blame if I felt its sting now. And yet I couldn't deny the fact that I was happy to see him, too. The sight of him lifted my mood so much I was almost able to ignore my deceit. I just had to hope that writing good things about the show would fix my past mistakes.

"I took your advice," he said. His eyes were impossibly blue that morning. "I came in with a plan for promoting the show in its new format, completely unscripted. Which is not the same thing as running an unedited show, of course. But even unscripted is pretty bold and crazy for reality TV. We're about to go where no show has gone before." He turned to Apollo, who was licking a patch of carpet. "I hope you're ready for it, buddy. This is all going to come down to you."

Watching Apollo act so much like a canine, running his tongue over the wall-to-wall carpeting, I saw Mason's confidence falter. I could almost hear him wondering how a dog could possibly carry a show about human love and relationships? He suddenly looked uncomfortable in his China-blue button-down shirt— another meet-the-bigwigs shirt. My fingers itched with the urge to jump in and help. He'd need to be fearless if he was going to pull this off.

"Don't worry about Apollo," I said, hoping I spoke the truth. "Love is in his nature." *Wait, what was I saying? I was the one who kept telling everyone that he was just a dog!* "He just needs you to set the stage for him and let him do his work. He's been waiting for this chance, I feel sure of it."

As if on cue, Apollo stopped sniffing and sat down across from the two of us so we three formed a triangle. He looked as if he'd joined us at a meeting.

Mason turned to him. "Yes, Apollo? You have something to add?"

Apollo barked, making us both laugh. "Actually," I said, "I came to see you about Apollo. I know you're deep in other things, but you've asked me so many times about Lucas's relationship with him—"

Mason jumped in before I could finish, leaning forward. "You learned something?"

I nodded and pulled the USB drive from my pocket. "I, uh—well, this is probably a completely inappropriate thing for an employee to do, but I had a hunch that things weren't right. Apollo just didn't seem as happy as he should, especially after his weekends away with Lucas. So I set up a nanny cam."

"A nanny cam."

"Yeah, you know, a spy camera. Motion sensitive." I handed him the little drive. "It taped this last night after I'd gone home."

Mason hopped up and plugged the drive into the laptop that sat on his desk. Seconds later, he was playing the recording. From my chair, I could hear Lucas's disembodied voice through the speakers.

"What are you looking at? Get out of the way!"

I looked at Apollo and wondered if I should cover his ears. He was staring at me with a strange intensity.

"No—over here!"

My heart was aching. How long had Apollo been enduring this kind of anger from Lucas? All his life? I knelt down and wrapped my arms around him, wishing I could protect him from everything that was harsh and mean.

"Sit still, dammit. Don't look like that. I'm not going to hit you. Shit."

Mason's shoulders were tense. I knew the clip was nearly over, so I stood. When he straightened up, our eyes met and I felt our thoughts mesh together. Watching this clip had been painful for us both. We shared the urge to protect Apollo, not only because we knew and loved him, but because he represented all dogs who led unhappy lives. If we could have helped them all, we would have. But that was impossible. The only answer was to start with the dog who sat in front of us.

"I need to see Lucas as soon as he gets in," Mason said. His look was level, serious—I knew he would treat this with the gravity it deserved. "Thank you for finding out the truth."

I bit my lip. He was thanking me for spying on my boss—yet he wouldn't thank me for spying on the show, even though I'd done both things for good reasons. I'd done one to help Apollo, the other to help the women of the world. Was there such a difference? There would be collateral damage in both cases. Lucas would face a reprimand, or worse. And my writing not only put jobs at risk—it threatened a project that was extremely close to Mason's heart.

How nice it must be for people who're always sure they're right.

Apollo

After my meeting with Mason and Sam, my eyes kept drooping shut. Sending out my thoughts is tiring work, and it's far harder when I cared so much about the outcome. I'd filled Sam with so many love thoughts I was surprised she didn't run over to Mason and start rubbing his belly. But she didn't. She's a tough case.

I did see her give Mason a long look that made me thump my tail on the floor. It was a careful look—she seemed to be examining not only his face and posture but the deepest part of his being. I thumped my tail because I knew that Mason could bear that kind of scrutiny and come out looking nobler than Lassie. If

Mason had four paws, he'd be the king of all dogs. Sam couldn't help but see that, now that she was looking.

She seemed reluctant to leave his office—something I took as another good sign. I hated leaving Mason's presence, too. Sometimes when I was falling asleep at night, after I'd sent out my love and spent some time with my rope, I let myself weave a golden little dream of a world where Sam, Mason, and I were together all the time. Sam and I moved out of my office, into Mason's. I had a bed underneath his desk, so if I fell asleep and woke up worried or unsure about where I was, I could open my eyes and see his shoes. His warm scent would be a part of me, twisted into my fur, and I'd never feel lonely. Sam would be there, too, to rub my tummy and speak in her gentle voice. I liked to imagine the sounds of their two voices intermingling above my head as I fell asleep. It was the safest feeling in the world.

After we left Mason, Sam and I went back to our office and sat on the floor. Sam seemed nervous, which was becoming normal for her. I was too exhausted to try to calm her down, so I lay on the floor and let her stroke my side while I recovered my strength. Of course, I knew I'd get my energy back faster if I ate something. Maybe something like almond butter. But Sam didn't have any.

The sound of Lucas's steps outside the door made me jump. I hurried into my crate—I knew Lucas didn't want Sam to spend her time petting me.

"Lucas," Sam said, scrambling up off the floor. "Good morning. Um, Mason said he wanted to see you."

Lucas grunted. "Did he say what about?"

Sam shook her head, looking guilty. It was a look I knew well by now. "Nope. Just said he wanted to see you right away."

After a second grunt, Lucas went out the door to our office. Two seconds later, I heard him next door in Mason's office.

Even listening as hard as I could, I only heard part of what was said next door. The door opened and shut, and Mason said something like "we have monitors in this building." I crept slowly out of my carrier, back to the middle of the floor. Sam sat back down, and I laid my chin on her thigh. She was listening, too.

We heard Mason say "—video of you interacting with Apollo . . . I'm deeply disturbed."

Lucas's voice was a note higher than usual. He was speaking in a rush, saying "—never laid a hand on him. I've never hurt him. I wouldn't do that."

"Not hurt you *physically*," Sam whispered to me. When Mason spoke again his tone was firm and low—an alpha's voice. I heard "tone of voice" and "unacceptable roughness." Lucas's voice got even higher. His stress made me feel uncomfortable, so I got up and paced around the room, stopping to bury my face in Sam's lap. Lucas. Thinking of him made my heart hurt. I knew Kim had wounded him—and the wound had been reopened when she called last night. Now he was in trouble with Mason. If only I could help him. If only he would let me.

Suddenly, Sam jumped up. She beckoned for me to follow, and we crept out into the hall, close to Mason's door. Sam clipped my leash onto my collar, and we stood there together, our backs to the door, listening.

"Here's what's going to happen," Mason way saying. "We're going to rewrite our contract. I'll get legal to work on it today. The new contract is going to make me Apollo's official guardian for as long as the show is filming. You won't see him, train him, or have any contact with him. Not during the week, not on weekends."

Lucas made a scoffing sound. "I'm not agreeing to that. I haven't done anything wrong."

"You haven't done anything right either," Mason said. "You'll agree to it because this is your business. Because if I make it known that you treat your animal stars this way, you'll never do better than low-budget ads and infomercials. Even the made-for-TV movies won't touch you. You know how freaked out Hollywood is about pissing off the animal welfare folks. I could call our person from Animal Humane and let them know what's been going on when they aren't here to monitor things. You may not have broken any of their rules, but we both know they won't be happy."

There was silence behind the door. I shivered. Lucas said some low things in an angry voice that made the air smell like metal even though he was on the other side of the wall. The growly noises twitched in my ears. Then I heard a chair being pushed across the floor. "Fine," Lucas said. "Write your damned contract. It'll be a relief to not have to come all this way every day. But your show is done. He only performs for me. Now you'll have no trainer whatsoever. You're totally screwed. I hope you know that."

Mason said something too quiet to hear. I only caught the end—"leave Apollo here and go now. We can talk about his future later, after we shoot the finale in Madrona."

Sam and I scooted away from the door. "Come on," she whispered, her voice tense. "Let's get out of here—quick!" We slipped down the hall, striding at our fastest pace. As we glided away, Lucas's metallic scent billowed out into the hall behind us.

"Keep going," Sam muttered. "Don't look back."

I turned my head and saw Lucas standing in the hall, watching us walk away. He looked the same way he had when he saw Kim with Dr. Danmore, as if every dog in the world had taken a nip at him. I wanted to run back to him, to lick his face and show him that I still loved him even if Kim had gone, even if his heart was broken. I couldn't, of course. Not only because I was leashed to Sam, but because Lucas would push me away if I tried. Instead, I turned my face forward and let my thoughts flow out with the beat of my paws, drifting back to Lucas.

You are loved. You are safe. One day you will be okay. I know you will, because I love you.

🖥 Samantha

I was in full-blown panic. My article deadline was coming up and I had nothing more than a vague rumor of good works and charity to work with.

But luck was with me. In the afternoon, Isabella came to take Apollo for some promotional shots, and she mentioned that he'd be posing with a rescue dog. At last, this was my big opportunity. After they left, I watched the clock, my heart thumping. I made myself wait fifteen full minutes until I felt sure that the photo shoot was under way. Then I grabbed a little blue canister of treats that I'd found deep in Apollo's leash box and flew out the door, moving fast so I wouldn't have time to rethink my plan.

I dashed down the stairs, pretending that I knew where I was going even though I had no idea. But if I couldn't get Mason to tell me about these great acts of charity, I was going to witness them for myself. One look at Apollo with a rescue dog or an at-risk kid and I'd have something to write about. Maybe I'd even get to talk with one of the beneficiaries.

I walked along the lower hall, pausing outside every door to listen for the click of a camera. Most rooms were completely silent, though a few had music coming from behind their doors. I hesitated near these, unsure if photographers would play tunes to get their subjects in the mood, but I was too timid to barge in. I scooted from door to door, feeling more jittery the further I went.

At last I heard Isabella's voice coming from a room a few doors down. I sprinted in that direction and got there just as the door opened. Rebecca popped out, and I slid to a stop just as she closed the door firmly behind her.

"Let me guess. Lost again?"

"Um, no, not this time." My face was burning hot. "I just—" I fumbled for the canister of treats in my pocket. "Isabella forgot to take these. Dog treats. She'll need them for the shoot." I motioned to the door and started to step around her. Rebecca blocked me, reaching for the treats. I pulled them back, out of her reach.

"Give them to me," she said. "I'll take them in."

"I can take them."

"No, you can't. It isn't part of your job."

"But I'm Apollo's handler. Anything that involves him involves me."

Rebecca gave me a cold look and lunged for the

treats again, surprising me. This time she snatched them out of my hand. "I'll take them," she said, her voice like iron. "And, as I think I made clear before, you belong upstairs. I'm sure I won't see you down here again. Will I?"

18

Samantha

On Thursday, I didn't see Mason at all. It was strange to walk by his office and know there was no point in stopping by under the pretense of giving him "Apollo time." Strange to stop myself from looking for him on the set. In fact, I hadn't realized I'd started doing those things until I no longer had the chance to.

What was happening to me? I needed a stiff dose of *Unvarnished* truth serum. It was all well and good to spend time with Mason—he was so easy and fun to be around. I liked talking with him, hearing his perspective on things. I was also impressed by the way he'd handled the Lucas situation. And yes, his handsomeness was a side bonus.

But I'd caught myself thinking about him far too often—more often than anyone should think about someone after just one date. I needed to stop my head from filling with visions of him when I lay in bed at night. Needed to stop feeling my heart swell when he was around. I couldn't forget that for 98 percent of us, there was no epic love story. There were just breakups, divorces, and long dreadful moments in a church, waiting for someone to tell you why your fiancé wasn't coming.

Richard. I still couldn't believe he was getting married. But strangely, Richard was beginning to feel less and less important. If I tried, I could probably drum up a good red-hot anger, but anger like that—which used to come so easily it had to be repressed—would take a lot of work.

"Maybe Richard should just do whatever he wants," I told Apollo. "Maybe I don't care anymore." And as I said the words, they settled on my shoulders like a heavy blanket. This was true. Richard was the past. I was busy enough trying to shake my head free of thoughts of Mason.

So it was probably a good thing that he was gone all day. He'd flown out late the afternoon before so he could be on the East Coast for predawn appearances on *New Day* and *Sunrise America!,* the most-watched morning shows in the country. Pilar showed me a clip of his *Sunrise America!* segment on her phone. I got a secret buzz from seeing him promote our idea—*a completely unscripted show! Tune in to watch Apollo work without a net!*—to the world. He was a great salesman, full of genuine excitement about the new show we were going to tape that Friday. I just hoped he wouldn't be too crushed when Apollo proved to be a wonderful, adorable dog—and nothing more. The editing team would earn their pennies this week, that was for sure.

*E*very spare moment I had, I was working on finding out more about the show's charity work. It was the only thing I could do to soften the blow of the article that had already run—and the one that was coming. I tried striking up casual conversations with everyone I could, sidling up beside sound techs and hairstylists, bringing up Mason and his dog-friendly donations. When that didn't work, I chatted with people in line at the café, saying anything I could think of that might get them talking.

"Don't you love what we're doing for those hospital kids?" I asked anyone who would listen. "I wonder if Mason wants Apollo to practice anything for the photo shoot with that charity he supports. What's it called again?"

Nothing. My questions met with total silence. Could Pilar have been completely wrong? I wasn't sure what to think. I was walking Apollo down the hall, my head lost in these thoughts, and I didn't hear Rebecca coming up behind us. She pulled her headset down around her neck and gave me a disapproving look.

"I need to talk to you," she said, steering us into the café. She sat primly on a metal-backed chair and waited for me to sit in the one opposite. Apollo lay down at my feet. "You never signed a confidentiality agreement," she said. It was a challenge, not a statement.

"No one ever asked me to," I replied. This was the defense I'd prepared. I hoped I sounded relaxed, as if I had no problem signing such an agreement. Inside I was cold and clammy.

"Will you sign one now?"

Crap. I was afraid something like this would come up. What could I do? If I signed it, did that mean the end of my columns? What about the advance money that I'd sent to my credit card company?

"How would that work?" I asked. "Would my contract be rewritten to include it, or what?"

Rebecca's jaw shifted to the side. "I don't think we'd need to go to all that. It's a stand-alone agreement. Everyone here has to sign one. You should have before you started."

I lifted an eyebrow. "Like I said, I would have if anyone had asked. They didn't. So why don't you bring it to me and I'll have my lawyer look it over." That was my other prepared line. I needed to stall as long as possible, and I thought the bit about the lawyer was good for a couple of days, if not a full week. My fictitious lawyer was a very slow reader.

"Your lawyer?" Rebecca made these two words sound like an incrimination.

"Mm-hmm. I'm a disaster with contracts and things. He's told me I should never sign anything without showing it to him." I shrugged my shoulders as if it was out of my hands. Delay due to mental incompetence.

"Fine." She exhaled a quick breath through her nose. "Now, about today. Mason e-mailed. He wants Apollo to go to the casting—that's downstairs at noon. He wants him to meet the potential cast members and weigh in on who should be hired for this week and next." She squinted down at her phone, apparently checking these ludicrous instructions. Then she looked up at me. "How is he supposed to do that?"

"I'm not sure," I said. Heck, I didn't even know how I was going to avoid this confidentiality agreement. "He's a clever dog. I'm sure he'll make his preference clear."

Rebecca snorted. "If he has one. He'll probably just go to the people who smell like food."

I looked her levelly in the eye. "Apollo's a lot smarter than you give him credit for."

Rebecca rolled her eyes. "Sure he is. Not that it matters. I'm sure you're unaware, but that *Telltale* article torpedoed our ratings. The show could be canceled if Mason can't get people watching again." She fixed her eyes on mine. "That's why I'm going to hunt down the person who spilled our secrets. Mason doesn't seem to have the heart to do it, but I do. I won't stop until I find her. And when I do, I'll let the whole world know about it. Starting with Mason."

I shivered. Damn this air-conditioning. And damn Rebecca with her curly hair and tight little jeans. She knew it was me. It was obvious from the way she looked at me that she knew, and pretty soon she'd be able to prove it. She got up and sauntered away, but I stayed, sure that if I stood I would collapse into a puddle on the floor. The exits were disappearing. All too soon, my jig would be up.

Apollo

Mason wasn't here. All morning, I'd listened for the sound of him opening his office door or talking on the telephone. I'd waited to sniff him somewhere on the set or catch sight of his shoes in the café—but nothing. He wasn't here. And if he wasn't here, that meant he was *gone*.

I tried to stay calm. Lucas was also missing, for the second day in a row. What was going on? Was a dangerous monster attacking people outside the studio building? I wondered if I should try to get away from Sam, so I could break out and hunt the creature down.

No, I should stay and protect Sam. That's what Mason would want me to do.

In the middle of the day, Sam and I walked down a series of hallways to a large room that had a row of tables at one end and two empty chairs set in the middle, facing the tables. A number of people sat behind the table in plastic chairs that squeaked when the people rocked forward or backward. They were talking when we came in.

"I heard that there are still ten people who haven't signed the confidentiality agreement," said a woman in jeans and high heels. She sounded aggressive, like she was on the verge of a growl. "You'd think Mason would just fire them all—better safe than sorry, right?"

I felt Sam go stiff beside me, so I wagged to reassure her.

"Probably he can't," said a man in a vest and tie. His shoes were black and shiny. "You can't just fire people without a reason. Though how can we trust anyone after this? I heard the share was less than *ten percent* this week. Those are doomsday numbers. They can find a thousand reality shows that'll do better than that."

The people jumped a little when they spotted us. Sam was letting off a miserable guilty-dog smell that made me want to lick her face. She stood very still as the woman in jeans bounced up to greet us.

"Apollo! Wonderful! And you must be the handler. I'm Janis, the casting director." She shook hands with Sam while I sat between them, panting. The woman scratched under my chin with long red nails. "Mason wants this little guy to have final approval on casting." She looked up at Sam. "Do you know what that means? How are we supposed to know if he likes the actors or not?"

Sam looked down at me. She still smelled like she was in trouble, but it seemed to relax her to focus on me, so I worked on drawing her attention with pants and ear twitches. I tried to look hungry, since I was pretty sure there was a bowl of M&M's on the table.

"I think it'll be pretty obvious when he likes them," she said. "He's easy enough to read. If he's indifferent, we should take that as a no."

The woman's face looked displeased. "If you say so. We'll carry on as usual—you let us know which people he likes. Let's just hope he doesn't fall in love with the ones who are stiff as a board."

Sam and I settled down on the floor in the corner of the room. She unhooked my leash, and I took that as permission to trot around and explore. I met each of the people in the plastic chairs, then I checked the carpet, the doors, and examined the underside of the table. I found some interesting smells, but nothing amazing— the plastic-chair people weren't dog people. No one even offered me an M&M.

After a minute of sitting quietly by Sam, the door at the far end of the room opened and a young woman in a very short skirt came in. I could tell she was chilled by the bumps on her skin, but she pretended not to be. She gave the plastic-chair people a nervous smile.

"You can go see her if you want," Sam whispered, motioning toward Short Skirt. I padded quietly up to Short Skirt—she looked down at me, but didn't offer a hand. Her perfume smell was so strong I couldn't get a sense of her at all, so I went back to Sam and sat down to watch. The plastic-chair people asked her questions that made her even more nervous, then she left and a young man came in.

The same thing repeated, over and over. Each of the

people who came in were either so nervous or so covered in cologne that I couldn't get to know them. Some of them stopped to pet me, but not for long. They seemed focused on what the plastic-chair people wanted. I started to wonder what I was supposed to be doing.

At last, Sam stood up. "We're going to take a quick walk," she said.

"But what about the auditions?" asked the jeans lady. "Mason wants Apollo to approve the final selections. And we're in a rush this week, since he wants to do some filming tomorrow."

"Why don't we have him look the finalists over at callbacks? This just isn't going anywhere. I think he should take a break—you can carry on with the auditions."

We went out into the hall. Sam seemed relieved to be out of that room, so I was also happy about it. I held my tail high as she turned us down a hallway that was lined with people in chairs. They were all holding pieces of paper, and some were muttering to themselves or making fake smiles into the air. Sam turned to me.

"Do any of these people interest you? We need two guests for the next show. Can you pick out your favorites?" She bent down and unhooked my leash again, something that never happened in the halls. I wasn't sure what I was supposed to do—with Lucas I always knew when he wanted something. With Sam I wasn't quite sure. She seemed to be giving me my own head, but what was I supposed to do with my freedom? What would make her happy?

I wandered down the hall, accepting rubs from anyone who wanted to give them. The people were all young, and nice to look at, with new clothes on that creaked and rustled when they moved. I gave them each a light sniff, but I didn't catch anything more interesting than food and car smells. I was about to start smelling the floor when I saw a set of wiggling fingers.

The fingers belonged to a young man with hair so short he looked almost bald. He wore heavy black boots with thick tread. And he was watching me—smiling in the quiet way some people have. Just looking, I could tell he really wanted to meet me.

I went right to him. He put his hands on either side of my head and bent down. "Hi, buddy," he said softly. "How are things? How's a dog today?"

I turned sideways and he rubbed my flank, sliding one hand down to my belly. I leaned against his legs. He smelled just as nervous as all the other people in the hall, but I could tell that I was calming him down. Rubbing my side quieted him the way chewing on my rope did for me. I was so pleased to be able to soothe him I would have stayed there forever, even if I hadn't detected a second, more interesting smell coming from him. The smell of love.

19

🦴 Apollo

My new friend told me his name was Sebastian. "And this is Faye." He smiled at the woman next to him. She had long blond hair, a tiny body, and a pretty face without much makeup on it. Sebastian nearly melted when he looked at her. The smells that came off him were nutty and deep, like almond butter. I had almond butter once, off Kim's finger when we were practicing to film a commercial. Almond butter is heaven.

Faye wore boots with heels so tall they made her hold herself like a Chihuahua, even when she was sitting. She seemed to like Sebastian, but her gray eyes were sad, and she kept her body rigid instead of leaning toward him the way he did to her. Yet, for all that, I caught a sweet scent coming from her, one that reminded me of lemons and laundry drying outside. She liked him, but something was holding her back.

As I watched Faye, I had a feeling that she reminded me of someone. Not her looks—she looked like most of the women we'd had on the show. They were all blond and thin like birds. No, it was the energy around her that felt familiar, and particularly the way she acted with Sebastian. It smelled like something I'd encountered—not exactly like, but very, very close.

I sat down so I could observe them more carefully. They were each pretending to read their piece of paper, but from time to time Sebastian would lean over and say something in low tones to Faye. Often she would smile, but it was a reserved smile—she was holding back.

"Run lines with me?" Sebastian asked. Faye nodded, and they resettled themselves in their seats so they were facing each other. Sebastian started in a low voice that sounded like it belonged on the radio. "How am I supposed to feel good about myself as a man when you're always nagging at me?"

Faye giggled.

"What's so funny?" Sebastian grinned at her.

"Why don't you use your regular voice?"

He winked. "My regular voice didn't make you smile," he said.

Faye's face lit up, but only for a second. With her eyes locked on Sebastian's, worry washed over her in a wave. And just like that, everything fell into place. I realized what she was feeling—she was afraid he'd hurt her. Not physically—people rarely do that. She was afraid he'd hurt her heart. And she would only think that if someone had before.

What really had me excited, though, what made my tail hammer against the floor, was my second realization. Because I remembered who Faye reminded me of. And that was thrilling, because it gave me a breakthrough in my number-one project, the one I felt destined to put right. Faye—nervous, wary, untrusting Faye—reminded me of Sam.

🖥 *Samantha*

I was watching Apollo from a distance. He'd attached himself to the pair at the far end of the hall, a stunning blonde and a young guy in Timberlands and a rugby shirt (an ironed rugby shirt, if my eyes didn't deceive me. How was that for mixed messages?).

What was it about them that drew him in? They seemed to be flirting, and I couldn't shake the feeling that he'd gravitated straight to the only people in the room who were romantically interested in one another. Everyone else was busy studying his lines or looking around for someone to impress. Only Apollo's pair was engaged in a genuine conversation—one that included long looks and blushes.

I was about to creep closer, to see if I could overhear their conversation, when my phone rang. I checked the number as I moved to a quieter area—it was a 323 area code, but I didn't recognize the rest.

"Hello?"

"Hi." It was a man's voice. My heart skittered around in my rib cage.

"Richard, I thought I told you I didn't want to talk. I don't have anything more to say to you."

There was a pause, then the voice spoke again.

"Uh, Sam. It's Mason."

A cold sweat broke out on my red cheeks. "Mason?" I squeaked. "Oh. Sorry. I thought you were someone else."

"Your other hot date?" he said in a joking tone. His voice had a slight edge to it though, as if he was 90 percent joking and 10 percent serious. Which struck me as so unlikely I dismissed it instantly. And decided to change the subject.

"I saw a clip of you on *Sunrise America!* You sold it really well."

"Do you think so?" I was surprised he had to ask. Did a man as famous and well polished as Mason really have doubts? "It's always so tough on live TV," he said. "Those morning show hosts are great, but they don't give you a ton of time for your plug. I hope I got it all out okay."

"Absolutely. I thought you were crystal clear." My blush was starting to subside, but my heart kept jangling like a Salvation Army Christmas bell. "I'm glad you called," I said. "I have a little conundrum with Apollo."

"What's that?"

I told him how Apollo had seemed uninterested in the people at casting. "But we're out here in the hall where everyone waits to be called for their audition, and he's met some people. A pair of people. They were sitting by each other, but I don't know if they came together or what exactly. Anyway, he's captivated by them."

"Do you think they have guest potential?"

I shrugged, even though he couldn't see me. "I don't really know what makes a good guest. They're certainly cute enough for TV, if that's what you mean."

Mason chuckled, then asked me to talk to Janis and tell her he wanted those two auditioned next. "And have her give them a long interview, really in depth, not just the five-minute job. If they have any promise at all, we want them. Tell her she can choose the backups—that'll make her feel better."

I promised to go see Janis as soon as I hung up.

"How's our star doing?" he asked with a warmth in his voice that made me feel like we were Apollo's parents, talking about our beloved boy.

"He missed you today. Every time we go by your office, he wants to stop and look inside."

"I hope Apollo isn't the only one who missed me."

My mind froze. For a long minute, nothing passed in or out—every synapse was stuck, trying to process the words he'd just spoken. He hoped I had missed him! And I had, I really had. But should I tell him that?

What popped out of my mouth was cagey and cautious. "We all missed you."

That earned me another chuckle. "Well, good. I'm glad to hear that. But, hey, Sam, there's something else I need to talk to you about." He suddenly sounded serious.

"Sure."

"Rebecca let me know that you haven't signed the show's confidentiality agreement yet."

I bit my lip and shifted the phone to my other ear. Damn. This agreement was going to ruin me.

"No, I haven't. I don't have a copy of it yet." *How long would I be able to hide behind that flimsy excuse?*

"And she said something about your showing it to your attorney?"

It was time to start flinging out lies. *Fast*. "Yeah. Well. I've signed some stupid things in the past and our attorney—he's a family friend—made me swear that I would never sign another contract without letting him read it first. It's not a big deal, just a habit I've had to develop because I never manage to read the small print. I've gotten into some bad spots with my overzealous signing hand."

"Was that with Richard?"

"What?" What was he talking about? Were my lies tripping me up already?

"You thought I was someone named Richard when you picked up the phone. And you sounded irritated. I thought maybe the bad contracts were with him."

"Oh. No. No, nothing like that."

A lame silence spread between us. My heart was still pounding from the whole contract discussion, and I felt the need to end this conversation as quickly as I could. Apparently Mason felt the same, because he said, "Okay—you'll talk to Janis, then? See if you can get her to sign those two on. If Apollo likes them, we'll give them a try."

When I hung up, I stood still for a moment, thinking hard. At the end of the hall, Apollo was still engrossed by the young couple. Somewhere behind the door, Janis and the rest of the casting team were interviewing would-be guests. All around me, nervous energy made the air feel full of static. All this movement encircled me, but my brain couldn't budge.

Finally, I looked down at my phone and dialed. Vern picked up on the second ring.

"Uh-huh?" I could hear him typing in the background.

"I have a big problem," I said, turning to face the wall. "They want me to sign a confidentiality agreement."

The typing stopped. "They do? When?"

"Any second—as soon as they have it ready for me.

I think I can stall on signing it till tomorrow, but then what am I going to do?"

Vern heaved a sigh. "Hollywood, man. They're crazy for this confidentiality shit. Like getting free press doesn't help them? Like they don't want us to cover their shows?" He rambled on, sounding less and less coherent as he spoke. Finally, I butted in.

"But what should I do? I don't want to get sued. I heard the agreement says I'd have to pay them over a million dollars if I tell show secrets. I don't have a million dollars!"

"Course you don't," he said indignantly. "It's a scare tactic. They're just strong-arming you. Have they threatened to fire you if you don't sign?"

"Well, no, but I don't want to be a holdout. Everyone's freaking out over that article you ran last Friday. If I don't sign, there'll be a massive witch hunt. They'll all hate me."

"Listen, sweetheart, they're gonna hate you by the time you're done writing your pieces. You're not gonna win Miss Congeniality here. What we have to do is keep you from getting sued."

I knew all that. Of course I did. But I still felt the clammy tightness in my lungs that signals an oncoming sob. I squeezed my eyes shut and tried not to think about Mason hating me. "Okay," I said, taking deep breaths to keep the tears at bay. "How do we keep me from getting sued?"

That night I sat in front of my computer, gnawing on my nails. I'd skipped dinner—I was too wired to eat. Jitters ran through me, making my knees bounce. I opened a blank document and stared at the blinking cursor. Where was Apollo when I needed him? I'd have given anything to be able to bury my face in his fur and feel my worries drift away.

Vern and I had reached a horrible conclusion. In order to protect the few hundred dollars I had in my bank account, I needed to file my last two articles with him before I signed that confidentiality agreement. I figured I had until Monday. They would give me the paperwork tomorrow, and I would need to deliver a signed agreement when I started work next week. If I did anything different, Mason would know I was the one behind the articles and the great hating-of-Sam would begin.

Vern had pointed out that I could quit as soon as the last article was filed. "If you can't share anything you learn after that, what's the point of staying?" But I couldn't imagine quitting the show before the season was over. Most important, I couldn't leave Apollo. If I disappeared, Mason would have to hire a stranger to care for him. I pictured Apollo, looking lost and lonely, walking his treadmill with someone new, and my heart clenched. I had to stay on. I just had to.

It was time, too, for me to admit another truth to myself, one that had been creeping up on me for some time. I couldn't let Apollo go back to Lucas. He was too sensitive a dog to be treated callously—I needed to find a way to free him from his current life. Of course, I had no idea how to do that. The only thing I'd come up with so far was to bring it up with Mason, to see if he had any bright ideas. He'd certainly worked fast when it came to revising Lucas's contract. Maybe he could think of a way.

With a sigh, I started typing. *"True Dog Love on The Love Dog Set,"* I wrote. Then I proceeded to write paragraph after paragraph about nothing. I took Pilar's rumors and spun them into long, rambling passages about Mason's philanthropic spirit and love of canines. I went on at length about the way he'd jumped to move Apollo's room. And I painted Apollo as every child's best friend. Then I sent the whole thing to Vern and slouched into the kitchen to microwave a bowl of soup.

Minutes later, Vern called. "What the hell happened?" he said in lieu of hello.

My stomach clenched. "What do you mean?"

"I mean your last piece was great and this one is shit. We can't run this."

I fumbled for a chair and sank into it. "You can't? I thought you said exposing good things would be fine."

"To an extent, sure. I mean, we can do good stuff if it's an ameliorating factor. As in 'Mason Hall sniffs paint but gives to dog charities,' that sort of thing. But this is all goody-goody blah-blah. And there's no substance to it. Do you even know what charity he supports?"

I confessed that I didn't.

"Well, there you go, then. I'm sorry, Sam, but we can't print this. It's crap. Utterly pointless. We need you to go back to the kind of stuff you gave us last time. Dirt. News. Secrets. You know what we need. If you can't give it to us, then you have to give us our advance back," Vern said, his voice suddenly rigid. "We didn't pay you for stuff we can't run. Give us something we can use. Otherwise, I think you know what we'll be forced to do. We'll have to sue you for breach of contract."

I lapsed into horrified silence.

"Look," Vern said, his voice softening, "why don't you write about the bad ratings? That's news. That's good dirt." After Vern hung up, I considered climbing into bed and hiding under the covers. But there was no point. Vern was right—I knew what I had to do. With a heavy sigh, I walked to the computer and sat down again. I tapped my fingers on the keyboard and bit my lip. "*Ratings Slump Throws* Love Dog *into Tailspin*," I typed. It was time to quit stalling. My advance money was already spent—I had no choice. And besides, another article wouldn't make Mason hate me any more. I was already sunk.

20

🦴 *Apollo*

Last night when I sent my love out to the world, I realized that my list of people was almost twice as long as it had been before I met Sam. Not only did I send my love to Sam now, I sent it to Kim. Lucas and Mason were still on the list, of course. And I'd added Curly Hair and Pilar and A.J. I spent an extralong time on Mason and Sam, because I wanted them to feel so much love they would naturally extend it toward each other. Sam in particular.

After I finished, I brought my rope out from the back of my crate and rested it between my paws. I had some serious thinking to do, and I needed my rope to engage my jaws so my mind could romp around.

I'd been living in this studio long enough to have a good sense of how things worked. Whenever Pilar brought guests around, I was going to spend time with them, so I knew I'd be seeing more of Sebastian and Faye. That was exciting—they were perfect practice for my work with Sam and Mason. As soon as I realized that Faye reminded me of Sam, I knew what I had to do. I'd work with Faye until I got her to trust Sebastian, and then I'd use whatever method worked with her to help Sam.

But what to do? I knew a fair bit about trust—any dog who's ever gone to a new home knows how to build a bond. Sometimes it's instant, like between dogs who both love wrestling. Or barking. A pair of barkers can become buddies in seconds. But if one of the dogs has been hurt in the past it can take days and weeks, sometimes months.

I didn't have weeks and months. If this week was like the others, I would only have a few days. A few days to form trust? Crazy! Crazy for any dog but me. I gave my rope a few good chomps. I was the Love Dog—this was my duty. I would figure out a way. To-morrow I would open Faye's heart to Sebastian and then I would help Sam love Mason. And all would be right with the world.

I woke up with my head on my rope and the answer on the tip of my nose. If I couldn't make Faye trust Sebastian by giving her days and weeks with him, I would have to help them bond through a special, shared experience. That was the way I bonded with Kim. On our very first trip to the dog park, a cattle dog got crazy and knocked Kim over. She landed on her back in a circle of dogs. I jumped into the middle and barked with all my might. The other dogs cleared off, and Kim hugged me for a long, wonderful time. She always trusted me after that. What I needed was something just like a dog park.

Sam arrived, looking exhausted with cloudy eyes

and hair in a messy ponytail. When I walked on my treadmill, she took a nap in a chair. Then Pilar appeared at the door.

"Hey, you two. They want you to go to makeup first thing. That's where they're filming the next segment." Pilar bent down to pet me.

"Where's Mason?" Sam asked, and I wagged my tail when I heard his name.

"He and Imogen are on the set, filming a segment with Sebastian." Pilar grinned. "They're playing shrink, trying to uncover an inferiority complex or something. Mason says we have to tape, tape, tape today, so they're capturing everything, even green room stuff. Guess he wants the editors to have reams of footage to work with."

She turned to go, but Sam jumped up and grabbed my leash. "Here, we'll walk with you." We headed off down the hall, moving quickly. "So, what do you hear from A.J. these days?" Sam asked.

Pilar shrugged and made a face. "Nothing. I've totally given up on him. I don't know what his deal was, but he obviously wasn't as into me as I thought."

"Maybe he didn't think he deserved you," Sam said.

That made Pilar snort. "Yeah, right. Like that ever slowed anybody down!"

We left Pilar and headed for the stairs, weaving this way and that to avoid people. When we reached the hallway at the bottom, A.J. nearly bumped into us. His hands were full of funny things—a beach ball, towels, champagne glasses, and a bouquet of flowers. He had a striped umbrella under one arm that clanged on the floor.

"Whoa, A.J.," Sam said, picking up the umbrella. While she did that, I checked A.J.'s scent. He smelled like longing, but in a faint way, as if he wasn't putting any effort into it. "Can I help you with that?"

"Naw." He took the umbrella back under his arm. "I got it."

"Are you okay? You seem kind of down."

He shrugged. "Nothing you can do about it. Not unless you can turn back time."

As he sauntered off, I had to give my heart a rough shake, the way I would a stuffed squirrel. His sadness had that creeping quality that could make everyone on the set feel mopey without knowing why. I couldn't afford to be distracted by his melancholy—not now that my biggest project was in play. Still, I wondered what had A.J. feeling so low. He reminded me of the way Kim had seemed when she came to apologize to Lucas—as if she wanted to fix things, but it was just too late.

The makeup area smelled like sugary, sneezy things. It was always crowded there because of the large chairs and mirrors, but today it was also crammed with legs. One cameraperson stood at each end of the hall and behind each of them was a sound person holding a microphone boom. Faye was there, sitting in one of the large chairs, and behind her was Sam's friend, the one who wore all the perfume. Sam waved at her when we arrived.

A short man with curly red hair seemed to be in charge. He told Sam that "we want Apollo right here, in front of Faye, so we can get shots of him looking up at her. Can you make him look up at her?"

Sam said she would try. She led me to a tiny patch of floor in front of Faye and asked me to sit and stay, then she took off my leash and slipped behind the sound person.

"Val, are you good?" the red-haired man asked. Sam's friend said she was. "Faye? All right, then. Let's roll." He pointed to the camerapeople, then stepped back by Sam.

Valerie cleared her throat. Then she looked into the mirror in front of Faye and tried to lock eyes with her. "So, Sebastian's pretty cute."

Faye nodded and looked unsure. I wagged my tail encouragingly. When Faye looked down at me, her shoulders relaxed a bit. Val started poking around her eye with a pencil, and Faye started talking. "He is cute. I don't know why—I'm just nervous about going out with him. I've been hurt before, you know?"

I wagged harder. Val nodded and switched to poking the other eye. "I do. Absolutely. My divorce was pretty much a cage fight. I still have the battle wounds to prove it."

"Then you know what I mean," Faye said, more energetically. "It's hard to jump back in there again with someone new. I'm half positive that the next guy I date is going to sleep with my best friend and her sister, just like my ex did." Behind Faye, the red-haired man's face blossomed with glee. Beside him, Sam was nodding her head. I shuffled a little closer to Faye. "I mean, he just ripped my heart out. I was so angry after I found out . . . I'm still angry. All I have to do is think of him, and all those feelings come right back. I really loved him. And now I hate his guts."

Behind her, Val fiddled with a big brush and something in a small box. Then she looked hard at Faye's mirrored face again. "I think you have to figure out where you went wrong the first time. Then you'll know what to avoid. With my husband, the problem was that I married a douche bag." She brushed pinkness onto Faye's cheeks. "Now I know not to do that again."

The camera crew started chuckling. Faye smiled and looked down at me. I was delighted that she was sharing her fears—talking always seemed to help people, kind of like the way chewing helps a dog. "But that's the trouble. My ex seemed perfect—wonderful—until I found out he'd been cheating for nearly a month. With my best friend!"

Val shook her head as she spread something colorful onto the back of her hand. "How could any guy screw around on someone as pretty as you? He should have been worshipping at your feet."

Faye shrugged. "I don't want that, I just want someone to stick by me, you know? To be in my corner. I want someone who can be a friend and a lover, who'll put up with holidays at my family's because he loves me that much. And I want to love him so much that I'll gladly go to his stupid office parties and wrap all of his Christmas presents. I want real love. And I don't want to be treated like shit anymore."

Val's hand paused beside Faye's cheek. "I know, sugar. We all do. But to find it, you have to take a risk. You have to jump off the bridge and trust that bungee to hold. Sebastian could be the very guy you're looking for. But you'll have to jump or you'll never find out."

Samantha

I watched Valerie and Faye in a state of numbness. Faye seemed to be my very own mouthpiece—she was expressing everything I'd felt since Richard's sudden at-the-altar dumpage. But she seemed so starry-eyed compared to me, with her dreams of lifelong love and family holidays. I sighed. Hepburn and Tracy. Lord Nelson and Emma Hamilton. Of course even I wanted to fall in love—and be loved—with all the passion of the great romances. But as I listened to Faye talk about her ex, I realized that my problem with Richard was exactly the same as hers. I had loved him—genuinely loved him. I knew that didn't seem possible for a person as cynical as me, but it was true. And as I looked back, I couldn't see what went wrong. Was Richard flawed? Did I choose poorly when I fell for him? Or was there something I did—or didn't do? I couldn't tell what had made it crumble. And if I didn't know where things broke, how could I ever leap into that void again?

The camera crew cleared out as soon as they were done taping. Valerie finished Faye's makeup while Apollo sat at her feet. Then Faye scurried away to have stills and head shots taken for the opening montage. I came up to Valerie and watched her capping lipstick tubes and cleaning brushes.

"That went really well, don't you think?" Valerie asked, her face flushed. "I've never been on TV before. Wouldn't it be awesome if this became a regular thing? I could be the Dr. Phil of the makeup chair."

"I see a spin-off already," I said, smiling. "You were fabulous. I bet they're going to use that whole thing." I spent some time twirling the brushes Valerie kept in a jelly jar. "So do you really believe what you said or was that just for the cameras?"

She raised her pencil-perfect eyebrows at me. "Oh, no, I meant it. He was a complete douche bag."

"Right," I said, laughing. "No question about that. But I mean what you said about taking a risk. Do you really think it's worth it?"

Valerie looked surprised. "Of course I do. It's the only way to find happiness. We aren't solitary creatures, you know. We were meant to live in groups—pairs at least. That's why we have all these complex language skills."

I thought about that as she put the eyeliner pencils in order. "But is it worth it? You just went through a miserable divorce. Do you really think it's better to have loved and lost?"

She turned and looked me in the eye. "Yes. Oh, Samantha, love is the most wonderful thing in the world. It's worth everything. Sure, it's scary. Life is scary. Opening yourself up to love is about taking a big bite out of life. It might work out beautifully or it might be a train wreck. Look at me—I've had the disaster marriage. And I also had a great first marriage that gave me two fabulous kids. I'm still friends with my first husband, and we're both grateful that we had those years together because we love our children. The point is that you don't know where life will take you. The key is to spend your time in the game instead of sitting on the sidelines."

I scrutinized her face, shocked to see that she really believed what she was saying. I ducked my head, feeling strangely embarrassed by my doubts, yet still aware of them running like a ridge down my chest. All this talk of love was making me feel sick inside.

Apollo

When I heard the bus pull up outside the studio, my tail started wagging. I knew what that meant—it was time to take a trip. We did this nearly every week, and we often went to the same park by the ocean. The park had everything—a beach, a pool, slides, and little cars that spun and ran on tracks. One time I sat with the week's guests in a spinning car while the crew filmed us. After that I threw up three times.

When we got off the bus, I was pleased to see the crew hauling their equipment down to the beach. That was my favorite spot, and it suited my plan perfectly. Sam kept me on a leash while people ran around fluffing Faye's hair and smearing something on Sebastian's nose. Mason wasn't with us, but the red-haired man had taken charge and was yelling out orders.

Usually when we came to the beach, I knew exactly what I had to do. Lucas would sit behind the camera and wave at me or click his clicker, and I would lie down or cover my nose with my paws or shake my head from side to side. Today it was all different. Lucas wasn't here, I hadn't practiced anything, and the whole atmosphere was open and free, as if the alpha dog had stepped away and the puppies were taking over.

The crew was gathered on the beach and on a tall wooden pier that ran out into the water. The red-haired man did more yelling, and when everything was the way he wanted, he shouted something in our direction and Sam unhooked my leash. I glanced up at her, then trotted off toward Faye and Sebastian, who were standing on the sand in their swimsuits. Faye was stiff, like a nervous dog—everything about her told me she wanted to run away from Sebastian. But she stayed, maybe because we were all there. I'd had times when I wanted to leave the set, but I didn't because it isn't right to leave the pack.

She and Sebastian stood there awkwardly—I had to

get them moving. I went closer to the water and made a spin move, enticing them to follow me. Sebastian tried to grab Faye's hand, but she pulled away and ran toward me. I raced down the beach, my paws sinking into the dry sand. When I hit the wet stuff, I slowed down so the humans could keep up. Sebastian and Faye caught up with me, and I ran us all around in a circle so they would stay close. I saw the border collies at Lucas's ranch do this with a dachshund once— herding by leading. It really works.

When I had them both close on my heels, I crashed into the water, pushing forward until my paws lifted off the sandy bottom. The pier made shadows on the water, and I panted as I paddled from shadow to glinting brightness, then into shadow again. Chills seeped through my fur, waking me up all over. I swam, letting off barks. Then I heard Sebastian shout.

"Faye! Aren't you coming?"

I swam in a circle so I could see the shore. Faye was standing in waist-deep water, the waves sloshing against her bare midriff. Even though the sun was shining, her skin looked bumpy with cold. She looked up at the pier, at the crew up on top, and took a few more steps toward me.

"Are you cold?" Sebastian asked. "You'll get warm once you start swimming." He reached out a hand to her. She looked at it, then up at the crew again. Then she took his hand and let him lead her into deeper water. I gave another bark and paddled myself around. At last we were all headed where I wanted to go.

Sebastian and Faye followed me farther and farther from shore. When I started to feel tired, I slowed down and let them come even with me. Faye, I noticed, was off to one side, breathing hard, while Sebastian was on the other. Her faced looked strained. I felt bad for putting her in this hard situation, but I didn't know any other way to make her trust Sebastian. I could feel his caring and concern for her coming off him like a warm glow—he was ready to do his part.

"Are you okay?" Sebastian's voice floated over my head. "Faye? Are you getting tired?"

I saw her nod, her eyes wide with worry. This was the moment. I moved a little deeper and saw that we'd drifted closer to the pier. We were fully under its shadow. An extralarge wave surged over us, pushing us closer to the pier's black legs. Faye made a worried little noise in her throat and tried to move away, fighting against the surf.

Let Sebastian help you. You can trust him. He's a good person—I know it. I closed my eyes and saw Samantha's face, and Lucas's. They each wore the same hurt as Faye—it draped over them and smothered them, like a coat of long fur in the summertime. It engulfed them until they didn't have the energy to reach for the hand that was offering help.

Another wave carried Faye closer to the pier. She shrieked and flailed, sending splashes into her face. She struggled against the water, but every movement forced her closer to the nearest piling. Faye started to thrash. Then, in a smooth motion, Sebastian held out his hand again.

"Here—take my hand. Let me help you."

Trust him. Sebastian wants to help you—he wants to care for you. You just have to let him.

Faye's pale face appeared between the waves. She stretched out her fingers, lunging for Sebastian. He grabbed her hand, drawing her toward him through the water. Curling his arm around her middle, he pulled her back into his chest and began hauling them both to shore, kicking powerfully under the water.

I paddled behind him, panting hard. The taste of salt filled my mouth, and my eyes squinted, trying to hold off the glare of the sun on the water. From the beach, I could hear the red-haired man calling up to the crew on the pier. "Did you get it? Did you get that shot? That was fantastic!"

21

Samantha

I don't know what Apollo did exactly. All I can say is that when Faye and Sebastian set out for their beach segment, she was as wary of him as a squirrel facing off with a Saint Bernard. When they stumbled out of the water, Faye in Sebastian's arms, everything had changed between them. Faye looked like she had found her safety zone. She clung to Sebastian, and when he stepped out of the waves and lowered his head, she kissed him as if kisses were breathing, like life itself. Theirs was a Hollywood kiss made real, a megawatt showstopper meant for no one but the two people involved. When they finally broke apart and saw the film crews on the beach, they both turned pink.

While Apollo and I waited for the beauty crew to finish blow-drying Faye's hair, I bent down and whispered into his ear. "What did you do? What happened to Faye out there? She's like a completely different person." I peered up at Faye, who was at that minute looking across the beach at Sebastian. Even when they weren't together, something seemed to hold them tangled in one another. "She's like a woman in love."

I knew how ridiculous this all sounded. I mean, seriously—what could Apollo have done to make Faye fall in love with Sebastian? And why did I think it was love, anyway?

I couldn't explain. I just had an overwhelming conviction that in the space of a fifteen-minute swim, Sebastian and Faye had gone from being just two people to being part of the 2 percent who'd found genuine love. The connection between them was overflowing onto the crew, the beach, all of Los Angeles County.

"Are you some kind of magician?" I asked him. Apollo wagged his tail and looked mysteriously blank. We looked on as Faye and Sebastian took seats on the beach, waiting for the camera crew to get in place. They sat side by side, talking in the quiet way couples do. Watching, I felt an odd twist in my gut.

"You might be able to create love," I whispered to Apollo, "but you can't make it last, can you?" He wagged again, stirring up sand, and leaned forward to smell my face. "No one can make it last. Love comes and goes, that's the deal, isn't it? We can fall in love all right. We just can't keep it." I sighed.

Apollo ducked his head under my hand, asking for rubs. When he looked up at me, I felt as if he was thinking something very hard, trying to get a message through telepathically. Suddenly a picture of Mason popped into my head. I blinked, but it stayed, vivid and warm. "Love is dangerous." I said this a little louder, to underscore the truth of my statement. Apollo crooked an eyebrow in a doubtful way. "Way too dangerous. If I got involved with Mason, it would end in disaster. He would find out the truth and hate me, or

he'd break up with me out of the blue. Something awful would come along and ruin it. Something always
does."

*T*hat afternoon when Apollo and I stepped off the
bus back at the studio, I felt like sledgehammers hung
from each of my limbs. Apollo, on the other hand, had
never seemed so peppy. And who could blame him? If
he'd been the star of the show before, now, in the crew's
eyes, he was a god.

"Did you see that?" the senior cameraman kept
asking everyone on the bus. "In twenty years of TV,
I've never filmed anything that real. Those two had no
chemistry at all when they went into the water. But
when they came out, ker-sizzle!"

Everyone was buzzing about the transformation
they believed they had witnessed—and since I felt the
same thing, I could hardly quibble. "Apollo's the real
deal," the field producers said. "He's a genuine love
dog. Our show should stay on the air for ten years,
we're that good. What other reality show can claim to
be actually *real*?"

We filed into the studio, and Apollo and I went to
our place in the wings where he stood ready to go on
set for more filming. He seemed tireless, while I felt as
if I could curl up on the floor of Grand Central Station and take a three-hour nap. What was wrong with
me? Why did seeing Faye so much in love make me
feel wiped out? I gazed out at the set with overcast
eyes. When I saw Mason sitting on the velvet chair,
prepping for the next scene, what energy I had fizzled
out of my feet.

Just then Rebecca bustled into our corner of the

wings, holding her clipboard like a wedge in front of her. She came to an abrupt halt in front of me.

"You have my confidentiality agreement?" I asked in a resigned voice.

"No." She sounded annoyed. "Legal had some big thing this week, so they haven't gotten to it. Yet. I'll have it Monday. You can fax it to your lawyer from Madrona. Mason needs it signed on Tuesday."

By Tuesday, I thought, my second article would be out. The show could very well be dead by then. Besides, by Tuesday the season would nearly be over regardless of what the *Telltale* ran or didn't run. What was the point of signing it in the show's last week? But I suppose the point was a symbolic one. Rebecca probably thought that signing it would demonstrate my loyalty to the show. That was just what I needed, someone prancing around trying to prove a point when I had one more article to write.

As she speedwalked away, I did a little crunched-brow thinking. It was such a bitter twist. Vern had hired me to write about how fake the show was. But I'd been pummeled all day with evidence that this reality show was that rare bird—genuine. Now Apollo really did seem to be some kind of love dog. Now the show's guests really were in love with each other. Now a relationship really had blossomed during the filming of the show, thanks in large part to Apollo. Bizarre.

Mason appeared at the entrance to the set. "Hey there!" He smiled brightly, looking more excited than ever. He came close to me, slipped a hand around my waist, and—I kid you not—kissed me on the cheek.

"There's the woman I need to thank." A second kiss—very sweet and slow—followed the first. I thought I might melt. "This is going beautifully. I heard what

Apollo did at the beach." Keeping one hand at my waist, he lowered his other and scratched Apollo under the ear. "You are one fabulous dog, you know that?" Then he released me, bent low, and stage-whispered in Apollo's ear. "Think you can work that kind of magic on Sam? Can you make her fall for me like Faye did for Sebastian?"

My face turned bright red, and I'm pretty sure all the air disappeared from the room. I couldn't look at Mason—I just couldn't. Fortunately Apollo saved the day by barking and rearing up on his back feet, his paws waving at Mason's legs.

"Wow, I've never seen him do that," I said, covering my blush by scrambling to collect Apollo's leash. "He's usually so well behaved."

"Maybe he's glad to be out from under Lucas's thumb," Mason said. I was grateful that he didn't make another reference to Faye or the magical moment at the beach. "Speaking of which, there's something I need to ask you. Do you want to take Apollo home for the weekend? He can't go with Lucas, obviously, and I think it would be best if you or I took him home. He doesn't know anyone else well enough."

A picture popped into my head of sitting home with Apollo, gazing into his eyes for hours and hours while I anguished over Mason. My heart quailed. I couldn't withstand that kind of onslaught, not without the kind of soul searching that would leave me wailing for relief. I loved Apollo, but I knew what he would require of me. Too much. Way too much.

"I, uh, I have a cat. Could Apollo go with you? I don't think she'd appreciate having a dog appear in her apartment."

"Sure." Mason nodded. "No problem, I'll take him."

He turned to Apollo. "Looks like you'll just have to work your magic here at the studio, buddy. And in Madrona." He swung back to me. "Oh, I forgot to tell you. Remember how you said you thought Apollo wanted another chance to work with Honey and Chad? Well, I got it worked out. They're going to be our guests for the finale. And you're all set to come to Madrona next week, right? I want Apollo to stay in a house, not a hotel. My parents said we can crash with them."

Gulp. "Your parents?"

"Yeah, don't worry. They're very low key. They know we'll be busy shooting, so we probably won't see much of them. And they love dogs." He tousled Apollo's head. "But you're good with the flights and everything on Monday? I want to get up there ASAP so we can have as many filming days as possible. Hopefully we'll catch a little good weather."

I nodded, since my throat felt a little too tight for speech. Rebecca had handed out itineraries a week ago, letting us all know about our flights and accommodations. The only surprise here was learning that Apollo and I would be bunking at the Hall residence. Terrifying. I decided to put the thought out of my mind and not deal with it again until I was on their front porch.

Apollo

Something exciting was happening between Mason and Sam. When they talked in the wings, everything about his body was angled toward her like a Lab with a tennis ball. His shoulders leaned toward her, his hips and chest were squared in her direction, and his eyes never left her face. The energy of the moment shot through me, making my paws feel hot and ticklish. I closed my eyes, wagged like crazy, and sent every thought I had to Sam.

But it didn't work. Not quite. I felt her coming close—she was standing on the top step, very close to the edge. This was the delicate moment, when she could go either way. She might get scared and shrink away. Mason and I had to convince her to jump.

Fortunately, I'd never felt such strong love flowing through me. The success of Faye and Sebastian had fueled me like ten cans of the world's best dog food—I felt like I could tackle anything. Love between the two biggest dogs at the dog park? No problem. Romances for everyone who worked at the studio? Easy! Getting Sam to take a chance on Mason should be as basic as wagging my tail.

While Sam waited in the wings, Mason and I went onto the set where Faye and Sebastian were already cuddling on the couch. I longed to jump up in between them and burrow my way under their hands, but I held back. I didn't want Mason to feel left out.

Mason took the velvet chair and asked me to sit at his feet, which I was happy to do. I spent some time scratching my shoulder, then I licked my paws. After a little while, some things were shouted back and forth with the crew, the bright lights came on, and Mason turned to the camera.

"Today," he said, "we witnessed a wonderful thing. We saw two people, Faye and Sebastian, fall in love." On the couch, Sebastian put his arm around Faye. As she tipped her head in close to his, she gave off the scent of wisteria and candle wax, mixed with Sebastian's nutty almond-butter smell. Love, that's what they smelled like. Love and happiness.

"Usually on *The Love Dog,* Apollo has his hands full—well, his paws full—trying to put broken relationships back together. But today he got to do something different. Working his own brand of love dog magic, he helped Faye overcome the scars of her last relationship. He helped her learn to trust again." I wagged my tail, hoping that the cameras were picking up my support of Mason. Everyone was listening to him, even the people in the very back of the audience.

"But if they want to make their relationship work, they're going to have to be honest with each other. They'll have to share the truth, no matter how embarrassing it is or how must easier it would be to just stay quiet. It's never too late to start being honest with one another."

Whatever Mason was saying, it must have been important, because half the audience was nodding and the other half looked like they might burst into tears. I spotted A.J., sitting in the third row, his face as pale as a Samoyed's. I considered the way he'd seemed earlier, like it was too late for him to fix things. And then I thought, *that's stupid*. Just because you've gotten in a fight with a dog one day, that doesn't mean you can't act better the next time you meet him.

So even though I was probably supposed to stay next to Mason, I decided to let my instinct take over. Instinct had worked for me with Faye and Sebastian, and everyone seemed pleased. Lucas wasn't here to fill the air with his angry metallic smell, so what did I have to lose? Maybe it was time to do what I thought was best and quit worrying so much about following the rules.

I sat up, stared right at A.J., and barked. My bark was loud, and it startled everyone in the audience—they weren't used to hearing me make noise. I'm a big dog and I can really woof when I want to. I saw people jump when I barked, and two P.A.s dropped their soda cans right on the floor. But most important, A.J. looked up. He looked straight at me. So I barked again.

People started to make noise around me. I saw Samantha running around in the wings with my leash—pretty soon she would take me off stage. If I was going to get through to A.J., I had to act now. I had to follow what my nose and ears and eyes were telling me. My heart told me to move.

Pushing hard with my paws, I jumped up and ran to the aisle, then squeezed myself down the row to where A.J. sat. He turned when he saw me coming, his eyes big and round.

Talk to Pilar.

It was hard to send him thoughts while I was moving, but I concentrated and just managed. *Go see her. Explain yourself. Tell her the truth and say you're sorry. Do it now.*

When I got to A.J., he reached out and touched me with a shaking hand, like he thought I might give him a static shock.

Go to Pilar. Talk to her. Do it now.

Slowly, A.J. nodded his head. Then he got up and went down the row in the other direction, away from me. I watched him go, feeling a calm settle over my heart. I didn't question that he was going to speak to Pilar. I knew he was. Love was awake and flowing today. First Faye and Sebastian, now A.J. and Pilar—I'd never had so much success.

Before my brain processed another thought, my paws

were moving me out of the audience seats. Sam appeared, waiting for me with my leash, Mason at her side.

"Apollo, what were you doing?" Sam's voice had a mock-scolding tone, as if she couldn't bring herself to really correct me. Probably because she knew I'd been helping her friend Pilar. Also, she looked distracted and guiltier than ever. She reached down and clipped the leash on my collar. Then she turned to Mason.

"Um. Look. There's something I need to tell you," she said. "Something important."

Samantha

When Mason stood on that stage and told the world that Faye and Sebastian would have to be honest with each other if they wanted their relationship to work, I felt like someone was using a plumber's snake on my insides. "They'll have to share the truth," he said, "no matter how embarrassing it is or how much easier it would be to just stay quiet. It's never too late to start being honest with one another."

His eyes were on the camera, but obviously he was talking to me. Directly to me. He must have found out about my *Telltale* articles. Maybe Vern hadn't protected my identity the way he'd promised, or maybe Rebecca knew someone who worked at the *Telltale* or something. Mason knew and now he was trying to get me to confess. Well, good. *Good*. I wanted to confess. Mostly. I wanted it all to be over, for my guilt to be out in the open. So what if I didn't get to go to Madrona to meet Mason's low-key parents? So what if I didn't get to see him anymore? I wouldn't once the show was over anyway, right? Right?

When Apollo started barking after Mason mentioned telling the truth, I felt ready to do it. I was on the high-dive platform, ready to jump. As long as no one got in my way, I was going to tell Mason the truth. All of it, unvarnished.

"There's something I need to tell you," I said. I felt sick to my stomach. "Something important."

"Okay, sure," he said. He smiled as if I were about to offer him sexual favors. Then the segment producer started shouting out questions and Imogen Blakely appeared at his elbow, wanting to talk about the filming schedule in Madrona. Mason gave me an apologetic, please-wait-a-minute smile, and I led Apollo away. Inside, I backed down off the diving platform, knowing that I'd never get the nerve to walk out there again.

Amazingly, though, I did. An hour later, after walking Apollo on his treadmill, we headed back to Apollo's room for a rest. Just as I was about to turn the knob on the door, I heard Pilar's voice coming from inside.

"—and you believed her?"

"Well, yeah." This was A.J.'s voice. "I mean, I had to, you know? She said she was pregnant. How was I supposed to know she was lying?"

"I don't know—you went out with her for a year. She was your girlfriend. Seems like you might have known she was a liar."

There was a pause. I wondered if I should step away from the door and give them their privacy. But then I looked down at Apollo, who was staring at the door with a strange intensity, his ears perked forward. Apollo wanted to stay. So we stayed.

"Look," A.J. said, "Hailey didn't start to get crazy until we broke up. I thought things were really done and over with us—that's why I asked you out. I really wanted to see you that night. Honest. But Hailey called that very afternoon saying she'd just taken the pregnancy test and could I come over. Of course I had to go. I didn't want to—I'm not ready to be a dad. But I wasn't going to flake on her."

"No, of course you weren't." Pilar's voice was subdued.

"Let me tell you, I was pissed when she told me the truth. She was never pregnant at all—she was just screwing with me. And by then, I figured it was too late with you. You were already so mad at me."

"Why did she tell you? I mean, she could have kept stringing you along . . ."

"She probably found some other guy she wanted to go out with more than me. Lucky break, I guess." He made a whistling sound, signifying a narrow escape. "Though she would have had to tell me eventually. She couldn't fake it forever. But she managed to screw things up with you, and I'm thinking that was her goal."

"She knew about me?"

"Uh-huh."

"Oh." Pilar's voice turned softer still. A quiet moment ensued. Apollo began to wag harder than I'd ever seen him wag before. When he whined at the door and pawed it, I drew us away. Pilar and A.J. seemed to have found love at last, too. I pushed on my solar plexus, wondering why their happiness made my heart hurt so much.

* * *

After fifteen minutes of soul searching and stiff self-talk, I strode us purposefully back to the set. I was going to tell him. I would just hold my nose and plunge. Then it would all be over, for better or worse.

"Mason," I said, working my way in between Rebecca and the prop master. "Can I talk to you for a second? In private? It's important."

"Sure," he said, looking sorry and stressed. I felt my resolve faltering. Maybe I shouldn't add this to his plate of troubles. Didn't he have enough going on, just trying to put together a reality show about something genuine? "Could you give me half an hour? Maybe get Apollo all packed up for the weekend at my place?"

I trundled off with Apollo, but inside I was climbing back down the high-dive ladder. I'd lost my nerve. There it went, fluttering off to the ceiling. *Good-bye, nerve. Hello lies, shame, and betrayal. It looks like you're here to stay.*

22

🦴 Apollo

I've flown on a plane twice and been to the airport three times. Flying is strange. It's very loud and dark, and there's always another dog—or a couple of cats— who yowl the entire time. But both times, I've been overcome by an intense sleepiness once I entered my crate. Sometimes I can't tell which of the sounds really happened and which ones were parts of dreams.

I woke up to see walls moving past the door to my crate. I felt dizzy, so I closed my eyes, and when I opened them, Sam was there. "Hey, Apollo," she said gently. "Was your flight okay? Do you feel all right?"

I managed a tail wag, even though my head felt heavy and wadded up like an old dog bed.

"I think he's still pretty woozy," Sam's voice said. I closed my eyes and let my chin fall onto my paws. "I hate giving him that doggy Valium. Are you sure it's okay for him?"

"No, I'm not at all sure." Mason's voice was full of concern. I tried to wag my tail in a salute to his presence, but I'm not sure I managed it. "But I guess I worry

more about the plane experience than the Valium.
What can it be like for him, flying in the belly of the
plane? He must be scared out of his mind."

My crate started to move again, and I think I fell
asleep. When I woke up, my crate was in a vehicle
that was traveling quickly. Windshield wipers made
swooshing sounds. Outside, other cars passed us in
wet waves that reminded me of the hose Lucas used to
fill our water bowls at the ranch. I licked my paws for
a while and started feeling more like myself.

From the front seat, the sounds of Mason's and Sam's
voices floated back, wrapping me up in a cloud of
warmth. It was so soothing to hear them speaking in
low tones that blended with the sound of the engine.
Lucas and Kim used to talk like that when we went to
film ads. Those were good times. I hadn't felt this
happy since those days—not until now. And I realized
that part of my wanting to build love between Mason
and Sam came from a secret hope that if they loved
each other, they would love me, too. That the three
of us would become a team, the way Lucas, Kim, and
I had been. Except this time, if I was vigilant, there
would be no Dr. Danmore. There would just be to-
getherness. A dog's perfect dream.

Thinking about my old life made me wonder again
where Lucas had gone. It wasn't like him to disappear
for so many days. He might vanish for a day or two,
leaving someone else to feed and water us at the ranch,
but he'd never been gone for more than a week. And
now I was somewhere else, in a place where the air
smelled heavy and damp, like the inside of a cloud.
Could Lucas find me here if he came looking? Would
he bother to hunt for me?

Inside, deep inside my belly, I think I always knew

Lucas would vanish completely one day. Without leaving me, he could never escape the memory of Kim and that day with Dr. Danmore. I had been there that day, and when Lucas looked at me, he saw that moment. I know he did. It wasn't his fault, or my fault, or anyone's fault. It was just the way things were. Sometimes dogs with a hard past are afraid of men in baseball hats. That doesn't mean that hats are bad or that the men are. The fear is just there. There's no sense in denying it.

"How was your weekend with Apollo?" Sam's voice said from the front seat. I heard my name and lifted my ears.

"Great," Mason said. "We had an awesome time. Went for a run in Griffith Park. I don't think he was too anxious, staying in a new place."

"He's a consummate professional," Sam said. "With you there, he probably thought it was an audition or something." She laughed. "Seriously, he loves you. I'm sure he had a great time. I never said this before, but I always had a bad feeling about his weekends with Lucas. I think he hated going home on Fridays. There was something in the way his shoulders sagged—and he was always so happy on Monday mornings, like he was back in his favorite place again."

"I've been thinking a lot about him," Mason said. His voice was low and serious. "About his future. No matter what happens to the show, I don't want him to go back to Lucas."

"No," Sam agreed. "That would be a disaster. I don't think Lucas loves him at all."

"There's definitely something weird there. But Apollo is a big earner for him. He won't give him up easily."

"So what can we do? I was hoping you might have a bright idea."

Mason sighed. "My only idea is the obvious one. Offer Lucas money. I'm just afraid he might want more than I can afford."

"Oh." Sam's voice suddenly sounded small. "Right. Of course you're right. Things always come back to money, don't they?"

"Not always," Mason said, laughing.

"For me they do. Or at least it seems that way. I have student loan debt up to my eyeballs. I probably shouldn't tell you this, as my employer, but before I took this job I was actually a paralegal. I was an idiot and got myself fired. If you hadn't hired me, I'd have been totally screwed. Even with this job, well . . ." Sam let her words fall into the air, and I sensed a sadness in her. And regret. "I hate being in debt," she said.

"You were a paralegal? Did you have to wear a suit and everything?"

"Kind of." Their voices took on a happier note, and I knew they were skipping away from the serious topic that Sam had introduced. I sighed. So often, she seemed close to making an important confession, but all she did was prance around the edges of whatever had her so deeply afraid. Delicate as she was, I was going to have to give her a push. And I needed to do it soon.

"So," Mason said in a hesitating way, "did you see the *Telltale* this weekend?"

"No." Sam's voice sounded far away. "Is there another article about the show?"

Mason nodded. "There is, but the idiots are lagging behind this time. They ran a whole story about how we storyboard our episodes, but the joke's on them, isn't it?" He turned to her. "We don't anymore. And anyone who saw me on the talk shows last week knows it."

"Well that's good," she said, sounding pleased. "So this one isn't such a big deal?"

"Oh, it's still going to screw us. It'll still eat the ratings, just you watch. Everyone should know better than to believe their stupid crap, but they'll still swallow it. Most people are sheep." Mason gripped the steering wheel tightly, then exhaled. "But I'm trying to focus on the things I can change, not the things I can't. The *Telltale*'s going to do whatever asinine stuff it does, whether I stress out over it or not."

"Too true," she agreed.

"But there is something in the *Telltale* that I have to show you. Something else." Sam stiffened and looked over at him, her eyes large. Mason reached down beside his seat and pulled out a folded newspaper. "Page six," he said, handing it over.

She unfolded it and gave a little gasp. "That's us?"

Mason nodded. "It's hard to tell—crappy photo, of course. But they ID'd me. You're the 'mystery woman.'"

Sam gave a shaky laugh. "Wow, I've always wanted to be the mystery woman."

"Yeah. I bet." They were both quiet for a minute while Sam looked at the newspaper. She seemed strangely relieved. "Look, I'm really sorry about this," Mason said. "I know this is nothing you ever wanted. They're like buzzards, they just swoop in and click—they don't really care who gets hurt. It's all about making a buck for them."

Sam took a deep breath. "I know this is part of what you have to live with. And I can see now why you're always wearing the hat and sunglasses."

Mason reached up and poked the bill of his hat. "They work better than you'd think. That's part of why I'm so excited to be working in Madrona. We'll be free of the media hounds there—no hat, no sunglasses once we cross the water. But seriously, I know you're not into mugging for the camera and all that—it's part of what I like about you. Fame isn't the number-one thing on your values list. And I am sorry that it happened."

"It wasn't your fault," she said. "Hollywood culture strikes again. And as you say, it'll be nice to be here. Nice for you to be unfamous for a while."

Mason grinned as he changed lanes. "On Friday you said there was something you wanted to talk to me about. We never got a chance—I'm sorry about that. Is it something we can discuss now?"

I saw a movement between the two front seats, right in front of the door to my crate. Mason had reached out his right hand and wrapped it around Sam's. Both of their hands rested on her knee. I panted into the damp air, waiting to see what would happen. Would she shake him off? My breath flowed in and out, in and out. Time was passing. She was letting his hand stay. My heart felt so full, it ached.

"No," she said. Her voice sounded strange—daring and scared at the same time. "That's okay. It's not important. "

Samantha

It was raining when we landed in Seattle. Mason said the weather was the reason we'd planned so many filming days for the location shoot—he needed extra time in case a big storm washed in from the coast. We could do some of the filming indoors, of course, but he wanted some outdoor shots if we could get them. The beach would be perfect. And the ferry was a great romantic setting, he said, especially on a clear day.

He'd surprised me by renting a van at the airport and insisting that he drive Apollo and me to his parents' house, to get our star settled in his new quarters. On the plane, he'd sat with the story producer, the red-haired director, and Imogen Blakely, presumably so they could sketch out the filming plan. But once we were off the plane, he'd appeared at my side and hadn't left it. I felt honored by his attention. And nervous about what this trip would hold.

Mason drove the van onto the ferry, a massive green and white metallic whale sitting in an even more massive gray plate of water. "Let's go up," he said after he'd parked. "As a tourist, you really have to see the view from the upper decks. It's pretty much mandatory. Apollo will be all right here in the van."

On deck, we found that the rain had slowed to what Mason called "a drizzle," something we rarely got in Southern California. A light mist dampened my face as I stepped onto the main deck and breathed in the clean air. Seattle, with its old brick buildings and towering skyscrapers, huddled against the shore that we were about to leave.

I stood at the rail, watching white-headed gulls swoop alongside the ferry. Below us, cars were loading, causing the deck to shake under my feet, which is why I didn't notice Mason moving behind me until his arms were around my middle. This was the closest our two bodies had ever been, and it left me unable to speak. So I simply stood and listened while he talked to me about his native land.

"You can't see it now, but Mount Rainier is down there." His face was beside mine, and I could see him jutting his chin to the south. "It's a big whopper—more than fourteen thousand feet tall, rising from pretty much sea level." I looked, but all I could see was a curtain of whitish-gray, as if the sky had sagged right there and needed propping up.

"There's a mountain? Where?" I joked. I closed my eyes, trying to memorize the feeling of his arms and the soft warmth of his breath on my cheek. Every second with him was precious, something I'd never experience again—not once he learned the truth. Time with him was like clutching at smoke.

The ferry's horn blasted behind us, and we both jumped and laughed. "Sometimes you can see orca whales here in Puget Sound," he said. He started pointing out islands, dark green lumps of land rising out of the gray water. When we'd flown in, I'd been surprised by the watery look of this place and the amazing amount of coastline curving into coves and inlets or wiggling around oval islands. I'd thought of the Northwest as soggy with rain—I hadn't thought of its feet as being wet, too.

The ferry landed in Madrona, a tight-packed little town on a hillside that slanted above the harbor. Mason ceremoniously doffed his hat and sunglasses, shoving them under his seat before he drove us off the ferry, the ramp clanking under our wheels. As we went, he pointed things out like a tour guide, obviously energized to be back among the cedars and firs. He rolled down the windows in the back so Apollo could get a good sniff of the place.

We left town behind and drove into the woods, then turned down a gravel road. Dark green boughs swept the ground, and as we passed they shed silvery drops from the recent rain. From time to time, we'd pass a rhododendron that was taller than I was, covered in light pink flower bouquets. At last we pulled into a clearing with a large rolling lawn, a fenced garden, towering white rhodies, and a Craftsman-style house with green shutters. Two gray-haired people appeared on the porch as we parked.

"Jack and Gloria," Mason said, introducing his parents. His mom stopped petting Apollo long enough to shake my hand and give me a grin that was oddly like Mason's. Jack wore a T-shirt that said Happy Pigs Eat Truffles, which made me think of my mushroom-growing mom. She would probably like these people, I thought. They were gardeners and dog people. And they were nice to strangers. They took Apollo and me inside and made us feel as if we had the run of the house.

While Gloria and Jack showed Apollo the backyard and the dog beds they'd scattered around, Mason took me on a quick tour. "Living room, dining room, kitchen," he said, waving to the basic living spaces. I noted the pictures over the mantel, showing a younger Mason with what must have been his brother, Zach, and I remembered the family's secret sorrow. *Thank God I never wrote about that. I'd never be able to face these people if I had.*

Upstairs we saw Mason's childhood room, which had since become Jack's office. "He's president of the county Audubon Society this year, so he has lots going on," Mason told me. "I'll sleep in here," he said, motioning to a hideaway bed. "You and Apollo will have the guest room."

Mason insisted on carrying my bag up to the little

gabled room at the top of the stairs. Its sloped ceiling peaked above a sleigh bed covered with a thick down comforter. Twin windows looked out over the garden.

"That's a mighty big tree," I said, pointing to the shaft of smooth orange bark that curved gracefully toward the sky. It seemed like a lame thing to say in a land filled with mammoth trees, but Mason nodded.

"It's a madrona. That's the kind of tree the town is named after. Pretty, aren't they? They really like it by the water, but this one's done just fine where it is, even up here in the woods. When I was a kid, I liked to use pieces of its bark as parchment paper. I even had a tree house in one." He fingered the scar on his forehead. "One of the steps in my ladder broke once and I got this cool scar."

I thought of Mason as a little boy, running around this yard, darting between raindrops, and a strange nostalgia came over me. He seemed so different here in his natural element—when I saw him in this room, I couldn't even picture him being on TV or working with network execs. Here he just seemed like himself, without any Hollywood glamour attached. In this place he was a son and a brother. A man. This place had nothing to do with ratings. This was real life.

*T*hat night, I lay in the sleigh bed feeling worse than wretched. *The closer you get to Mason, the worse this is going to be,* I told myself sternly. *You need to tell him the truth. Rip off the Band-Aid. Let the blow-up happen and slink away into the night. And don't use your worries about Apollo's future as an excuse to keep quiet. You know Mason will take care of him. He won't send him back to Lucas—you know he won't.*

Get up. Just get up and tell him.

I tossed and turned. Rain went *tippa-tip-pat* on the roof and tumbled down the windowpanes. I felt physically snug—warm and well fed by Gloria's vegetarian lasagna. But my conscience was a miserable mess. At the foot of my bed, Apollo gave a groan and stretched his legs. I got out of bed and went to crouch beside him.

"What do you think I should do?" I asked. I rubbed his silky belly until he sighed with contentment.

Go tell him. Tell him the truth.

"Is that really what you think or is that just my conscience speaking?"

Apollo blinked and looked me squarely in the eye. My hand froze as the thought came, louder, into my brain. *Go see Mason. Talk to him.*

"Wow, okay. That was intense." I licked my lips, shuddering at the idea of actually doing it. "It'll be cold out there. And he might be asleep. I should be asleep, and so should you—we'll have a lot to do tomorrow."

Apollo stood up and walked to the door.

"Okay, okay. I get the message. Just let me grab a sweater."

A minute later, Apollo and I stood outside Mason's door. I wore my paisley pajama bottoms, a cotton sweater, and the wool socks my mom had convinced me to pack. "Nice fashion statement," I whispered to Apollo. "Valerie would be proud."

Apollo, I swear, sighed faintly out his nose and lifted his toward the door. "All right, all right. I'll do it." I took a deep breath, raised my fist, and knocked.

Mason, in a T-shirt and boxers, was quick to answer the door. I saw his laptop, phone, and piles of notes spread out on the bed—he'd clearly been up working.

"Oh, sorry," I said. "If you have work to do—"

"No, no—come in." He held the door wide and motioned us both in, sweeping the papers into a pile. I settled uncomfortably on the end of the bed, very conscious of my pajama bottoms. Mason sat down in his boxers, and then I was more conscious of those. "Do you need anything? Towels? More blankets?"

"We're fine," I said, grateful that Apollo chose that moment to sit at my feet. I buried my fingers into his fur, trying to ignore the icy feeling that was running from my heart to my belly. "I just wanted to talk to you. About that important thing I mentioned before."

Mason leaned forward, resting his elbows on his knees. I could see the hard muscles in his legs and the reddish-brown hairs covering his skin. Heat seemed to come off his torso, through the thin fabric of his shirt. "Yes, okay. Let's talk. Is it about Richard?"

"Richard? What—no. No, why would you think it was about Richard?"

He glanced up at me. "When I called that day, you thought I was Richard. I figured . . . well . . ."

"What? What were you thinking?"

"That you had something going with this Richard guy and were trying to figure out how to let me down easy."

"Let you down easy . . ."

He looked down at his hands. "You know, tell me that you weren't interested. I've probably come on a little too strong—I figured you wanted me to back off."

Well, that was unexpected. As I tried to get over my apoplexy, I stared at Mason's hands. They were such gentle-looking hands—large, strong, agile. Handsome hands on a beautiful man. A beautiful, surprising man. A man my heart kept leaping toward.

I should have turned to face him and told him about the *Telltale*. Or I should have gotten up and left, or at least changed seats to the desk chair behind the bed. But I didn't. Instead, I leaned toward him, tilted my face toward his, and kissed him.

Mason met my kiss, his lips warm and parted. His hands—those same handsome hands I'd just been staring at—slipped around my back, leaving a trail of tingles on my skin. I leaned toward him, drawn by the sudden heat in my core.

I gasped as his lips moved to that secret spot between my ear and my jaw. I arched closer, sliding my fingers along his back. Kisses lit up the nerves all down my neck, making my skin burn.

Then, suddenly, he pulled back.

"I'm sorry," he said gruffly. "I just have to know. Are you in love with Richard?"

Rain lashed the window. I looked into his clear blue eyes, startled to realize what he was really asking me. He wanted to know if I was toying with him. Was I kissing him now, but planning to run back to someone else when the whim struck? He was trying to protect himself.

"No," I said, meeting his gaze. "But I was. For a long time. Richard and I were engaged, and we almost got married. But he broke it off. He, uh—he never showed up to the church."

"You're kidding."

"Nope, not kidding. It was all set, I was in the dress,

the works. He called my sister on his cell to say he wasn't coming."

Mason looked appropriately stunned. "Wow. What an asshole."

I nodded. Asshole indeed. "I was really angry for a long time. I could hardly see straight. He said he wasn't ready to get married, but I was pretty sure he just wasn't ready to marry me. And then he called a few weeks ago to say that he was getting married to someone else. That hurt, it really hurt. After that I tried to convince myself that I didn't care about love. I figured I would never find it and I told myself I didn't care."

"But what do you feel now?"

What a question. The room—the world—felt very silent as I pondered the answer.

"I would like to find love," I said quietly. "But I'm afraid."

Mason's posture relaxed. "Sure. Of course you are." He grinned. "I am, too."

I laughed. "Then why are you smiling?"

"Because we're in the same boat. Because it sounds like Richard has no shot with you at this point. And because Apollo wants us to get together, and he always gets what he wants."

"He does from us," I agreed. We both bent down and rubbed Apollo behind the ears.

"Wait, though," Mason said, "if you didn't want to talk about Richard, then what was it?"

My heart gave an uncomfortable squeeze. I'd come here to tell him the truth, but now that I was facing him, I couldn't do it. I wanted the joy of this moment—I wanted to take the risk Valerie talked about, to jump off the high dive with both feet. Despite all my noisy denials, I wanted this desperately. And I dreaded the way Mason's face would crumple when I told him the truth. I couldn't bear the way he would see me after he learned what I'd done.

"I can't," I said, surprised to hear a catch and a sob come out of me. I put my hand to my mouth and pressed hard, shaking my head. "I can't. I'm sorry. I'm so sorry."

I sprang up off his bed and ran out the door, down the hall, and back to the solitary safety of my own room.

—23—

🦴 *Apollo*

I tried to sleep, but rain and worry about Sam kept waking me up. Plus it was strange sleeping outside my crate. I could hear Sam's breathing from where she lay up on the bed, and I liked listening to her quiet exhales. It's hard to sleep when you want to keep listening to such a wonderful sound.

In the morning, Jack and Gloria spent fifteen full minutes petting me, then they took me outside. The rain was gone and sun glinted off the wet grass and branches. I romped all around, into the woods, across the grass, out to the mailbox with Gloria to get the newspaper. Jack took me down a trail to a steep ravine lined with ferns. It smelled incredible—rich and ancient, sprinkled with delectable animal smells. I nosed around in the pine needles for a long time, until Jack waved me back to the house.

I watched Sam carefully that morning. We'd had a breakthrough the night before in Mason's room, I felt sure of it, but at the end she'd gotten scared and run away with her tail between her legs. Now she seemed more fragile than ever. She wouldn't look at Mason, not even when he made her a cup of that tea she drinks. She said some appreciative-sounding words, but that was all. No look, no smile.

It wasn't long before the three of us jumped into the van and went to work. I rode with my head out the window, watching for dogs. I saw five—*five!*—before we parked the van and went to a big square lined with cobblestones. The crew was there, and it was exciting to see them again. Sam had me sit next to a copper dog statue while Mason stood beside me.

"This is Spitz, our town hero," Mason said while the cameras made their whirring noises. "Madrona is a town that loves dogs, and this dog was our most famous canine citizen. He saved two children from drowning right here in the harbor. Today his statue is the town meeting place."

Sam walked me around the square a few times, then we went back to meet this week's guests. Even before we got to them, I recognized their scents—I couldn't stop wagging. It was Honey and Chad! I was so excited to see them I almost jumped up on them. A second chance to bring them together—I felt like the luckiest dog in the world.

Of course, once I settled down to work, I saw what a challenge this would be. Honey and Chad didn't speak to each other; they just looked at Imogen and Mason and waited for instructions. Honey kept her arms crossed around her middle. Chad stood with his legs apart, trying to look as large as possible. I thought I'd made some progress with them the last time they were on the show, but it looked like all my good work had worn away.

We all stood around for a while, then went to a beach

where I really got to work. I hadn't had much time to study Honey and Chad, but at least I had some sense of their personalities. Chad had a lot of top-dog energy, I decided. When I'd growled at Honey before, he'd jumped to protect her. That was the alpha's job, to guard what he thought was his. And Honey, from the way she held herself—bending toward Chad, but with her arms and elbows crossed between them—wanted his alpha attention. She admired him. But she wouldn't put up with his being distracted. He had to focus on Honey or lose her to another top dog.

The beach was covered in golden sand, just like the beach I was used to, but when I trotted up to the water I was startled to find it icy cold. I shivered and raced along the wet sand until I got warm, dashing past volleyball players and little kids with shovels and plastic pails. I couldn't take these two swimming like I did with Faye and Sebastian. I'd have to figure out something else.

The crew took up a lot of space on the beach, and soon other people gathered around to watch, and the more people came, the more excited Honey was. She started to make little twitchy movements, like an Australian shepherd who's waiting to have his ball thrown. I ran up to her, barking.

"What is it, Apollo?" she asked, speaking quickly. Her face was flushed, her arms swinging. I barked again and raced down the beach. Chad hung behind, looking sullen, but Honey scampered after me. I led her past the kids with their buckets of sand, down to the volleyball players. There was a group of young men on the far side of the net—I aimed straight for them.

"Hey!" they said, "check out that dog."

"Whoa, are those cameras? Are we on TV?"

I stopped in the middle of the collection of men. Honey caught up with me, breathing hard. Almost in one motion, the men stood up, all their attention on Honey.

"I hope he didn't ruin your game," she said, smiling at them. She reached down to pet me while they stared at her swimsuit. I wagged in the sand and let out another bark, trying to keep the energy up. Not that I needed to. The men were so fixed on Honey that they started trying to edge each other out by angling closer and closer to her.

Heavy feet ran up from behind us.

"Hey, Honey." Chad pushed into the middle of the group and slid his hand under Honey's elbow.

The men in the circle glared at Chad. Honey beamed at them, then turned her golden smile to Chad. "Hey," she said, her voice warm and low. "These nice guys were just about to teach me to play volleyball. Weren't you, guys?"

The men nodded. Chad stepped in closer to Honey and put his hand on the small of her back. "The camera beckons, sweetheart," he said. "You're too big a star to waste your time with volleyball." He reached down and caught her hand. As Honey followed behind him, she looked down and winked at me. "And," Chad muttered as they walked away, "you're way too pretty for those idiots."

After that, Chad gave Honey his total attention all afternoon. The crew followed them everywhere—on the big metal boat to the city, through a fish and flower market, to a restaurant at the top of a building. Honey sparkled and glowed, and my latest project seemed completely fixed.

That night, Jack and Gloria made dinner for Mason

and Sam, then we all took a walk in a park filled with wild rabbits. When we got home, Sam went straight to her room where she called someone named Vern on the phone.

"I have a big favor to ask," she said. "I need out of my contract. I can't go through with it, not now. The show is too good, it's too honest—I don't feel like I'm telling the truth anymore." She was quiet for a minute, then she jumped up and walked to the window. "I gave you two articles—let me just pay you back a third of the advance." With a quick turn, she walked to the door, then back to the middle of the room. "Please, Vern? Please."

She sank onto the bed, her forehead on the palm of her hand. Her voice was sagging. "Yes, of course I know that I signed the contract. And that what I'm suggesting is a breach of contract. And yes, I know that backing out will mean you never pass my name on to *Enchanté*. I get it, I get all that. I just want to be done. Let me pay back what I owe and walk away."

Sam's mouth flattened into a thin line as she listened to sounds coming through her phone. "Okay. All right. I'll think about it overnight. But I won't change my mind. I'm not writing any more exposés for you, breach or no breach."

With a sigh, she clicked her phone and sat down, her knees jouncing up and down. "I am in such a tight corner," she said to me. She rubbed her forehead with her thumb and two fingers. "I'm broke, in debt, and completely screwed. Any second, this whole thing is going to blow up in my face. Do you know how close I was to telling Mason everything last night?" She shook her head. "Shit. I should have. I know I should have."

Sam got down on the floor and wrapped both arms around my middle. She buried her face in my fur. "I'm so screwed. So very screwed. Apollo, what am I going to do?"

Samantha

I'm a horrible, horrible person. I mean really, what decent human being could live under Jack and Gloria's roof, enjoying their evening meals and morning steel-cut oats and even consider being a "source" about Mason Hall's home life? But that Vern, he knew all my weak spots. I could be an *anonymous* source, he said. I could share only good, happy, glowing things—he promised this time. And the *Telltale* would launch my writing career.

Still, it wasn't worth it. That's what I told myself, lying in that sleigh bed, listening to the birds practice their morning operetta outside. Even if everything I said was positive, Mason would know I had been the source. No one else possibly could be. And Mason didn't like publicity—he'd told me as much himself.

Even though I hadn't taken Vern's offer, I could hardly look Mason in the eye that morning. And, frankly, he made it worse by being so kind. I didn't deserve to have a hot mug of Earl Grey waiting for me when I came downstairs in the morning or to have someone carry my bag of leashes and brushes out to the van as we headed out. I deserved to be kicked in the shins, not consulted about radio station choices.

I tried to avoid all contact with my handsome friend, but Mason had a funny way of making me forget my best intentions. Before I knew it, I was laughing at his stories about elementary school bullies and the disastrous speech he gave in high school debate. It was a gorgeous day. The sky was cerulean and cloudless, and sunny daffodils nodded their heads along the side of the road. For someone who was used to the arid openness of Southern California, the thick greenery snuggled close like a blanket. Evergreens towered over vine maples that shaded heaping mounds of underbrush. Greens piled on top of each other—the lime green of new leaves, the deep, dusky shade of the pines.

"How do you survive in L.A.?" I asked Mason. "It's so different from here."

He gave me a shrug and a smile—a motion I was coming to understand meant that he was getting by, muddling through. "It's where the work is. No one makes reality shows in Seattle. Unless one comes on location—and then we play Russian roulette with the weather. Not that TV is the end all and be all."

"Don't you want to stay in television?" I was surprised. Most people with a showbiz career clung to it with an ironlike grip.

"Not necessarily. I like hosting things, making everything run smoothly. But the paparazzi are a real drag. And I don't like having to bow to what the network wants all the time. There has to be more to life than the ratings share, right?"

"So what would you do? In an ideal world?"

"I don't know." He flashed a grin in my direction. "Move up here and make some goofy kids show with lots of dogs in it? I have a few ideas knocking around. And it is nice to be back home."

"Well, today is certainly beautiful."

Mason looked up at the Olympic Mountains, which today were sharply drawn with clean white caps. "Yeah.

It rains a lot here. But when it's clear like today, there's no prettier place on earth." He drove in silence for a minute. "What do you think of it here?" There was a cautious note to his voice, as if he was a little afraid to hear my answer. It frightened me, hearing him put such weight on the question. And at the same time, it gave me the kind of secret delight that I wanted to capture and keep in my pocket, like a charm for happiness.

I tried to make my voice light as I answered. "It's great. So nice to breathe clean air for a change."

Despicable people don't deserve to have anyone care what they think of a place. Despicable people deserve to fly back home, all alone and unloved.

*T*hat day we filmed in three locations—at the Glimmerglass Café, in the Space Needle's rotating restaurant, and on a trail that ran through Madrona's forests to the beach. The café was charming, filled with posters for Woofinstock, the town's big annual dog festival. They actually let Apollo into the restaurant, where he spent a blissful half hour sniffing noses with a white German shepherd named Zoë. She even posed for a few promo shots with Apollo.

As the day wore on, the crew became more and more on edge. At the end of the previous day, Honey had seemed ready to leap into Chad's arms, and a field crew had spent all night with them at their hotel, just in case they had a midnight hookup. Instead, Imogen reported to Mason in a whisper, they had a big fight over dinner. Honey had spoken with her agent and learned that she'd been chosen to do voice work for a commercial. She was bubbling, slightly delirious, and the more she talked about it, the more sullen Chad had become.

"What's the matter?" she finally asked. "I thought you'd be happy for me."

"I am," he said in a grouchy voice. After ten minutes of Honey's prodding, he finally confessed what was really bothering him. "You have it all together. I don't think you really need me."

Honey had protested, but Chad didn't believe her. "You could have any guy you want," he said. "What do you need me for?"

After relating all this, Imogen shook her head. "These two—what a mess. First Honey is all weepy, thinking Chad doesn't appreciate her the way he should. Then, after Apollo fixes that by making him jealous of the volleyball guys, Chad has *his* nose out of joint. To tell you the truth, I don't think either of them are worthy of Apollo."

It was late afternoon by the time we started filming the trail segment. First the crews got their setup shots of Chad and Honey hiking with Apollo in the lead. They had them take two water breaks and filmed what amounted to cold silence between the two guests. Apollo was strangely subdued, considering our exciting surroundings. I expected him to run down the trail, tail wagging, but instead he hung close to Chad and Honey, staring at them keenly. He looked as if he was communicating with them, shooting them thoughts with his eyes.

The trail led through waist-high ferns and spindly salmonberries, down a long hill to a secluded beach. When it reached an end, there was a four-foot-high drop-off between the trail and the beach below where storms had washed the bank away. A barnacle-covered rock stood a few feet off, and Chad nimbly jumped from the bank to the rock, then scrambled down to the rocky beach. Apollo, being a dog, jumped straight down. Honey quailed at the top of the drop-off, then finally sat on her butt and shimmied her way down the dirt until her feet landed on the beach. One of our crews was in a boat offshore and another stood off to the side on the beach, catching shots of Apollo wading and Honey pointing out the way the sunset cast a pink glow on the Olympics.

They stayed as the evening turned dusty blue, then Imogen told Honey and Chad that it was time to head back. She sounded weary, probably thinking about all the work they'd have to do, trying to edit this severed relationship into a story with a happy ending. Chad clambered up his rock and jumped across to the trail while Apollo clawed his way up the dirt bank. Honey stood on the beach, looking at the bank, trying to see a way up.

She tried kicking a foothold with her boots in the dirt face, but the pocket crumbled and she slid back down, scraping her knee. Her second try was worse—she lost her balance as she slid back to the beach and stumbled against Chad's rock, cutting her elbow on the barnacles. Tears sparkled in her eyes as she looked up the trail to where Chad and Apollo had vanished.

The camera crew couldn't help her. The director couldn't help her. This was the kind of difficulty that reality TV was made of.

"Chad! *Chad!*"

Honey brushed tears out of her eyes.

"Chad!"

Her voice disappeared into the woods. Minutes ticked by. The sun was gone and darkness was falling. Chad had the only flashlight.

"Chad, come back." Honey's voice was a warbly whisper. "I need you."

Just then, a bark sounded deep in the woods. Chad's footsteps echoed on the trail as he raced down to Honey, Apollo at his heels.

"What happened?" he asked as he stopped at the edge of the bank, breathless. Apollo sniffed Honey's face.

"You left me," she said, sounding forlorn. Behind her, the cameraman shifted his footing, careful to pick up every emotion that flitted across her face. "I was trapped down here. I called and called. You were too far away."

"I'm sorry, baby," Chad said softly. He crouched down, his face full of concern. "I guess I forget that you need my help sometimes."

"I need you all the time," she said. "Even if I'm doing okay, I still need you."

Apollo nudged Chad's hand. He reached out and rested his palm on her cheek and they stood still for a long moment, while the sky shifted from lavender to violet behind them. Then Chad straightened, reached down for Honey's hand, and pulled her to the top of the bank. While Apollo sat at their feet, the two shared a long kiss. Then another. And another. When they finally turned away, up the trail, Apollo stayed where he was for a moment, panting at the camera. Then he, too, turned and padded up the trail.

The camera crews burst into spontaneous applause.

* * *

🦴 Apollo

I've had dreams like this. One I remember in particular—there was a huge, meaty bone lying on the grass at the end of a long field. I was running, my paws beating against the ground, but no matter how fast I ran, I couldn't get any closer to that big bone. As I ran, hands kept throwing smaller bones in my way. I could have stopped for any of the little bones, anytime, but I wanted the big one, the one at the end. The one I couldn't get to.

I'd had success after success with my practice people. Pilar and A.J., Faye and Sebastian, Honey and Chad—they were all happy and in love. I didn't doubt their happiness—I could feel it the way I felt the wind whisking over my nose. Their love was adding to the world balance, and everything looked a little brighter because of it.

But those successes were the little bones. They were nice, if that was what you were after. But I wanted the big bone at the end of the field. I wanted love between Mason and Sam.

How to get it? I'd tried everything. I'd sent Sam a million messages, thoughts that she seemed to be ignoring on purpose. I'd encouraged Mason at every turn, and he was responding beautifully. But it wasn't enough. Sam was one of the toughest cases I'd ever encountered. And I only had one thing left to try.

It started to rain as we drove home in the dark. In the front seat, Mason's voice was full of excitement.

"It totally worked! Can you believe it? You were so right, Sam. I should never have doubted you. Apollo is the real deal—he *made* the show this week. Made it.

You were absolutely right. He *is* a love dog. Who would have guessed? Who knew there was even such a thing?" He chuckled.

Beside him, Sam was quiet. *Sad,* I thought. *She's sad. She must want the big bone, too, and there's some reason she can't have it. Or some reason she thinks she can't have it.*

Jack and Gloria weren't home when we got there. Mason started moving around in the kitchen while Sam took me out into the backyard. It was raining hard, so she wore a raincoat with my leash slung around her neck. She didn't hook it onto me—this wet land was full of freedom.

I sniffed the perimeter of the yard, watching Sam out of the corner of my eye. I only had one trick left to try, and its success depended on Sam's following me when I made my move. Wagging my tail so Sam could see me, I slipped down the trail Jack had shown me the other day. Drops of water flew off the ferns and salal, soaking into my coat. It was hard to see in the dark, so I followed the dirt smell of the trail and trod carefully. The path angled downhill, switching back and forth when the going got steep.

"Apollo!" Sam's voice sounded far behind me, so I slowed down and took a moment to sniff at a place where a cedar log had rotted away. Rain beat against my head. The dirt under my paws was slick. "Apollo! Come!"

It hurt me physically, like a little pinch, to ignore a command, but I did it. Images of Lucas flashed in my mind as I sat there in the dark woods. Lucas's sadness was so much like Sam's. My muzzle itched with a need to grab that sadness and shake it until it snapped in two. I wanted it gone, destroyed, ripped apart like a stuffed toy. I shook myself, sending water around me in a spray, and kept working my way down the path.

"Apollo—where are you?"

Sam sounded closer. She would just be hitting the steep section of the trail, where it wound down toward the ravine. I was tempted to go back to her, to give up and take us both back to the house—to warmth and dryness and Mason—but I didn't. This was my last try. I had to give it a chance.

"Apollo!" It was hard to hear her through the rain. The wind blew a gust that made the trees moan. "Ap— Ohhh!"

I heard a thud and the sound of branches breaking. Something was sliding down into the ravine. I let out a bark and raced back toward Sam, crashing through sharp sticks and brambles. I couldn't smell, couldn't hear. Leaves flipped into my eyes, blinding me. My paw landed on a fallen branch and skidded. I scrambled, but my back paws hit something slick and slid out from under me. I was falling, faster and faster through the dark.

Samantha

When my feet started to slide, I fell backward, banging my tailbone against something hard. Branches smacked my face as I careened down the hillside. I couldn't see anything—just felt pain and terror as I bumped my way downward. I tried grabbing at branches, but nothing held—everything ripped out in my hand. My breath shot out of me as I careened downhill, out of control.

Then I was sliding through space. My insides shot upward and flipped over. I hit bottom, landing in water, iciness soaking through my jeans and my shoes and socks. Everything was black—I could just barely make out my hands, still gripping plants that I'd pulled out in my fall. My knee ached like it had hit a rock. Sobs shook my chest.

"Help," I said feebly. "Please help." I tried to stand up and slipped again. Tears were flowing down my face. My knee really stung. Where was Apollo? "Apollo! *Apollo!*"

I heard a whine somewhere above me. "I'm coming, Apollo," I called, standing up with more determination. My foot slipped off a rock, and I banged my ankle. "Shit, shit, ow!" I started crying again. Or was it just rain washing down my face?

Then a beam of light cut through the blackness overhead. "Sam? Sam, are you out here?"

"Mason—Mason!"

The beam swung in my direction. "Sam, are you okay?"

"I think so." I waved, then pointed up the hill. I had to shout to be heard over the pounding rain. "Apollo's up there somewhere—I can't see him."

Branches snapped as the light bobbed down the hillside. I heard Mason speaking softly, then he called out to me. "Apollo's fine, he's here. I'm coming down for you."

As I watched him make his way down the muddy slope, I felt overcome with emotions—relief at being rescued, gratitude toward Mason, and overwhelming guilt. He was too good a guy to be deceived by me for one more second. I had to tell him the truth. Here, to-night. And that's when it dawned on me. In keeping my secret from Mason, I was doing just what Richard had done. I was holding back the truth because I didn't want to rock the boat, because I was enjoying the status quo and hated for anything to change. Richard had liked dating and he'd liked being engaged. So even though he hadn't been wildly in love with me, he'd dragged his feet, not speaking up until the last possible second.

How was I any different? I wasn't. I was enjoying my time with Mason. Frankly, I was loving it. It was the most precious thing in the world to me. But by keeping my secret, I was being just as cruel to him as my altar-panicked fiancé had been to me.

Mason reappeared on the hillside above me. In the glow of his flashlight, I could see the steep slope I'd fallen down and the icy puddles that had soaked my feet. He skidded and slipped down toward me, then stretched out a hand which I took, thankful for the strength with which he pulled me up the hill. Rain beat into both of our faces, and when a limb crashed to the forest floor somewhere behind us, I jumped. Mason squeezed my hand, still towing me uphill. When we got to the top, Apollo was waiting, his tail beating sideways like a windshield wiper. Mason pulled me close against his raincoat.

"Are you sure you're okay? No broken bones?"

"No, I'm okay. Just scared. And Mason, I—" I broke off and buried my face in the warm patch of skin above his raincoat zipper. I wrapped my arms around his waist and hung on tightly, giving myself one moment—just a moment—to be totally wrapped up in him. I'd never felt so safe. Then I pulled myself away.

"Mason, I have to tell you something." In the dark, I couldn't see his face, and that helped me carry on. "I'm the mole. I'm the spy. I wrote the articles for the

Telltale, the ones about the show. It was me, all me. I'm so sorry."

I stood there for a second, hoping for a miracle. Maybe he already knew. Maybe he'd laugh and say, "Oh, Sam, that's no big deal. I knew it was you, and I don't even care—"

"What? What do you mean? *You* wrote those articles?"

No, he hadn't known. And yes, this was going to be just as awful as I'd feared.

"I—oh, God—I needed the money, and I—I'm so sorry, Mason."

"But—" Confusion swam in Mason's eyes. "Those articles almost killed the show. They almost ruined everything." He held his hands up in an empty gesture, his eyes full of disbelief. "Everything!"

"I know." I was sobbing, my tears blending in with the rain. "I know they did. I never meant for it to happen. I tried to fix it—I tried again and again—but it was too late. I couldn't take it back." I looked at him, hoping for a hint of warmth or forgiveness, but what I saw on his face made me take a step back. "I'll leave," I stammered. "I'll just go." I turned and started toward the house, my shoes squelching water.

"Damn right, you'll go," he shouted at my back. I picked up my pace, jogging away from him. Apollo barked at my retreating back. "How could you do that? How could you sell us out, Sam? You know what, you're fired! Did you hear me? Fired!"

I wished the rain would drown out his voice so I wouldn't have to hear anymore. But I could still hear well enough to catch his last words.

"Don't come back. Don't ever come back!"

—24—

💻 Samantha

I cried all the way back to Los Angeles. By the time I arrived at my apartment, I was a husk of a human, barely able to see well enough to get my key in the lock. I stumbled in, waved at Zephyr, and fell face-first onto the couch. There I stayed for two days until my family tracked me down.

First Mom called. Twice. Then Cassie called. Then, on Tuesday night, they both arrived at my door.

"C'mon, Sam, let us in," said my sister, peering through the mail slot. "I can see your socks sticking off the couch. We know you're there."

I hoisted my miserable self up to sitting and shuffled to the door.

"Wow, what happened in here?" Cassie whistled as she looked around my mess of an apartment. "And I thought my place looked bad."

Mom came to sit beside me on the couch. "Honey, are you okay? You didn't answer our calls, so Cassie and I thought we'd pay you a visit. Just in case something was wrong."

"Yeah," said Cassie, plunking down in the chair across from us. "Because the last time you went AWOL, you'd lost your job. And the time before that, it was Richard. A visit from us is your punishment for not answering your phone. So tell us—what's going on?"

What could I say? How could I sum up my *Love Dog* experience for people who hadn't lived it with me—and then get them to go away?

Of course, on the other hand, having them leave felt like a reward, which I didn't deserve. And confessing to them seemed like penance, which I did. I'd been thinking a lot about penance in the past few days.

"I did a horrible thing," I said, pushing my face into my hands. "A shockingly bad thing."

"Sweetheart, did you get fired again?"

Well, yes, I did. But that wasn't the worst part. I sighed. "Do you know the tabloid the *Telltale*?"

"No," said Mom.

"Sure," said Cassie.

"Well," I said, turning to Mom, "it's a gossip magazine that prints stuff about Hollywood and the stars. You know—who's divorcing whom and who looked bad at the Oscars. Plastic surgery nightmares. That sort of thing." Mom nodded. "About a month ago they hired me to write some articles for them."

"Oh, but Sam, that's wonderful!" Mom leaned forward and squeezed my knee.

Cassie was more clued in. "Wait, you were writing for a tabloid? That doesn't sound like you, Sam. I thought you wanted to write short stories."

"I do. But no one wants to buy my short stories. Heck, they won't even publish them for free. I was really broke and my student loan payments were due . . . and my editor at the *Telltale* promised this would be a step on the ladder to bigger things." I explained how Vern had seen the blog and asked for more of the same—but specifically about *The Love Dog*. "So I went on the show as a spy. I went to work there looking for dirt. I wanted to reveal the show for what I thought it was, a total sham." I ducked my head, avoiding Cassie's gaze. Knowing how she felt about the show, I figured she wasn't pleased.

Mom was the first to speak. "I can see how you wanted to prove your point, sweetheart, but it's not like the show was doing anyone any harm. It's just TV."

A part of me wanted to explain to her that it *was* doing harm, that by leading people to believe love was the kind of thing that could be fixed by the wave of a wand—or a furry tail—the show was doing them a real disservice. It was setting up a false hope, like promising kids that the homework fairy was going to swoop in and take care of their algebra. It was fantasy. It wasn't real.

But the heat had gone out of the argument for me. When I thought of love, all I could see was Mason laughing in the van, Mason sitting on his bed in his boxers asking me about Richard. Mason's flashlight coming toward me in the dark. Having Mason Hall care for me was a fantasy. And it was also real. So who was I to say that no one else deserved to dream?

"It seemed like a good idea at the time," I said lamely. "But it was the worst decision I've ever made. Everyone on the show hates me now. They just hate me."

I started to cry, which is amazing, since I shouldn't have had an ounce of tear-making liquid left inside me. Mom moved in to give me a hug. While we sat there, with me weeping, Cassie got up to sort through the mail piled up under my mail slot. When I finally dried off, she sat back down in the chair across from us and held up an envelope with my bank's logo on it.

"It totally kills me that you tried to take down *The Love Dog*, Sam. You know how much I adore that show. But looking at this, I can see why you took *the Telltale* job. I just hope they paid you enough to make it worth it."

I snuffled against the back of my hand. "That's the worst part. I owe them money now. I was supposed to write them one more article, but I can't. Not now." I turned to Mom. "You understand, don't you? I've been so awful—I just can't hurt the show anymore. I know it's too late to fix anything by not writing more, but I can't do that last article. I just can't."

"Wow," said Cassie softly. "That really sucks." She looked down at the pile of mail in her lap. "Hey, is this really from Mason Hall? Himself?"

I was up off the couch in a flash. The envelope was large and brown with my address written on it in blocky male letters. My hand shook as I tore it open. I pulled out the pages, then covered my mouth to prevent my wail of despair from reaching the four corners of the earth.

In a fit of anger, probably hoping to get back at me—and twist the knife a little deeper—Mason had sent me the confidentiality agreement.

 Apollo

I failed.

I pushed Sam too hard, too far. It had seemed like such a good idea to run off in the rain that night. I thought I could make it all work like it had with Faye and Sebastian. Extreme moments build trust, I know they do, but something went wrong with Sam and Mason. Something exploded between them, and it doesn't look like it can ever be right again.

What really put me off my kibble was the fact that there, right there at the end as we stood in the rain, Sam changed. For that moment when she stood with Mason, the most wonderful smell shimmered off her—like oranges and maple syrup and cinnamon. It was the strongest love smell I'd ever experienced. It made me woozy—so woozy that I didn't notice she had gone until it was all over.

So now I know that she loved Mason. And she didn't just love him a little—she loved him with the deep, life-tie kind of love that dogs feel for their families. She loved him the way the stars love the moon, always clustering around it through the long night. Sam and Mason's love was the greatest I'd ever worked with. But it was broken. Broken like a good chewing stick.

Mason didn't sleep that night. After Sam left—after she caught the taxi in front of the house and drove away into the night—he spent hours sitting at the kitchen table, talking to himself. Sometimes he talked in my direction, but his tone was so nasty, I knew he wasn't speaking to me—he was just letting the words pour out. They were angry, angry words. Mason's anger wasn't metallic like Lucas's—it was thudding and sharp, like the rocks on the beach that will cut your paws. It made me whine inside, so I moved under the table and sat near his feet. I kept my mind blank and just breathed, in and out, letting it come in as anger and go out as whatever I could manage. Disappointment. Sadness. Air.

Somewhere in the morning I realized that I hadn't sent my love out that night, and that felt horrible because I knew Sam would need it more than ever. It took me a long, long time to send it because my heart was so ruffled. Mason's outbursts didn't help any.

I hoped the other people on my list would forgive me for sending most of my love to Mason and Sam. I spent a particularly long time on Mason. Poor, poor Mason. His heart was deflated. He kept saying the same words over and over again, the same thing he asked me as he put down my breakfast.

"Why would she do that, Apollo? Why would Sam hurt the show like that? I thought she loved us. I thought . . . Oh, buddy, aren't you going to eat your breakfast? Come on, Apollo—it's good stuff. See?" He shook my bowl. I turned away and returned to my seat under the kitchen table.

That's how it was. Mason and I flew back home, we slept at his house, and we went back to the studio. But he couldn't stop asking that same question. I fell into an exhausting routine—sending my love to him and Sam when I was awake, then drooping into a deep sleep that seemed to last for days. I was excited to return to the studio because I thought Sam would be there, but she wasn't. My room was empty, and for the first time I hated its carpet and coffee smell. It smelled abandoned. I spent my time in Mason's office instead, asleep underneath his desk.

There was one bright moment in our days at the studio. On Wednesday, the first garbage day, Mason and I went to a meeting of cologne-smelling people in the fancy conference room, the one with the leather chairs.

The people were full of praise and warm-sounding words for Mason, but he didn't care. He just looked at the floor, nodding along with what they said. He might have been thinking of sloppy Joes. Or bacon. But I knew he was thinking of Sam.

After the meeting was over, we sat at his desk for a long time, staring at the empty room. Then the phone rang and Mason spoke into it. His tone became very serious. When he hung up, he looked down at me. "Well, this is it, buddy," he said. "Make or break. Keep your paws crossed."

I panted, and he rubbed my ears while we waited for the visitor to arrive. Footsteps sounded in the hall. I caught a whiff of scent, jumped up, and ran to the door. It swung open, and Lucas walked in.

I knew instantly that he was healed. Not only was his metallic odor gone, but a warm new aura—like dog biscuits and hot cider—flowed off him. Love! Lucas had found love! I beat the floor with my tail until dust rose out of the carpet. Lucas looked at me and actually smiled. Then he winked, and turned to Mason.

"You know, two weeks ago I wouldn't have returned your call."

"What changed your mind?" Mason came around his desk and reached out to shake Lucas's hand.

"I started seeing someone. She works here on the show—Valerie Martz. You know her? Yeah, you can't miss her. Anyway, I guess she filmed a segment with Apollo last week. She was super excited about it— she'd never been on TV before. But what she couldn't stop talking about was Apollo. She said from the moment he walked into the makeup room, she could feel the love pouring off him. It's crazy, but she thinks he does have some secret love power."

Mason leaned back against the front of his desk. "I think she's right."

"Well, I'm not ready to go there," Lucas said, crossing his arms, "but I will give you one thing. He's a sensitive dog. He takes things hard—always has. I know it's been tough for him, living with me since my divorce. He really feels things, you know? And I haven't always been the easiest person to live with. He was there when all the shit went down with my ex-wife, and I guess I've had a hard time forgetting that. I know I wasn't a very good person to him—you don't have to say it. Anyway, when Valerie kept talking about his secret love powers, it got me thinking that living with me is no good for Apollo. I've kept him all this time out of spite, because I was pissed at my ex, you know? But now that Valerie and I are together, well, that's just not so important to me anymore."

Mason nodded, his mouth in a hard line. "It's easy to do stupid things when you're angry. I'm glad you've changed your mind."

An hour later, Mason and Lucas shook hands again, then Mason said, "I'll give you a minute to say good-bye," and left through the door. Lucas looked down at me for a long time, his arms still crossed. Then he squatted down, his eyes on the floor.

"I'm really sorry I was such an asshole," he said. "I just—anytime I saw you, I always saw Kim, you know? And it"—he shook his head and took in a quavering breath—"it just burned me out inside. I couldn't take it. So I'm sorry. I never meant to let you down. But I think this'll be better for you. Mason really likes you. It's not just about the show for him. He'll take good care of you. And he'll do it forever—he promised.

"And I'm doing one more thing, because I think you

would want me to. I'm letting Kim take all the rest of the animals to her place. She's the real trainer, the one who understands how dogs think. She's going to buy me out, and I'm selling the ranch. I think I need to work around people more, so I don't get too lonely. Lonely isn't a healthy place for me to be. You would know—you've had to deal with me at my worst. I'm sorry, Apollo. I really am. And I hope you have a wonderful life with Mason."

I listened attentively, letting Lucas's words float over me. I just felt so relieved. For years I'd been trying to help him release Kim from his mind. I knew he would never find happiness until he could walk away from the memory of that day with Dr. Danmore. But for all the times I tried to help him, for all the nights I sent my love out to him, I was part of the problem. Every time I wagged my tail or walked down the hall beside him, I brought Kim right along with us.

And now here he was, glowing with his toasted biscuit smell, all hints of whisky and cigarettes gone. I knew because I'd sniffed the back of his pant legs and shoes while he was talking to Mason. The apple cider odor went through and through, deep into his bones. It was the greatest thing I'd ever smelled. I might have failed with Mason and Sam, but at least I'd gotten out of Lucas's way at last. He hadn't needed me. But he'd found love, and that was all that mattered.

Samantha

I sat down at the computer and stared at the screen. Zephyr perched near me, threatening to walk across the keyboard if I took my fingers off it for even a second. I arched them over the middle row of letters, took a deep breath, and started typing.

An Open Letter to Apollo, the Love Dog
by Samantha Novak
Dear Apollo,

I was wrong. I was wrong, wrong, wrong—so wrong, I couldn't have been any more wrong. And I owe you an apology.

Nine months ago I had my heart broken, and in the deep despair that followed, I started to rant. I ranted on a blog, telling anyone who would listen that love was a fairy tale spun by the people who make Valentine's Day cards and candy. Love, for most of us, was an unattainable dream—one we'd be better off giving up on. I was bitter, I was hurt, and worst of all, I believed exactly what I was saying.

It was in this spirit that I wrote two articles about the reality television series The Love Dog. *I worked on the show, and what I saw going on there (standard reality TV fare like storyboarding and hiring unemployed actors as guests) looked to me like proof of my platform. Nothing could fix a broken relationship—certainly not a blond dog named Apollo.*

But since the Telltale *published those articles, I've had a change of heart. And I mean a serious change of heart. Because it turns out that there is a love dog. His name is Apollo, and he's the star of this very same reality TV series.*

How do I know he's a true love dog? Because once the show stopped doing all the things that made me call it a fake, everything became very, very real. And once it was real—once Apollo was behaving however he wanted while the cameras rolled—love bloomed on the set. It bloomed on-camera and off. Guests had their relationships repaired, new lovers learned to trust one another. Even members of the crew were affected.

Even I was affected.

Yes, jaded and bitter as I am, I was swayed. I had joined the show's staff in order to expose it as a fake, but I've come away as Apollo's staunchest believer. Because in spite of all the walls I put up around myself, I fell in love. I fell truly, madly, hopelessly in love, all thanks to Apollo.

Once again, my love is sadly one sided. He is understandably hurt by what I wrote about the show, and because there is no relationship if only one person's in it, ours no longer exists. I cry about this, and wish I'd behaved better. But this time I'm not bitter. I won't rail against love or coach other women to be suspicious of anyone who uses those three little words. This time I know better. Apollo showed me that love can exist—does exist—for all of us. We just have to be brave enough to keep on looking.

I hit "send" and went into the kitchen to start a pot of soup. When I came back, I had instant messages from Livy and Essence. After a deep breath, I clicked them open.

That pretty boy's cute bum got to you, didn't it? Livy wrote. *If I could reach across the ocean, I'd slap you silly. You've gotta shake out of it and snap back. We can't run all that on* Unvarnished. *It's a load of steaming crap.*

I don't know. Essence's message popped up. *If Sam*

*has had a change of heart, then her heart's changed.
We aren't here to censor her.*

I'm really sorry, I typed. *I understand if you don't
want me to post it. It's just something I feel compelled
to do. But if you say no, I'll abide by that. And I know
it goes without saying that I'll have to leave the blog.
Again, I'm so sorry.*

Damn right, you're sorry! A sorry excuse for an
Unvarnished *blogger. Really, Sam. I expected better of
you,* Livy wrote.

I nodded, reaching out to stroke Zephyr's back. I'd
expected better of myself in so many ways. *Sorry, Livy
and Essence,* I wrote. *I guess this is good-bye.*

No, wait, Sam. This was from Essence. *I think we all
have a right to change. Our mission has always been to
tell our readers the truth, right? And this is your truth.
Maybe the truth for me is that I met a guy over the
weekend who's smart and funny and sweet as can be.
Maybe that's true. I shouldn't have to pretend I'm being something I'm not, not on* Unvarnished. *We always
said we were dishing out truth serum. Whatever the
truth turns out to be.*

In the end, they let me post it. And we agreed to part
ways without any hard feelings, which was more than
I'd dreamed was possible. I read through my piece
again, made a few edits, and posted it. There. The
readers would be shocked, but so be it. It had felt
like my duty before to warn them off love, but now I
knew I owed it to them to tell them about my change
of heart. Love wasn't bad—it was just risky. And people had the right to weigh the risks for themselves.
What was the line? A ship in a harbor is safe, but that
is not what ships are built for. Exactly.

When I'd finished posting, I saved my article and attached it to an e-mail to Vern. This was it—my final installment. I doubted the *Telltale* would print it, and I'd have to repay their advance using money I didn't have. But at least my conscience would be clear. I shook my head. *Too little, too late, Novak. You couldn't have made this decision weeks ago?*

When I was done I sat still and closed my eyes, trying to squeeze out the visions of Mason that kept popping up when I let my guard down. In a sudden rush, I put the computer to sleep and stood up, moving away before I Googled his name again. I was just trying to hurt myself, hunting for photos of him with other women. I suppose on some level, my psyche wanted me to see evidence that he'd moved on, so I could entertain the thought myself.

−25−

🦴 *Apollo*

I was so excited, my paws itched. Mason and I stood outside an apartment building, looking up at windows and the tops of palm trees. He'd dressed himself carefully, trying on three different shirts until he found the right one. Then we'd washed the car. And he talked to me in a nervous, nonstop way as we drove here. That was how I knew this was important.

But even after all that preparation, we almost left without going inside. Mason stood looking up while I sniffed the grass and peed discreetly on a patch of agapanthus flowers. He fiddled with the neck of his shirt. Salty nervous smells were beginning to blend with his clean soapy scent, so I decided to step in. I let out a bark. Then I trotted up the paved path to the doors and barked again.

Thankfully, Mason took my hint without my having to send thoughts to him. I was glad, since sending thoughts was exhausting, and I guessed I would need plenty of energy for whatever was coming. We moved in through the doors, then stood in front of an elevator while Mason shuffled his feet and looked over his shoulder ten or twenty times. The elevator doors opened, and he peered down at me.

"Here goes nothing, right?" I wagged. "Okay. Good luck to us."

We got out of the elevator and stood in front of a wooden door while Mason bounced on the balls of his feet and whistled softly under his breath. Then he took a long inhale, raised his fist, and knocked.

I heard sniffling sounds and the shh-shh of slippers on a wooden floor, then the door opened. Sam! I jumped toward her, crashing into her shins. She folded herself down around me so I could lick her face, rubbing myself against her. She smelled clean and wonderful—toasted almost—like she'd just been soaking in hot water. I wished I could climb onto her shoulder and stay with her for days—wished I could smell like her, look like her, *be* her. But at least I was touching her. That was mighty good.

After a minute, she straightened up and stiffened, looking at Mason. He said some mumbly things "—hope we aren't bothering you—" "—I thought we should talk—" while I trotted further inside. Samantha's place was far smaller than Mason's house. Here there was just one small room-plus-kitchen and two doors. Sam touched her hair and pulled on the neck of her bathrobe, saying something about getting dressed, then she disappeared behind one of the doors. Mason put his hands into his pockets and looked around while I continued my exploration.

A saggy couch sat in the front room. It was my favorite, the kind that's lived in several different apartments, not like Mason's stiff leather one. Sam had plants and books and a guitar in the corner, but not much else. There weren't orange trees in mosaic pots like Mason had, or carved wooden elephants, or rooms full of furniture that no one ever sat on. Mason had one room we never went into that housed one big table. No dog beds, no treadmills—just that one table.

I'd just finished looking around when Sam came back out. As she opened the door, a small gray face peeped out and blinked. I blinked back. It blinked some more, looking at me with bewitching green eyes—paralyzing me. I sat down, frozen. The creature slinked further out of the doorway, wrapped its fluffy tail around its feet, and sat. I sat, too. Whatever it was, I couldn't take my eyes off it.

Behind me, I heard Sam and Mason settle stiffly on the couch. I knew I should be helping them—that's the reason I had come—but the green-eyed one had me in its thrall.

"I want to explain," Sam said suddenly, at the same time Mason said, "I saw your article."

Sam made a throat-clearing cough and spoke again. "I just need to tell you this. I know you hate me—*I* hate me. I can't believe I did such a horrible thing. But before I knew you, before I came to the show, I was in a really dark place when it came to love and relationships. I didn't even realize it until a few days ago, but I was kind of out of my mind."

Out of the corner of my eye, I saw her shift her body to face him. "I've told you what happened with Richard. But I didn't say how angry I was at him for a very, very long time. So angry I couldn't see straight."

"I know. I found the blog. It—it kind of explains everything."

Sam made another uncomfortable sound. "Did you read much of it?"

"All of it. Every one of your entries."

"Oh." She paused. "And you saw the article. My retraction."

"I did." Mason's voice was very soft. I glanced over my shoulder and saw that his eyes were fixed on Sam as if she were a red bird in a field of snow. "Did you mean that?"

Her head bobbed up and down. "I did. I really did. I'm so ashamed of what I wrote for the *Telltale*. I had no business doing that. That's not me—it's not the kind of thing I would ever do, except that I needed the money. I'd lost my job and I owed so much on my student loans and my rent . . . They came to me before you gave me the job. And, as you've probably figured out, I—I came in under false pretenses. I'm so sorry."

Mason sighed. "I think, deep down, I always knew it might have been you. I guess that's why I never gave you the confidentiality agreement. Because I was afraid you might not sign it."

"What do you mean, you never gave it to me? I thought it got slowed down in the legal department."

"Rebecca gave it to me before we left for Madrona. I had it in my bag the whole time. Something just kept me from putting it in your hands."

"Oh." They fell quiet. I started to breathe hard—this was the moment when they needed my help! I should be there, sending them prompting thoughts, bringing them closer together. Without the right nudge, they might fall apart again. Mason would walk out the door and he and I would never return.

Panic burbled in my stomach, making me feel sloshy and upside down. I wanted to go, but this green-eyed magician had me rooted in place. I couldn't leave, couldn't blink. But I could make noise. Shifting back and forth on my paws, I let out a whine.

"Apollo!" Sam jumped up off the couch. "Oh, shoot—I didn't know Zephyr was out here." She scrambled around toward us. The second she appeared, the green-eyed creature arched its back, transforming into a humpbacked, bristling dervish. I jumped up and let out a bark of warning. Sam and Mason needed to know that an attack might be imminent. But Sam did a surprising thing—she sacrificed herself, scooping up the creature in her arms and whisking her into the back room.

The second it was gone, I felt released, as if I was off leash for the first time in years. I ran over to Mason, who rubbed me up and down and bent his head toward mine.

"I think she might still like us, buddy," he whispered. "Lend a hand with her, yeah?"

I licked his face. When Sam came back out, energy surged through me. This was my moment! Golden love light was washing all around us—I just had to capture it. And first I needed to get us all to a different setting. Sam had been speaking like an unworthy dog, rolling over to show Mason her belly. She'd finished that, and now it was time to put them back on the same level. The easiest way to do that was to get us all up and onto our feet.

I trotted to the door and let out a bark. Then I pawed at it and nosed the crack.

"Apollo must need to go out," Sam said, coming toward me. Mason followed with my leash and seconds later we were moving down the hall, back into the elevator. When we burst outside, into the sunshine, I knew I'd made the right decision. Sweet spring smells circled through the air. Far over our heads, the palm trees flounced their bushy heads. I spotted a stone bench at the foot of the palms and led us that way. Once the people were settled, I lay down at their feet and pretended to smell a patch of grass by my paw.

"So," Mason said, rubbing his knuckle against his chin, "I have to say that this has been pretty hard for me. I wanted to be pissed at you. Really, royally pissed. But what you wrote in the *Telltale*—well, even I have to admit that it was all true. You didn't make anything up. We were storyboarding. We did hire actors. Apollo did have to do exactly what Lucas told him. Just because other shows did the same thing doesn't mean it wasn't true about the *Love Dog*. Knowing that—that you weren't lying—made me angrier than anything for a while. I wanted to hate you, but I couldn't. Not completely, anyway."

Sam looked down at the ground. I knew she was ashamed, and the danger in feeling ashamed is that sometimes people are so hard on themselves they can't let anyone else forgive them. So I closed my eyes and focused on sending her my thoughts. *You aren't bad. You're a kind, kind person. Let Mason care for you. You deserve it.*

Slowly, she lifted her head. Her eyes met his and they held there as I breathed in and out, in and out. She was letting him love her. I could feel it warming the ends of my fur. I wanted to wag, but I held my tail completely still, afraid to spoil the moment.

"And what was even worse," he said, "was that you fixed the show. You turned the *Love Dog* from an ordinary, C-grade, run-of-the-mill show into one of the best shows on television—ever. Looking back, I can see that when you joined the show we were doing exactly what I feared most, pumping out television that was just okay. We were doing the same thing as all the other reality shows. We were complacent, and it was your change that turned the show into something exceptional. Those last two episodes of the season were television magic. People will be talking about them all summer long. We already have advertisers lining up to buy spots for next season and none of that would have happened if you hadn't run those articles. So even when I was furious at you for having done it, I had to be grateful to you, too. That was pretty hard to take."

He shifted closer to her on the bench. His hand ran up to hers and slipped around it. Her fingers curled against his. "It was almost as hard as hating you and loving you at the same time."

An overpoweringly wonderful smell—of sugar and fresh-cut grass and midnight rain—flooded the air. My tail started wagging despite my best efforts to hold it down. I eased forward and nudged Sam's other hand, the one Mason wasn't holding. She put her fingers on my head, her gaze still locked on Mason's.

"I've been hating myself and loving you," she said quietly. "And that's been pretty damn tough, too."

Mason took a deep breath. "I think it's time you stop," he said. Then he laughed. "Hating yourself, I mean. You can keep loving me. All you want."

He leaned forward and she leaned forward, and they kissed, folding together in a whirl of delirious scents. Overhead, the palm trees nodded their approval. The wind blew the cut blades of grass down toward them, and the sunlight was stronger all around their bench. I could barely breathe. This was the greatest victory of my career—of my life. It was so beautiful, all I could do was watch.

—26—

Three Months Later

🦴 Apollo

I trotted out onto the studio set, my hair flying behind me, one eye on the camera. Mason sat in his velvet chair, and I moved straight toward him, finding my seat to the right of his feet. This was the way we liked to sit at home—it felt as natural to me as swallowing. When his hand settled on my head, I opened my mouth and smiled.

Mason spoke to the couple on the couch while I peered at them intently. They were having problems, these two. I'd chosen them out of a roomful of couples because of the salty, cindery smells coming off them. They were older than our usual guests—gray haired and flat-shoed—but I was excited to work with them. The woman was speaking to Mason, and as she talked, I sensed a shift in her, a faint molasses smell that warmed and warmed the more she spoke.

"He retired three months ago, and I can't get him to leave the house!" she was saying. Mason nodded. I panted. "We used to laugh and talk about things, but now there's nothing to say. Nothing to report. No news to share."

I looked at the man. He was staring at the coffee table, his face crumpled. He was the one I needed to work on, the one who was frightened. Not of her, I didn't think. But frightened. *You seem very brave and gentle and wise. Power is in you. Don't be afraid. You're stronger than you think.*

We finished talking and came off the stage. Sam met us, clipboard in hand, a headset curved over her dark hair.

"Great job, you two!" She gave Mason a bright smile and squeezed his hand, then she bent down and kissed me on the head. Mason and I both glowed from her attention. "That was fabulous work with Helen. I think what we need next is some one-on-one time with George and Apollo. Maybe outdoors?"

"It's where he's at his best," Mason said. "Maybe they should go fishing on the pier. Helen said George used to do that with their sons." He ran his arm around Sam's waist and pulled her in close. Then he looked down at me. "What do you think, buddy? Back to the beach?" He turned to Sam. "Let Apollo and me handle this one so you can get some writing done, okay? I know you want to get the revisions on your short story turned in early."

I wagged, looking up at my two people. They were my whole heart, these people. Every day I spent with them filled me so full, it was easy to send my love out to the world. I lay down at night, cuddled on the foot of their bed, while Sam rubbed my belly and Mason stroked my ears, and I was so full of happiness the love just bubbled out of me. I sent it to Pilar and A.J., to Faye and Sebastian, to Honey and Chad, to Curly Hair and Mason's parents and everyone I knew at the studio. I sent it to Kim, and I sent it to Lucas and Valerie. I sent love to the world, to the universe, and I never felt tired.

Now I looked at them, unworried. I knew they would give me time with George. They always did. My work at the studio had changed—now I had hours and hours to spend with the guests. I could walk with them on the beach, hike in the hills, sit on the set, or ride in the car. I could nudge them and wag at them and send my thoughts to them until they revealed their problem and I could get busy with the fixing. This was the way it would go with George. I was excited to get started.

But as much as I wanted to work with George, I couldn't forget my other secret desire. Because now that I'd finished my greatest project—mending the love between Mason and Sam—I had a new plan. A new project I wanted to tackle. That green-eyed creature from Sam's apartment had come to live with us at Mason's. Every time I saw it, it locked me in the same hypnotic stare I'd experienced that first day.

This was the mystery I wanted to crack. I worked in the day on the guests at the studio, but when we got home, I invested my time in the green-eyed one. I would make friends with this strange being. I would show it that I meant no harm. I was the Love Dog. This was my destiny.